THE
LAST
GOOD
DAY

OTHER JOANNE KILBOURN MYSTERIES
BY GAIL BOWEN

Deadly Appearances
Murder at the Mendel (U.S.A. ed., *Love and Murder*)
The Wandering Soul Murders
A Colder Kind of Death
A Killing Spring
Verdict in Blood
Burying Ariel
The Glass Coffin

THE
LAST
GOOD
DAY

A Joanne Kilbourn Mystery

GAIL BOWEN

M&S

Cloth edition published 2004
Mass-market paperback edition published 2005

Library and Archives Canada Cataloguing in Publication

Bowen, Gail, 1942-
The last good day : a Joanne Kilbourn mystery / Gail Bowen.

ISBN 0-7710-1468-6

I. Title.

PS8553.O8995L38 2005   C813´.54   C2005-902559-X

We acknowledge the financial support of the Government of
Canada through the Book Publishing Industry Development
Program and that of the Government of Ontario through the
Ontario Media Development Corporation's Ontario Book
Initiative. We further acknowledge the support of the Canada
Council for the Arts and the Ontario Arts Council for our
publishing program.

Typeset in Bembo by M&S, Toronto
Printed and bound in Canada

McClelland & Stewart Ltd.
The Canadian Publishers
481 University Avenue
Toronto, Ontario
M5G 2E9
www.mcclelland.com

1 2 3 4 5   09 08 07 06 05

To Alison Gordon, the best friend
Canadian mystery writers ever had

CHAPTER 1

The cosmos should send forth a sign when a good man approaches death, but the night Chris Altieri joined me in the gazebo to watch the sun set on Lawyers' Bay, there was nothing. No fiery letters flaming across the wide prairie sky; no angels with bright hair beckoning from the clouds. The evening was innocent, sweet with summer dreams and the promise of life at a cottage in a season just begun. It was July 1, Canada Day. The lake was full of fish. The paint on the Muskoka chairs was crayon bright; the paddles, sticky with fresh varnish, were on their hooks in the boathouse; and the board games and croquet sets still had all their pieces. September with its tether of routine and responsibility was a thousand years away. Anything was possible, and the gentle-voiced man who dropped into the chair next to mine seemed favoured by fortune to seize the best that summer had to offer.

Bright, successful, and charming, Chris Altieri was, in E.A. Robinson's poignant phrase, everything to make us wish that we were in his place. Yet this graceful man wouldn't live to see the rising of the orange sun that was now plunging towards the horizon, and when I learned that he was dead, I wasn't surprised.

I was a newcomer to the small community of Lawyers' Bay, renting the cottage that belonged to my friend Kevin Hynd, who was spending the summer exploring the mystical Mount Kailas in Tibet. My trekking days were over. Kevin's cottage, on a lake seventy kilometres from Regina, with good roads all the way, was adventure enough for me, as it was for my daughter Taylor, my son Angus, and his girlfriend, Leah. We'd been at Lawyers' Bay less than a week – long enough for me to master the idiosyncrasies of the motorboat and the ancient Admiral range in the kitchen, not long enough for me to know much at all about my new neighbours, the privileged group who, until he walked away, had been Kevin's law partners and who were still his friends. When they met twenty-five years ago in law school, they called themselves the Winners'

Circle; the name stuck, but Kevin hadn't mentioned whether the group's members saw it as a source of pride or irony.

So far I had met the members of the Winners' Circle only in passing. My family and I had arrived the previous Sunday afternoon, when the partners at Falconer Shreve were just packing up to go home. I'd spoken briefly to Delia Wainberg, the sole female partner in the firm, but the others had only had time to wave and call out a welcome before they headed back to the city and the demands of a high-powered law practice.

The Canada Day party that Falconer, Shreve, Altieri, and Wainberg threw every year to celebrate our nation's birthday was legendary in cottage country, and I had counted on it as my chance to get to know my new neighbours better. There'd been no shortage of opportunities. I'd water-skied with Falconer Shreve's juniors and clients, kayaked with Falconer Shreve friends from the city, and played beach volleyball with the cottagers who lived on the other side of the gates that separated Falconer Shreve families from the lesser blessed. Faces glowing with the soft sheen of summer sweat, we fortunate few had spent the last twelve hours savouring the newest, the fastest, the finest, and the freshest that money could buy.

By anyone's standards, it was one hell of a party, and there had been enough revealing glimpses of the people who were paying the bill to satisfy my curiosity. The first came in early afternoon, not long after the party started. People had donned bathing suits and were gathering along the shore to swim and water-ski. Zachary Shreve and Noah Wainberg had fired up boats and were idling off-shore waiting for customers. The teenagers, mine included, were lining up when Blake Falconer's wife, Lily, strode to the end of the dock and called out to Zack Shreve.

"Let's go," she said. He gave her a short wave of acknowledgement and they were away. Lily's performance was nothing short of virtuoso. She was in her early forties, but she skied with the abandon of a sixteen-year-old who believed she was immortal. It was clear that Zack had driven the boat for her before. Periodically, he would do a shoulder check and she would give him a hand signal indicating that he should go faster. Lily took the jumps at speeds that I knew were dangerous, but she never faltered. It wasn't long before the party guests stopped whatever they were doing just to watch her. I was standing beside Blake Falconer at the end of the dock. He followed his wife's progress without comment, but he didn't appear to exhale until she finally signalled to Zack to cut the motor and she sank into the water.

As Lily swam the few metres to shore, I turned to her husband. "That was astonishing," I said.

"Somehow Lily always manages to survive," he said, then he walked to the end of the dock to offer his wife a hand.

There had been other revelations. During the swimming races, my ten-year-old daughter, Taylor, discovered to her delight that the only other children staying at Lawyers' Bay were two girls a year older than her, and after five minutes of squealed exclamations over shared passions, the trio had bonded as effortlessly as puppies and gone off in search of food to inhale and boys to taunt. Later, there was a more poignant moment. While I was waiting for my turn to water-ski, I drifted over to watch Delia Wainberg's husband, Noah, help parents supervise the toddlers who had decided to venture into the lake. To see him knee-deep in water reassuring a slippery three-year-old with water wings and attitude was to understand the patience of the saints. Hugging her knees to her as she squinted through the smoke from her cigarette, Delia watched from her towel on the beach. When she called out to her husband, Noah turned expectantly. "Hey," she said in her appealing husky-squeaky

voice. "They should make water wings for adults
– something to keep us from sinking."

"That's what I'm here for, babe," Noah said.

Her husband's gentle gallantry sailed right past
Delia. "Actually, I was thinking about Chris," she
said. "I'm worried about him."

"I should have known," her husband said softly,
then he bent to guide the child he was holding
towards the safety of her mother's arms.

Delia Wainberg wasn't the only partner anxious
about Christopher Altieri that day. The men and
women of Falconer Shreve were good hosts, laughing, chatting, urging guests to refill a glass, replen-
ish a plate, enjoy themselves. But it was apparent
Chris's state of mind worried those who knew him
best. Despite repeated attempts to draw him into
the fun, Chris remained alone and unfocused, the
spectre at the feast.

When Chris and I arrived simultaneously at one
of the washtubs of ice and drinks that had been
placed strategically along the beach, Zack Shreve
seemed to appear out of nowhere. He fished soft
drinks out for Chris and me. "The skiers keep on
coming, Chris," he said. "I need somebody else
along in the boat. Interested?"

Chris's smile was sweet. "Maybe ask one of the
others," he said. "I'm not too sharp today." Then he

walked away without another word of explanation.

"Something wrong there?" I said.

Zack's eyes were still on Chris. "He just got back from Japan. Could be jet lag – at least that's what we're hoping."

"Because jet lag goes away," I said.

"Right," Zack said absently. Suddenly, he seemed to realize I was standing there. "Hey, I'm not much of a host. Want me to open that Coke for you?"

"Thanks, but I've been opening my own Cokes for a few years now."

"I have other talents," he said. "Sit next to me at the barbecue tonight, and prepare to be dazzled."

"I'd like that," I said.

"Me too," Zack said. "Now, if you'll excuse me, I'm going to offer a little aid and comfort to my lugubrious friend and partner."

Zack Shreve's brand of aid and comfort apparently left something to be desired. When, late in the afternoon, Chris and I were matched in a tennis tournament, he suffered a meltdown. He was forty-five, ten years younger than me, and his game showed flashes of a brilliance I could only dream of. But talent without concentration had been no match for doggedness, and I was beating Chris handily when he suddenly dropped his racquet and strode off. It was an unnerving moment, made even more worrying when Chris didn't appear at dinner. According to Zack, Chris was simply exhausted, but I was relieved when he appeared in the gazebo that night after the barbecue.

His eyes were anxious. "Your daughter told me where I could find you. I hope you don't mind me following you out here."

"I don't mind," I said.

The corners of his mouth twitched towards a smile. "Your daughter said you had come to the gazebo to straighten up."

"Taylor's not known for her discretion," I said. "I was suffering from too much sun and too much wine. Nobody to blame but myself."

"So you're not perfect," Chris said.

"Not even close," I said.

Chris inhaled deeply. "That makes it easier," he said. "Look, I'm sorry I was such a jerk today."

"It was pretty clear there was more on your mind than tennis."

"Thanks, but absolution shouldn't come that easily. I hope you'll give me a chance to make amends." He offered his hand. When I took it, I felt the thrum of connection. Apparently, Chris Altieri did too. Before he withdrew his hand, he pressed mine. "Kevin said you'd be a good person to talk to."

"When were you talking to Kevin?"

"Tonight when you were all having dinner."

"He found a phone on Mount Kailas?"

Chris offered another of his disarmingly sweet smiles. "Actually, he was in Delhi. We agreed years ago that somehow we'd always make it to the Falconer Shreve Canada Day party. Kevin may have had to phone it in today, but he still gets marked present." Chris gazed at the party across the water. "For us, this is holy ground," he said.

The scene was seductive. A small band had been hired to smooth the transition from the barbecue to the fireworks, and the music evoked a Proustian rush of memories of other summers. People were dancing along the shoreline, and their silhouettes, thrown into sharp relief by the blaze of a bonfire, were dreamily romantic. The lights strung across the branches of the willows had been arranged so artfully that their twinkling seemed a natural phenomenon, like the pinpoint illumination of fireflies.

It was impossible not to feel the crystalline beauty of the moment. "It is lovely," I said.

"Don't forget the people," Chris said. "No matter what you've heard, they're the best."

"Worthy members of the Winners' Circle?" I asked.

He lowered his head in embarrassment. "Sopho-moric, huh?"

"Kevin tells me you got together at the end of your first week in law school. Your sophomore year wasn't that far behind you."

"We *were* young," Chris agreed. "Zack Shreve was only twenty. He'd blazed through his under-graduate degree. He was the baby – although given what he's become, it's hard to believe he was ever a self-conscious kid."

"I sat with him at the barbecue," I said. "It was a rush meeting him face to face. Until today, he was just someone I'd seen on the news – Zachary Shreve, defender of the defenceless."

"The media love him," Chris said dryly. "Don Quixote in a wheelchair. But Zack doesn't waste his time tilting at windmills. He chooses cases he can win, and when the little guy gets a big settle-ment, Zack gets a big cheque."

"Big cheques benefit all the partners, don't they?"

"Our bank accounts, yes. Our immortal souls? Not necessarily."

"You disapprove of what Zack does."

He shrugged. "That doesn't mean I don't love him. I love them all. If I didn't, I wouldn't have cut short my trip to Japan so I could be here today."

"That is devotion," I said. "So what took you to Japan?"

"I was on a pilgrimage," he said, and his voice was flat. It was impossible to tell if the comment was ironic.

"It seems to be the summer for racking up good karma," I said. "You and Kevin both."

"Maybe we should have inquired about a group rate," he said.

"Did you find what you were looking for?" I asked.

He hesitated. "No," he said finally. Somewhere close to shore a fish jumped. "Isn't it amazing how even when things are at their worst, there are reminders of the goodness of life?" The sentiment was celebratory, but in the sinking light, Chris's face was haunted.

"Is it that bad for you?" I said.

Chris didn't respond. Seemingly, he was absorbed in the lustre of the roses floating in the low bowl at the centre of the table. "I've always been graced," he said. "Now the grace has been withdrawn. When I told Kevin that tonight, he said I should talk to a priest, but I can't do that and I can't talk to my partners."

"So Kevin suggested you talk to me," I said.

"If you don't mind," Chris said.

"I don't mind." I leaned towards him. "Chris, why do you think the grace has been withdrawn from your life?"

"Because I've sinned." This time there was no mistaking his tone. He was clearly suffering.

I turned my attention to the roses and waited.

Christopher tented his fingers thoughtfully. "Kevin says you're not judgemental."

I smiled. "That must be why he gave me a break on the rent."

"Must be." Chris's face grew grave. "Let's test your limits. Has anyone you loved ever had an abortion?"

The question shattered the perfection of the evening. "No one I loved," I said finally, "but women I was close to. My roommate in college, other friends. I know the wound goes deep."

"Does it ever heal?" he said.

"Truthfully? I don't know."

Chris turned to face me. We were so close, I could smell the liquor on his breath. It hadn't occurred to me that his confessional moment had been fuelled by alcohol. He wasn't drunk, but he was unguarded. "I was with a woman," he said. "She became pregnant with our child . . . with what would have been our child."

"She had an abortion," I said.

"She had an abortion because of me," he corrected.

"You forced her?"

Pain flickered across his face. "I gave her no option."

"But afterwards you had second thoughts," I said.

"It was beyond that. I was mourning something…" He extended his hands palms up in a gesture of helplessness. "I just wasn't sure what it was."

"And that's why you went on the pilgrimage."

He nodded. "I'd joined this chat room on the Internet. It was for people like me who couldn't deal with how they felt after an abortion. One night someone mentioned an article in an old *New York Times Magazine* by a woman who'd suffered a miscarriage while she was in Tokyo. She went through hell, but finally she found an answer. She discovered the Japanese have a name for a child that's lost before birth. They call it *mizuko*, 'water child,' because it's a being who is still flowing into our world."

"A beautiful image," I said.

"And an acknowledgement that what was lost was real," Chris said quietly. "There's an enlightened being, Jizo, who watches over the mizukos. The article mentioned a Buddhist temple in Tokyo where they performed Jizo rituals."

"And you went there."

Chris's face grew soft with memory. "It was incredible, Joanne. Rows and rows of tiny stone statues of mizukos. Their features were so perfect. Most of them were wearing little red caps that their mothers had crocheted for them. They'd left presents for their unborn children too – toys and bags of candy. The article said gifts were the custom, so I left a little truck for my mizuko with his statue." Chris's voice broke. "I said a prayer, then I left a letter telling him I was sorry and that I hoped he'd find another pathway into being."

The warm summer air was vibrating with the hum of crickets and the wishing star had appeared in the darkening sky. Canada Day. But in that moment, Chris Altieri and I were half a world away in an ancient shrine that offered comfort and hope to those who grieved, but from which he'd come away empty-handed.

"The ritual didn't work for you," I said.

"I didn't deserve to have it work."

"Why not?"

"The woman who wrote the article had a miscarriage, and a miscarriage is no one's fault. What I did was unforgivable."

"Nothing is unforgivable," I said.

Out of nowhere, a voice, peremptory and loud,

called out to us. "There you are. I was concerned."

Chris slumped. "My law partner," he said, "come to deliver me from temptation. You must have scared them, Joanne. They sent in the big guns."

When I turned in the direction of Chris's gaze, I saw Zack Shreve coming down the path. Seeing that he'd caught our attention, Zack waved jauntily.

I touched Chris's hand. "We can go back to my cottage if you want to talk," I said.

"Thanks," he said. "But I shouldn't draw anyone else into this."

In the silence I could hear the wheels of Zack's chair grind inexorably through the pebbles on the walk. Nothing could stop him.

"Everyone makes mistakes," I said. "It's only human."

Chris's smile was bleak. "I don't feel human," he said. "I feel like my mizuko – as if I don't belong anywhere." He left the gazebo and sprinted up the path that led back to the party. As he passed Zack, he bent and kissed the top of his head. It was an extraordinary gesture, but apparently it didn't touch Zack's heart. The senior partner of Falconer Shreve rolled up the ramp that made the gazebo, like all the buildings at Lawyers' Bay, accessible.

"So did our lugubrious friend open up to you?" he asked amiably.

In the enclosed space of the gazebo, I was struck by Zack's physical presence. As a result of an accident, he had been paraplegic since childhood, and as if to compensate for lower limbs that stubbornly refused to respond to his will, the upper half of his body was a coiled spring. His torso and arms were heavily muscled, reflecting the power of a man who quite literally pushed himself for seventeen hours a day; his head was large and his features were those of a successful actor, memorably drawn and compelling.

He flicked the switch that turned on the gazebo's overhead light, dimmed it, then wheeled past me to the window that looked onto the lake. When he turned and beckoned me to join him, his voice was silky. "It's a good night to be alive, isn't it?"

The view from the glass-walled gazebo was panoramic. Lawyers' Bay was an almost perfect horseshoe, and the gazebo had been built on the tip of the horseshoe's west arm. Lights twinkled from the distant shores that enclosed the lake and across the bay the party was in full swing.

"Yes," I said. "It's a good night to be alive."

Zack sighed contentedly. "That raises the question that brought me here. On this night of nights, why is Chris Altieri so miserable?"

"Why don't you ask him?"

"Because I'm interested in your opinion. Chris's tête-à-tête with you lasted ten minutes." Zack checked his watch. "Actually, it was shade less than ten minutes. Still, time enough for a man to reveal his darkest secrets."

I stood. "I'm going back to the party," I said.

"I'll come with you."

"Be my guest," I said. "But you'll be wasting your time. This is between Chris and me."

"No longer an option," he said pleasantly. "The moment you came through those gates at the entrance, you were part of all our lives."

"I don't remember taking a blood oath," I said.

Zack waved his hand dismissively. "Nothing that dramatic," he said. "We're not the Cosa Nostra, just five friends from a provincial law school who enjoy one another's company and take our obligations to one another seriously."

"I take my obligations seriously too," I said. "And it's time I went back and handled them."

"You're going to talk to Chris."

"If he wants to talk to me."

"You might want to rethink that decision."

"Meaning . . . ?"

"Meaning you're part of our little community now. Kevin invited you in. Except for those who've joined us through marriage, you're the first outsider to become part of life at Lawyers' Bay." He plucked a perfect rosebud from the bowl on the table and handed it to me. "As you've no doubt noticed, ours is not a hardscrabble existence," he said.

"I've noticed," I said.

"And your family has noticed too. It was a real stroke of luck that your son and his girlfriend got that job running the Point Store."

"You had something to do with that?"

Zack shrugged. "We just got the ball rolling. Kevin said the kids were having trouble getting summer jobs, so we arranged for them to meet old Stan Gardiner, the owner. Angus and his girlfriend did the rest. Stan said they were the only couple he interviewed who knew shit from shinola."

A mosquito landed on my hand, and I swatted it. "Any more surprises?" I asked.

"Lily Falconer's nanny has been given a hand-some raise to keep an eye on your daughter this summer," he said. "There, I've emptied my bag. No more secrets."

"Why would you do all this?"

"We wanted to make sure you enjoyed your holiday," Zack said.

My late husband had been a lawyer, so I knew

the value of keeping my lip buttoned. I twirled the perfect rose and listened to the crickets.

"Ah," Zack said. "The significant silence, forcing your opponent to say more than he intended to."

"Somehow I doubt that a charter member of the Winners' Circle would fall into a trap that easily," I said.

"You're scornful of our group?"

"Not of the people," I said. "Just the concept. I'm not a huge fan of elitist clubs."

Zack's laugh was robust. "The Circle was hardly elitist. It was just a group of law students who came together because they were scared and smart and socially inept. It was good for all of us. When I was invited to join, I was like a drunk discovering Jesus. Dazzled. Born again."

Despite everything, I found myself responding to Zack's candour. I taught at a university, and I'd seen my share of twenty-year-olds who hid their insecurities behind a carapace of brash egotism. "Undergraduate life can be brutal," I said.

Zack's profile had the chiselled authority of a king's on a coin. "I wasn't trying to elicit sympathy, Joanne. I've made a career out of defending lumps of foul deformity. I've never seen myself as one of them. Not that the temptation wasn't there."

"Because of what happened to you."

He raised an eyebrow. "Accidents happen. Smart people make the most of them. And smart people don't take no for an answer."

"You don't give up, do you?"

"Not when the stakes are this high."

"Well, if you're not going to give up, why don't you fill me in?"

Zack beamed. "All I ever asked for was a fair hearing. So, some context. Guilt is a powerful force, Joanne. It plays havoc with the judicial system. People are always confessing to big things because they're tortured with guilt about little things."

"And you think that's what Chris did here tonight."

"I've caught his act before," Zack said acidly. His face softened. "Chris is a thoroughly decent man, but at the moment he can't be trusted. He's hit a bad patch in his life. He was forced to do something that was necessary but morally repugnant. Not to put too fine a point on it, it's fucking him up. For his sake, for all our sakes, forget everything he said to you."

"Okay," I said.

"Just like that?" Zack said.

"Just like that," I said. "I don't know what's going on. If I involve myself, I could do more harm than good, and Chris said he didn't want to draw anyone else in."

Zack's head shot around. "Did he explain what he meant?"

"No."

"And you didn't push it. You surprise me," he said. "But you also make me understand why Kevin was willing to trust you." He gestured gracefully at the ramp to the gazebo. "Shall we rejoin the festivities?"

"Sure," I said. "When it comes to fireworks, there are no second chances."

By the time we got back, the party was rocking. The bonfire was burning hot and high, the music was pounding, and the dancers' movements had taken on a shank-of-the-evening abandon. My son Angus and his girlfriend, Leah, were on a bench near the fire. Hair still wet from swimming and hands gripping cans of beer, they were huddled under a beach towel, laughing at some private joke. When he spotted Zack and me, Angus waved and pointed at Taylor and her new friends, Gracie Falconer and Isobel Wainberg. The girls were up to their ankles in the lake, giggling and shrieking as the water splashed their shorts. Rose Lavallee, the tiny ageless woman who was Gracie's nanny, had planted a folding chair at the water's edge and was eyeing them fixedly.

"Everybody's happy. Everybody's safe," Zack said. "Now why don't we get a drink and join the others."

There were perhaps eighty people at the Canada Day party. No one appeared to be in charge of seating arrangements, yet as the first rocket spiralled into the sky and rained down its shower of fiery stars, my kids and I found ourselves alone with the Falconer Shreve families in what was, indisputably, the choicest location on the beach. It was an exercise in self-selection that would have interested a sociologist. Taylor wasn't a sociologist, but she was a keen observer. "How come no one's here but us?" she asked.

"Because it's our party," Zack Shreve said. "And that means we get the best of everything."

Maybe so, but as I looked at the faces around me, it seemed that getting the best of everything didn't bring happiness.

Dressed in a black T-shirt, slacks, and sandals, Delia Wainberg was a striking figure: sapling thin, with pale, pale skin, piercing cobalt-blue eyes, and wiry black hair so wild it seemed electrically charged. When I'd driven through the gates to Lawyers' Bay for the first time, it had been Delia who had waved me over to welcome me. It was hard to imagine a less likely representative of cottage life.

She was painfully intense – even jumpy – but she had a Cheshire cat grin that was infectious.

That night the Cheshire cat grin was nowhere in evidence. As she surveyed the world through the screen of blue smoke that drifted from her cigarette, Delia clearly didn't like what she saw. As soon as Chris Altieri walked onto the beach, the root of her preoccupation was obvious. She went to him immediately, and when her efforts to engage him in conversation failed, she ground out her cigarette and slid her arms around his waist. It was as if she believed that if she held on tight enough, she could keep him safe.

A stone's throw away, Noah Wainberg tended the bonfire and listened as his daughter and her friends fizzed with gossip and dreams. Kevin had told me Noah was the unofficial handyman of Lawyers' Bay, the one to call in the middle of the night if the toilet wouldn't stop filling or if the new flat-screen TV short-circuited the wiring. In a world fuelled by high-powered, high-paid talent, Noah had made himself indispensable. He was the fix-it man.

He was also an artist. The grounds of every home at Lawyers' Bay were blessed with Noah's wood carvings. Large and roughly hewn, these images of animals, real and fanciful, surprised you by their power. To look at his work was to feel, for an instant, the deep and numbing love that can drive a man to make art. His love for his wife also appeared to be deep and numbing. That night, as he piled logs on the bonfire while she obsessed over another man, it was impossible to read the feelings that lay behind his fire-reflecting eyes.

Their daughter, Isobel, was her mother in miniature, tightly wound and passionate. At eleven, she was already a worrier, her young brow knit in a permanent frown. I'd noticed at dinner that she had a number of tics: a need to align her knife, fork, and napkin just so; an obsession with keeping her clothes and her person spotless, and her hair, electric like her mother's, tightly braided. Despite all this, she was good company: intelligent, articulate, and sensitive.

While Isobel crackled with fretful intensity, her best friend, Gracie Falconer, loped through life with a bounce and a grin. She was, in every sense, her father's child, big-boned, auburn-haired, ruddily freckled, and effortlessly charming. Like her father, she seemed able to shrug off the slings and arrows without breaking a sweat.

It was a gift Blake Falconer must have been grateful for that night because his wife was clearly and publicly furious with him. At some point between Lily's water-skiing tour de force and dinner, the Falconers had apparently quarrelled, and their simmering war had drawn furtive glances all evening. Blake's efforts at peacemaking now were greeted with stony silence, and when he tried an offhanded hug, Lily removed his hand from her bronze shoulder with icy distaste. "I said I'd handle this, and I will," she said, and she looped her long black hair into a knot and stalked off to join Rose Lavallee.

Gracie watched her mother walk away, then wandered over to her father. Together, they tilted their heads to follow the trajectory of a pink and purple rocket. It was so spectacular that Gracie reached out exuberantly to hug her father.

"Cool," they said in unison; then laughed at the moment.

"Why can't she ever just see how nice everything is?" Gracie asked.

Blake shrugged and gave his daughter a rueful smile. "That," he said, "is a question I've asked myself for years."

As always, the fireworks were over too soon. The last star arced across the sky, the last lovely parabola of light faded, and the night was suddenly dark and cheerless. For a beat, we stood uncertainly, breathing in air wisped with smoke and pungent with bug spray. Then people began to fold blankets, collapse chairs, and say their goodbyes.

"Why does it have to be over so soon?" Taylor asked plaintively.

"Do you like riddles?" Chris Altieri's voice startled me. I had no idea he'd slipped away from Delia and joined us. He'd caught Taylor by surprise, too.

"Where did you come from?" she asked.

"I wanted to stand where I could get the best view of the big finish," he said.

"It was neat, eh?" Taylor said.

"Very neat," Chris said. "But you didn't answer my question. Do you like riddles?"

"Sure — as soon as someone tells me the answer," Taylor said. "My brother's a lot better at stuff like that than I am."

"Okay," Chris said. "Here's one to try on your brother. What three words can make you sad when you're happy and happy when you're sad?"

Taylor scrunched her forehead, gave it her best shot, and abandoned hope. The entire process was accomplished in less than a minute. "I give up," she said.

"I give up," Chris repeated thoughtfully. "Nope, those are not the three words I had in mind."

Taylor rewarded him with a laugh. "So what is the answer?"

Chris dropped to his knees so he could look at

my daughter face to face. "The three words are 'Nothing lasts forever.' Pretty good, huh?"

"Yeah," Taylor said. "I bet even Angus won't be able to figure that one out." Suddenly her interest was diverted. She leaned close to Chris so she could see his face more clearly. "You've got a cut," she said. She extended her finger tentatively, touched his eyebrow, then examined her fingertip. "It's blood."

Chris touched his eyebrow and checked his finger. "So it is," he said.

"What happened?" Taylor asked.

"I walked into a fist," Chris said.

Scuffles that ended in a bruise or a cut were not outside Taylor's realm of experience. "Well, you should clean it up and put some Polysporin on it," she said. "It makes it heal faster."

"Sounds like good advice," Chris said. "Thanks." He turned to me. "Are you an early riser?"

"My dog is. He and I run on the beach at five-thirty."

"Mind if I join you?"

"I'd like that," I said. I stepped closer. "Despite that accidental walking into a fist, you seem to be doing better."

Chris grinned and shrugged. "Nothing lasts forever. Remember?"

The cottage we were staying in was at the tip of the east arm of the horseshoe that was Lawyers' Bay. Built in the 1950s by Kevin Hynd's parents, Harriet and Russell, it was a dwelling with a thousand charms, and that night after Angus headed for his room above the boathouse and Leah and Taylor had gone to bed, I entered my bedroom with a sense of homecoming. I slept in the bed Harriet and Russell had shared, surrounded by photos of other summers at the lake and shelves of books containing their personal favourites: Virginia Woolf for her, Louis L'Amour for him. Everything I could wish for, yet that night as I slipped between the sunfresh sheets, I couldn't sleep. The windows were open, but no breeze stirred the filmy curtains. Oppressed by heavy air and sharp-edged memories, I tossed, turned, and finally picked up my pillow and headed for the screened porch.

Rectangles of light from the other cottages around the bay pierced the darkness. Apparently, I wasn't the only one struggling with sleeplessness. The opening notes of Bill Evans's incandescent "Waltz for Debbie" drifted from Zack Shreve's cottage. As I listened, I took the measure of my neighbours' blessings: money, success, health, and for troubled nights, a law partner who played piano with fluid beauty. Yet somehow this wasn't enough. I carried my pillow to the couch, lay down, closed my eyes, and pondered the universal truth that lay behind Gracie Falconer's question to her father: Why couldn't people just see how nice everything was?

I don't know how long I slept before I was jerked awake by a beam of light and the screech of tires peeling along the gravel road that led past our cottage to the boat launch. My first thought was that some kids had fuelled their Canada Day celebrations with one too many kegs, but the explanation didn't wash. Lawyers' Bay was a gated community. Nobody got in but us.

My heart pounded as I waited for a sign that the wayward car had headed home. But I heard nothing. When the splash came, there was no mistaking its significance. The car hit the water with a dull thud, and life moved into fast-forward. I jumped up and headed for the lake. It wasn't long before Angus caught up with me. Standing on the road in his jockey shorts, my son didn't look like a hero, but he had a hero's coolness. "I called 911, Mum, but it's going to take them a while to get out here. You and I will just have to do what we can."

The red roof of the car was still visible when Angus and I arrived on the scene.

"That looks like Chris Altieri's MGB," Angus said. There was no time to check out his assessment. The vehicle had apparently built up enough momentum to sail through the air before it hit. There was a sharp drop in the level of the lake bottom about ten metres from shore. The car had reached that point, and the dark waters were greedily swallowing their prize.

Before I could stop him, Angus dove off the dock and swam towards the spot where the car had gone under. In a heartbeat, he vanished too. Frozen with fear, I stared at the place where he'd disappeared.

When – finally – he surfaced, I could hear the panic in his voice. "I can't get to him, Mum."

"Is it Chris?" I asked.

"I guess so. I don't know. I need help. I can't open the door. Maybe if you spell me off . . ."

I didn't hesitate. I threw off my robe and dove in. The water had a familiar fishy-weedy smell, and in one of those synaptic leaps that fracture logic, I remembered another lake in another time when my friend Sally Love and I, poised on the cusp of adolescence, would go skinny-dipping, thrilled as cold water surrounded the new contours of our changing bodies.

That night, the only thrill was of terror. The world below was murky, and I could find my way only by touch. When a weed slithered against my leg, my fear was primal. Finally, my hand found metal. Blindly, I sought a handle. Like a beginner learning

Braille, I kept moving my fingers hoping to unlock the mystery. All I could feel was impenetrable steel. Finally, lungs on fire, I shot to the surface, and Angus went under again. We alternated dives until, exhausted and frustrated, I faced the truth. When Angus ducked to go back under, I grabbed his shoulder. "No," I said. "No more. It's over."

We swam to shore and clambered up the boat launch to the dubious safety of dry land. Shivering and breathless, we gulped air and stared ahead. In the distance a siren's shriek pierced the night. Help was on its way. I inched closer to my son.

Above us the uncaring moon moved through the sky, drawing a bright ribbon of light across the smooth expanse of water that covered all that remained of Christopher Altieri. The man of water had gone home.

CHAPTER 2

From the moment I met her, I had been a fan of Angus's girlfriend, Leah Drache. She was smart, funny, and original – a young woman with a blond bob and shiny brown eyes who charted her own course, but embraced anyone who chose to travel with her. The night of the drowning she was invaluable. The paramedics had convinced the police to let Angus and me go back to our cottage to towel off and get into dry clothes before they questioned us. Leah didn't hover, but she knew what we needed, and she offered it: hot tea with plenty of sugar, the softest towels, the thickest sweatshirts and socks. She seated everyone in the kitchen, the room farthest away from the room in which Taylor, innocent of the night's events, dreamed her summer dreams.

The RCMP confirmed my fear that the driver of the MGB was Chris Altieri, but beyond revealing his identity, they were tight-lipped. The officers who took our statements were smart enough to simply let us talk. They were professionals who recognized human limits, and they knew my son and I were on the edge. They also knew where to find us when the need for tough and close questioning arose.

After they left, Angus stood up, wrapped himself more tightly in his towel, and said he was leaving for his room over the boathouse. Leah was a woman who valued her space, and that summer she had opted for a room of her own in the cottage, but she loved my son and her tenderness as she reached for him brought a catch to my throat. "You shouldn't be alone tonight," she said. "I'll come with you." I went to my solitary bed envying them.

The physical exertion of the doomed recovery efforts had taken its toll, and I slept deeply. When I awoke, light was pooling on my bedroom floor and the scent of roses hung in the air. For a sliver of time, I was blissful; then with the suddenness of a cloud blocking the sun, Chris Altieri's face flashed into my consciousness. It took an act of will to plant my feet on the floor and take the first step that would begin the new day.

When I came into the kitchen, Leah was at the sink, rinsing dishes. She was wearing khaki shorts and a sleeveless white cotton blouse that showed off her tan. There was something achingly lovely about the way in which she performed this most commonplace of tasks, and I was grateful to her for offering me an anchor to moor me to the worka-day world.

She poured us both juice. "Rose Lavallee picked Taylor up about ten minutes ago. She thought the girls shouldn't have to see police all over the place, so she's taking them to Standing Buffalo. She's bringing them back at three-thirty." Leah handed me my glass. "Her sister's going to teach them how to knit."

"Our neighbours seem to take care of every-thing," I said.

Leah's brow furrowed with concern. "I'm sorry, Jo. I should have listened to Rose. She said I should wake you up to see if it was okay for Taylor to go, but I figured that, after last night, you'd want to sleep."

"You were right," I said, relenting. "And it'll be handy having a knitter around the house. This family goes through a lot of scarves and mitts." I sipped my juice. "How's Angus?"

"He seems okay," she said. "I'm glad we've got

the grand opening of Coffee Row today – keep him distracted."

"Your elderly gents are not going to lack conversational topics," I said.

Leah's smile was thin. "Half the town is probably out there already, sitting on the picnic benches, trading grisly details."

Coffee Row was Leah's answer to a quandary that had developed the week she and Angus started managing the Point Store. Stan Gardiner still lived over the business, and whenever the bell tinkled, announcing that a customer had come through the front door, Stan came down to visit. His continuing presence created a problem in both diplomacy and logistics.

The number of items cottagers believed essential to their existence had grown exponentially since the 1940s, when Stan's father had opened his store, but the square-footage inside the building hadn't increased. Despite Stan's best efforts, stock teetered on shelves and spilled onto the ubiquitous and universally despised display racks. Stock and fixtures weren't the only problems. A pitched battle had developed between the old men who had been meeting in front of the pop cooler at the Point Store since they were pups, and the sleek young matrons who presided over the huge summer homes that crowded the lakeshore. In a phrase, the issue was squatters' rights: the old men were for them, the young matrons were against them.

The situation into which Leah and Angus walked was fraught, but Leah had been quick to propose a solution. Her idea was simple: set up a few picnic tables under the old cottonwood trees at the side of the store, offer Stan's friends refreshments, and give the sleek matrons who were ready to pay top dollar for free-range chickens and anything labelled organic a clean, well-lit place in which to shop. Stan himself had selected the name for the new place. It would, he said, be called Coffee Row, because there was no point sticking a fancy name on something when you could call it what it was. The news that Coffee Row would be opening the Tuesday after the long weekend had been the number-one topic among the Point Store's customers for days. Chris Altieri's death meant there would be another story.

My son's girlfriend had a rare ability to scope out a situation, and that morning she was quick to take my measure. "I'm assuming you'd rather not talk about last night," she said.

"Anything but," I said. "Is everything under control for the grand opening?"

Leah pursed her lips. "Well, we're getting there. But I could use a little help with the refreshments. Since it's a special day, we're serving sandwiches: bologna and egg salad. Speaking of which . . ." She went to the fridge and removed a large ceramic bowl heaped with hard-boiled eggs. "Time for me to get crackin'."

We groaned in unison. "Nothing beats egg humour," I said.

Leah set the bowl on the table between us, and we began.

I had just finished peeling the last egg when Angus came in. He lolled against the doorway with his face screwed in an expression of distaste. "This place smells like farts. What are you guys doing?"

"Making lunch," I said, holding the bowl out to him.

Angus grabbed an egg. "Thanks," he said. "I'm starving."

"Got time to give your old mother a hug?" I asked. Leah took the bowl, and I drew my son close, savouring the coolness of his body and the dampness of his hair. Last night had been a sharp reminder that the threads linking us to those we love are fragile.

"It's okay, Mum," Angus said, breaking away. "I'm still here."

"Which is great," Leah said, "except that you should have been at the store twenty minutes ago. Got to wipe down those picnic tables, babe. Got to put on the oilcloth."

"Oilcloth?" I said.

"Mr. Gardiner had a bolt of it in his barn," Leah said. "It's brown-and-white checked – very retro."

"In that case, I'll love it," I said. "I'm pretty retro myself."

Leah picked up a pastry cutter and began moving it smartly through the bowl of hard-boiled eggs. "Come to the opening," she said. "Free food, and all the rotten coffee you can drink. I wanted to get beans from Roca Jacks, but Mr. Gardiner says his friends have been drinking floor sweepings all their lives and the good stuff would just confuse them."

It was a tempting invitation, but after Leah and Angus left, the energy seeped out of me. Heavy-limbed and gritty-eyed, I had the sense I was inhabiting a body that had been punished hard and long. As I sat at the kitchen table, staring at my coffee, my Bouvier, Willie, nudged me. His message was clear. We usually hit the beach by 5:45 at the latest. We were very, very late.

Willie followed me to the bedroom and stared as I pulled on shorts and a T-shirt. When I reached for my runners, he began to circle, then he directed me to his leash and the door. Bouviers do not rate high on the dog-intelligence scale, but when it came to his run, Willie fired up all the circuits.

It was a hot morning with a haze that hinted at the possibility of rain. Willie barked at the birds chilling out in Harriet Hynd's bird bath, then dragged me towards the horseshoe of beach that surrounded the bay. We were both committed to the routine, but it appeared Willie's dedication was of a deeper order than mine. The last sight I wanted to see on that tranquil July morning was the spot where Chris Altieri had died, but neither death nor trauma deterred Willie. As he had since we arrived, my dog headed straight for the dock beside the boat ramp.

The vehicles used in the investigation had chewed up the beach badly, and the dock was muddy and lashed with weeds, but the lake itself was as flat and benign as a plate. My throat tightened. I jerked Willie's leash. "Time to go," I said.

Running helped. It was a haiku day, worthy of seventeen syllables of celebration, and my endorphins were pumping. Survival seemed possible until I spotted the gazebo. I froze. Willie cocked his head, awaiting the next development. I reached down and gave him a reassuring pat; then, obeying an impulse I didn't understand, I led him along the beach towards the overhang of land where the gazebo had been built.

One of Noah Wainberg's most eloquent pieces hung like a figure on a ship's prow from the base of the structure. The carving was of a woman, seemingly a prisoner, her hands tied behind her back, her legs long and graceful, her breasts full, her face gentle but filled with an ancient and private sorrow. I had jogged past the carving for a week, but I had never seen it from this angle, and it was compelling. I reached out and touched the curve of her arm. Sun-heated, the wood was warm as flesh.

"Noah used my body as his model for the piece." The voice was husky and low. It was Lily Falconer's. I turned to face her. She'd been jogging, too. Her face was slick with sweat and her long hair had come loose. It fell against her shoulders – brush strokes of black against the glowing bronze of her skin. Her shorts and halter were the colour of pale jade, but they too were sweat-stained. "I need to talk to you," she said.

I gestured towards the gazebo. "Maybe we should go in there, get out of the sun."

She shook her head vehemently. "No. Let's just go down to the beach." She reached down and snapped off Willie's leash. "Your dog wants to play in the water."

Free at last, Willie bounded into the lake. Out-manoeuvred, I followed him.

When we came to the beach, Lily dropped to the sand and lay on her back, arms flung wide, palms up, legs sprawled, eyes closed. She was absolutely without self-consciousness. As I looked at her toned body and endless legs, I knew that if I had a body like hers, I wouldn't be timid either.

She didn't waste time on preamble. "I heard that you and your son tried to save Chris. We're all grateful for that."

"I wish the outcome had been different," I said.

"If wishes were horses, then beggars could ride." There was an edge in Lily's voice, the pragmatist correcting the dreamer. "Chris is dead, Joanne. All we can do now is keep things from getting worse."

A seagull swooped down and snagged something from the water. Willie, unaware that his mission was futile, paddled to the spot where the bird had been.

"I agree," I said. "Has something happened?"

Lily pushed herself up on her elbows and met my gaze. "There's a police officer named Alex Kequahtooway who wants to talk to you. From what I understand, you won't need to be introduced."

Her announcement had the force of a punch in the stomach. She was right. Inspector Alex Kequahtooway and I didn't need an introduction.

For three years, he had been my lover, and our parting had not been amicable.

"No," I said. "The inspector and I are acquainted."

"Then you know you can trust him."

"I know I can trust him professionally," I said.

A hint of a smile passed her lips. "Well, that's all that matters here, isn't it?"

"Lily, what is it exactly that you want me to do?"

"Tell the truth," she said. "Answer the questions you're asked but don't introduce anything extraneous. Alex says —"

"*Alex?*" I said.

"We go way back." She wiped her forehead with the back of her hand. "That sun's hot."

"Maybe we should move."

In a movement as fluid as an athlete's, Lily stood up. For a beat, she stared at the horizon. "No, we're finished here. Just remember that none of us knows for sure just what happened last night. Don't say anything that will muddy the waters."

I scrambled to my feet. "I'm pretty good at keeping my focus," I said.

Lily's grey eyes bored into mine. "Good," she said. "That'll make it easier all around, won't it?" She picked up the leash and whistled. Willie had not distinguished himself at obedience school, but he came to Lily immediately. She rubbed his head, snapped on the collar, and offered me the leash. "Chris's death was an accident," she said. "A terrible, terrible accident." Her tone was without emotion — like that of a schoolgirl reciting by rote words that were beyond her comprehension.

When Willie and I got back to the cottage, Alex Kequahtooway's silver Audi was in the driveway. I swore softly. I was depleted, without resources to examine a night that was still a fresh wound. There was something else, and it did not reflect well on me. The accident and its aftermath had battered me to the core, but apparently my vanity had survived. As I walked by the Audi, the rear-view mirror was in easy proximity, but I didn't bend down to give myself a quick once-over. There was no point. I knew I looked like hell.

Alex was sitting in one of the rockers on the front porch. I hadn't seen him since Christmas. He'd been involved in a difficult case then, and I'd chalked up his pallor and weight loss to overwork and stress. But the man in the rocker was suffering from something beyond too many late nights and too much caffeine. His eyes were closed and his head was resting against the wicker back of the rocker. His lethargy was a shock. Alex had always been driven, a dynamo who could grab a few hours' sleep and

function well. That morning, he looked as if something had hollowed him out. I called his name.

When he heard my voice, he opened his eyes and
then raised his head slowly. "You're okay?" he said.

"I will be," I said.

"And Angus?"

"He's remarkably resilient – as you well know."

"Jo, how did you and the kids get mixed up with
these people?"

"I explained that to the officers we talked to last
night. We're renting a cottage here for the summer."

"And your landlord is Kevin Hynd, the hippie
lawyer."

"I see him more as Kevin Hynd, the loyal friend,"
I said.

Alex flushed. The reference to loyalty had been
a zinger. We'd broken up when Alex had become
involved with another woman. Despite the hit, he
soldiered on. "The storefront law business must be
booming if Mr. Hynd was able to take off for parts
unknown," he said.

"They're known to me," I said. "Kevin is in
Tibet, half a world away from Lawyers' Bay. He's
not connected with this."

"Maybe not," Alex said. "But patterns are always
provocative. It would be interesting to know why

Mr. Hynd keeps walking away – first from a partnership in a highly lucrative law practice, now from his storefront office. Something seems to be making him uneasy."

"This conversation is making me uneasy," I said. "If you have questions about last night, I'll answer them. Otherwise, I'm going inside to take a shower."

"Okay, let's get started." Surprisingly, Alex made no movement to get his notebook and pen. "Something in your statement caught my eye. You said you were sleeping out here last night. Any special reason?"

"It was hot. It had been a full day, and my mind was racing. Monkey thoughts, my yoga instructor would say."

"You're still going to yoga?"

"Inner peace takes time."

Alex smiled. "You seem to be moving in the right direction. You look good, Jo."

The air between us was heavy with things unsaid, but I was in no mood for a trip down memory lane. "We were talking about the accident," I said.

The warmth went out of Alex's face. "All right, then why don't you take another run at your story? Somehow, it just doesn't feel right to me."

My account of what had happened the night before was truthful and, except on one point, meticulous. As I had in my first interview, I hurried over my conversation with Chris Altieri. When Alex didn't challenge me, I thought I was home free. I was wrong. He might not have been super-cop any more, but he hadn't lost his touch. When I'd finished, he took out his notebook and uncapped his pen. "Interesting," he said. "Now why don't you tell me everything you know about Christopher Altieri."

"There's not much to tell," I said. "Twenty-four hours ago Christopher Altieri was just a name to me – there must have been dozens of people at that party who knew him better than I did."

"You're probably right, but so far we're coming up empty. The peripheral people – clients, friends, other cottagers – are anxious to help, but all they say is that he was a great guy. The people who should have known him best – the juniors in the law firm, the partners and their spouses – aren't saying anything. That leaves you."

"And I have nothing to say."

The life had come back into Alex's obsidian eyes. "I think you do," he said. "I hear you had a one-on-one talk with Mr. Altieri last night."

"You'd be wrong to attach any significance to that," I said.

"Would I?" Alex made no attempt to hide his skepticism.

"It was a party. Lots of people were having one-on-one talks."

"But you were the only person who had a one-on-one talk with the man who was about to die."

"Alex, if you're asking me whether Chris told me anything that explains the way his life ended, the answer is no. Nothing else is germane. Why don't you just let him rest in peace?"

For an awkwardly long time, we held one another's gaze. Alex looked away first. "I wish to God I could let this rest in peace, Jo, but I can't."

In all our time together, I had never seen Alex appear frightened, but in that moment I knew there was something he was afraid of. "Alex, what's wrong?"

He didn't answer. Instead, he walked to the window and turned his back to me. "When I was growing up, I was out on this lake every day, swimming, canoeing, fishing, playing hockey. I knew it the way I knew my own body. These people have changed everything – cleared away all the brush, gouged the hills, bulldozed paths, transplanted the grasses that were here to places where they thought some indigenous grass might make them look culturally sensitive. Everything's for appearance.

This land means nothing to them. It's just another playground."

Suddenly I was furious. "Alex, you sound like a retread from the sixties. You hated living at Standing Buffalo. You left as soon as you could. You went to police college in the city, you got a job, and as far as I could see you never looked back."

"Maybe that was a mistake," he said softly. "Maybe we all would have been better off just staying where we were."

"Who is this *we* you're talking about? You've never divided the world into them and us before."

"Maybe that was a mistake too."

"Were you and I a mistake?"

Pain knifed his face, but he didn't offer any reassurance that our three years together had been worthwhile. "Just be careful, Jo. You may be new to Lawyers' Bay, but I'm not. I know these people. If anything comes up, you've got my number."

"Yes," I said. "I've got your number." The bitterness in my voice surprised even me.

A cloud of dust almost obscured the silver Audi as it sped up the road, but I was still able to see that, instead of heading straight for the highway, the car turned into the Falconers' driveway. I had a pretty good idea about the purpose of Alex's visit. Lily

Falconer had been born and raised on the Standing Buffalo reserve too. Alex's epiphany that blood was thicker than water had clearly prompted him to remind Lily that, in this world, there were two camps, and the wise stayed with their own kind.

Showered, splashed with my Mother's Day extravagance of Bulgari, and wearing a polo shirt, slacks, and sandals, I arrived at Coffee Row just as the festivities were about to begin. There was a buzz when I arrived. I had, after all, been part of the drama the night before, but my star was eclipsed the moment Leah poured the ceremonial first cup of java and presented it to Stan Gardiner. No doubt about it, this was a big event. The photographer from the town paper was there, so were the reeve of the municipality and the three candidates contesting the riding in the next provincial election. Clearly, the combination of free food, bad coffee, and a homegrown tragedy was impossible to resist. Stan had made certain that his guests were seated at the picnic tables intended for them. Latecomers had to make do with sitting on the grass. No one – not even the sleek young matrons – seemed to mind. The risk of a grass stain was a small price to pay for inside dope on the tragedy.

I'd planned to help serve the food, but a gaggle of pre-teen girls beat me to the punch. Cheerful as bees, they glided among the tables in their bright summer shorts and tops, offering sandwiches and cookies, teasing and getting teased. I was less merry. Even bologna and mustard on Wonder Bread couldn't banish the images of the night before. There was something else. Out of deference to my involvement in the tragedy, a sprightly gent with a walker had offered me his place at the picnic table nearest Stan and his friends. Eavesdropping was unavoidable, and what I heard did not improve my mood. The situation was as sizzling as the day, and as they hosed one another down with their theories, Stan Gardiner and his friends were gleeful.

Stan himself opened the discussion. "A lot goes on down there at Lawyers' Bay that they don't want people to know about. Why else would they have put up them gates out front?"

The question may have been rhetorical, but that didn't stop the man on Stan's left. After a meditative pull on his Player's Plain, he floated an answer. "Sex, drugs, and rock and roll – that's what they're into." He sucked back another lungful, cackled himself into a coughing fit, wiped his mouth smartly on his hanky, and continued. "Key parties, wife swapping, cocaine – they do it all."

The man across from him made a moue of disgust. "Jesus, Morris, if you don't cut out cigarettes, they're gonna kill you."

"I'm eighty-five, George," the smoker said reasonably. "Something's going to kill me."

"Better sooner than later," George said. "When you spew garbage like that about a decent man you make me impatient. That Chris Altieri was a nice young fella. When he was at the lake, he used to drive into town to Mass every day – real religious."

Morris was unconvinced. "You don't go to church every goddamned day unless you've done something wrong. If that Altieri guy was such a choirboy, why was that Indian cop sniffin' around here all winter?"

George was judicious. "A cop isn't just a cop. He's a man, too. And a man can have reasons to sniff around that don't have anything to do with his job."

"I get your meaning," Morris said.

"So do I," Stan Gardiner said. "And enough's enough. There are women and children around. One thing I know, nobody sniffed around when Harriet Hynd was alive. She was a lady through and through, and Russell Hynd was a gentleman. No gates on the bay in their time."

Coffee Row was still on full perk when I left. My cottage, empty of children and responsibilities, was

mercifully stimulant free, and I welcomed the tranquillity. I was bone-tired, and I needed to be alone.
As they always seemed to, the members of the
Winners' Circle had anticipated my needs. Taylor
was one of the delights of my life, but that day I was
relieved that Rose Lavallee had taken my daughter
under her wing. Rose was so tiny that she could
have bought her clothes in the pre-teen department
at the Bay, but there was no doubting her common
sense and reliability. I made myself a cup of Earl
Grey, picked up Harriet's copy of *To the Lighthouse*,
and read until the mid-afternoon shadows danced
across the ceiling. By the time the kitchen clock
struck three, I had wearied of the grace with which
Mrs. Ramsay presided over the seashells, bird skulls,
and conflicting needs of her sons, daughters, and
friends. I wanted a protagonist in my own image, a
woman who was grateful none of her kids were
around to watch her sulk over an old lover who
apparently had wasted no time before he began
sniffing around for a shiny new replacement after
he'd dumped her.

Annoyed by my self-pity, I put Mrs. Ramsay
back on the shelf and went to the kitchen to check
out the possibilities for dinner. Rose was bringing
Taylor home at three-thirty. Knowing my daughter,

she'd be keen for a swim. If I got dinner started, she and I could take our time at the beach.

I might have been unlucky in love, but I was lucky in the kitchen. I'd been at the farmers' market the day before and picked up a basket of tomatoes, some fresh basil, and a block of Taylor's favourite white cheddar. I had a loaf of wild-rice bread in the freezer. Taylor loved smoked tomato soup. A mug of soup and a grilled cheese sandwich would be just the ticket after we came back from the lake.

I'd just finished chiffonading the basil when Rose and the girls came in. Isobel Wainberg was carrying a Zellers bag from which only the tips of her knitting needles protruded, but Taylor and Gracie were waving their handiwork like flags.

"Look at this," Taylor said, shoving six inches of a hyacinth scarf towards me. "Isn't this great? The very first thing I ever knitted. Rose's sister, Betty, says I took to it like a duck to water."

Gracie swung her creation from side to side. Her knitting, large-looped and irregular, flopped dispiritedly. She laughed. "Betty says I have many other talents."

"You do," Isobel said loyally. "You don't always worry about doing everything perfectly. That's a talent."

"And," Taylor added, "you can shoot hoops better than Angus. Now, who wants to eat?"

The girls raced to the kitchen, leaving Rose and me behind. "Can I get you something?" I asked. "Some tea or a cold drink?"

Rose looked critically at a loose button on her sundress. "I appreciate the thought," she said, "but you don't have to entertain me. I'm happy just to sit."

"Me too," I said. "And thanks to you, I got to sit all afternoon. Taylor obviously had a great time."

Rose snapped off the errant button. "I'll take care of you when I get home," she said, popping the button in her pocket. She turned her attention to me. "That girl of yours surprised me today," she said. "She's a free spirit, and free spirits are hard to rein in — not that you want to. All the same, it makes it easier for everybody when they find something that they like to do. Your girl really concentrated on her knitting. She's got an idea that she wants to knit a bedcover made of squares. She drew what she wanted so Betty could help her with the patterns. They were interesting — all different kinds of fish and shells. Your girl has a knack."

"Taylor's birth mother was an artist," I said. "Her name was Sally Love. She was brilliant, and when we were growing up, she was my closest friend. After she died, I adopted Taylor."

"So the gift was passed down. It isn't always," Rose said. She picked up the knitting that Gracie Falconer had abandoned and smiled at the loose, loopy stitches. "You can tell a lot about a person by the way she knits. I taught this one's mother. From the first day, she never dropped a stitch. She never has."

We were silent, listening to the laughter drift from the other room. "So you've known Lily for a long time."

"All her life," Rose said. "We're from the same reserve."

"And Alex Kequahtooway?"

Rose's jaw tightened. "I know him," she said.

"Were he and Lily friends when she was growing up?"

"On a reserve everybody knows everybody," Rose said. Her mouth snapped shut like a coin purse. Clearly there'd be no more revelations coming my way today. "Remember that old saying, 'Curiosity killed the cat'?" she said.

"My grandmother used to tell me that when I was sticking my nose in where it didn't belong."

"Well, I'm saying it to you now." Rose picked up Gracie's knitting and Isobel's Zellers bag. "Thanks for the visit. It's good to get to know new people."

CHAPTER 3

I n the days before the funeral, the partners of
Falconer Shreve stayed at the lake, grieving,
planning, and cleaving to one another. It was rare
to see any of them alone. The weather had turned
hot, and Lawyers' Bay was enveloped by a kind of
hazy unease as we waited for the heat to break and
for the funeral that would rescue us from the limbo
into which Chris Altieri's death had banished us.
Life went on, but there was sadness in the summer
air. There was also uncertainty. The police hadn't
yet ruled out the possibility that Chris's death had
been an accident; however, their search for a suicide
note had proved fruitless. Without a Rosetta stone
to unlock the mystery of why a man who had everything to live for would choose to die, questions
persisted, painful as a troubling tooth. Why would a

man who loved his friends so deeply leave no explanation for an act that he knew would plunge them into confusion and painful self-examination?

And given that Chris Altieri's death was a suicide, why were the police investigating the tragedy with such thoroughness? Alex Kequahtooway's silver Audi was much in evidence. More than once I saw it turn into Lily Falconer's driveway. It never turned into mine. On Coffee Row, rumours grew like mushrooms after a three-day rain. Distracted, the people of Lawyers' Bay went through the motions of life at a summer cottage, and I came to know my neighbours.

Taylor, Gracie, and Isobel had become inseparable, and that meant Rose Lavallee and I were drawn together too. From the moment I met her, I liked and trusted Gracie's nanny, but Taylor was one of the joys of my middle age and I wasn't about to miss a summer with her. And so when Rose and the girls went off on adventures, I tagged along, and after her initial surprise, Rose seemed to welcome my presence. When the girls decided they wanted to learn how to dive from the tower, Rose and I took on the task together.

The arrangement worked well. At seventy, Rose had a face that bore the chisel marks of time, but her body was wiry, and what she didn't know about dealing with young girls wasn't worth knowing. She was, Taylor confided, very strict about bathing suits. That summer, prepubescent girls who still had trouble keeping track of their retainers were wearing the skimpiest of string bikinis, suits designed to entice with provocative peeks at budding breasts and belly-button rings. My daughter and I had had a stormy exchange on the second floor of the Bay about how much of her was going to be on display that summer. When I saw Gracie and Isobel in their functionally cut navy Spandex one-piece suits, I knew Rose was my kind of woman.

The diving lessons turned out to be a boon for me as well as for the girls. Climbing the tower, testing the spring of the board, then plunging into the dark, inscrutable waters and counting on muscle memory to guide me back into sunlight proved to be surprisingly therapeutic. And Rose was good company: silent unless something needed to be said. Neither of us returned to the subject of Alex, Lily, or the old days at Standing Buffalo. At some level, we both recognized that our friendship was too new and too fragile to withstand a blast from the past.

That didn't mean that blasts weren't in the offing. One morning, just after Rose and I had swum back from the tower and were sitting on the dock watching the girls, Blake Falconer appeared. His red-gold hair was cut scrub-brush short for summer, and his skin was ruddy with the sunburn of a weekend sailor. In his shorts, runners, and University of Saskatchewan sweatshirt, he had the breezy confidence of a man who had spent his college years being envied by men and longed for by women. Not the kind of person who usually made my Christmas-card list, yet Kevin had told me that, next to Chris, Blake was his closest friend.

He tossed us a smile. "You can take off now, Rose," he said. "Joanne and I can watch the girls."

Rose adjusted the strap on her ancient turquoise Jantzen. "I'm staying put," she said. "Visit around me."

Blake's eyes widened, then he laughed. "You and my wife," he said. "The only two women I know who find me utterly without redeeming features." He pointed to my towel. "Mind if I sit down?"

"Not at all," I said. But I did. He sat close, so close that I could smell the sharp citrus of his aftershave and see how the sun burnished the red-gold hair on his arms and legs. Too much proximity. I inched away.

Blake didn't seem to notice. "We haven't been able to reach Kevin to tell him about Chris," he said. "Lily thought there was an outside chance he might have been in touch with you."

"I would have told you," I said. "I know you and Kevin are close."

"That's nice to hear right now." Blake's voice was gravelly. "It was always Kevin, Chris, and me against Zack, Delia, and Lily."

I thought I'd misheard. Lily wasn't a partner. She wasn't even a lawyer. She managed the office.

Without taking her eyes off the diving board, Rose reached over and tapped Blake's shoulder. "Button your lip," she said.

"Yes, ma'am," Blake said, and he touched his thumb and forefinger to his mouth and made a tweaking gesture.

"Keep it that way," Rose said. Something she saw on the lake displeased her, and she frowned. "Your daughter's entry was a little sloppy," she said, glancing over at Blake. "She'll have to fix it or she'll never be as good as she could be." Rose stood and brushed the sand from her thighs. "Remember to watch your mouth, mister," she said, then she strode towards the lake – a trim figure of rectitude in a slovenly world.

Blake watched her with a rueful smile. "Not much point hanging around since I've been issued a gag order," he said. He stood up. "If you hear from Kevin, let me know. We should be the ones to break the news about Chris. We might be able to keep him from blaming himself."

"Why would he blame himself?" I asked.

"Same reason we all do. We're Chris's family. We should have been able to pull him back from the edge."

"The last time I saw Chris, I thought he *had* pulled himself back from the edge," I said.

Blake's blue-grey eyes were searching. "What do you mean?"

"When I talked to him after the barbecue, Chris was in bad shape, but after the fireworks he seemed better. He asked if he could run with my dog and me in the morning. He even taught Taylor a riddle: 'What three words make you sad when you're happy and happy when you're sad?'"

Blake's voice was a whisper. "And the answer is . . . ?"

I swallowed hard. "Nothing lasts forever."

"It just keeps getting worse, doesn't it?" Blake said, then he walked off without waiting for my reply.

After lunch at our cottage, Rose and the girls went over to the tennis court to hit balls, and I cleaned up and took Virginia Woolf out to the rocker on the porch. Taylor's cats, Bruce and Benny, were already curled up in their cat beds; Willie sniffed them incuriously, then flopped down by my feet. We were all settled in for a lazy afternoon when the first clap of thunder came. The cats ran inside and Willie's ears shot up. By the time the second clap of thunder sounded and lightning split the sky, Rose and the girls were through the door.

"Now what?" Taylor said.

"Dry clothes," said Rose.

"And an afternoon off for Rose," I said. When she started to protest, I raised my hand. "I insist. The girls can spend the afternoon here. I have no plans, and we have a cupboard full of board games. I know I saw Monopoly in there and Trivial Pursuit and Risk."

Gracie was towelling off her explosion of curly red-blond hair. She peered out from under the towel. "I'd forgotten about the games," she said. She tapped Isobel's arm. "Remember how Kevin used to let us play with all his old action figures when the adults played Risk?"

"That was before," Isobel said.

"Before what?" Taylor said, always alert to nuance.

Isobel and Gracie exchanged a quick look. "Before the adults stopped having fun," Isobel said.

"I'm for Monopoly," Gracie said quickly. "But if

we're going to get in an entire game before the rain stops, we'd better bounce. Monopoly takes about a thousand years."

Willie and I spent the afternoon on the porch contemplating the rain and listening to the whoops of delight and misery that erupted in the living room as real-estate empires rose and fell. We were content. When I glanced up and saw Noah and Delia Wainberg walking down the road towards our cottage, I felt a frisson of annoyance.

"Company, Willie," I said.

His glance was mournful. Seemingly, he was no more eager to entertain than I was. But the Wainbergs were Isobel's parents and our neighbours, and as they trudged through the rain, it would have taken a harder heart than mine not to welcome them. Delia was wearing the same black slacks and T-shirt she'd been wearing at the fireworks, and she was even more tightly wound than she'd been that night. Her short black hair was spiky, as if she hadn't thought to comb it. She was pulling nervously on her cigarette, the way serious smokers do when they're about to enter what they fear may be a no-smoking zone. Clearly, this was a day when it wasn't much fun being Delia Wainberg.

As they neared my house, Noah Wainberg extended a large strong hand towards the back of his wife's neck and kneaded it. At his touch, Delia's head dropped to her chest and her shoulders relaxed. Husband and wife did not exchange glances, but it was a moment of exquisite intimacy. So often that week it had appeared to me that the awkward, amiable giant, Noah, was simply an extra in the high-powered drama that starred his wife and her partners. I'd been wrong. Noah was an essential supporting player.

I invited them inside and offered fresh coffee. When Isobel heard her parents' voices, she came running. "I don't have to go home yet, do I?"

Noah held his arms out to her. "No, Izzy. Your mother and I are just here on an errand. You can stay until Mrs. Kilbourn boots you out."

Isobel beamed at her father, blew a kiss his way, and ran back to Monopoly. In his gentle presence, Isobel was sunshine, a child of smiles and lilting laughter. With her mother, she withdrew, as if to shield herself from something sharp and spiny that might, at any moment, be flung at her from Delia's direction. When she left the room without acknowledging her mother, neither of them seemed to notice the slight.

The Wainbergs turned down my offer of coffee, but when I asked if I could get them anything else, Delia looked so longingly at the tiny shoulder bag in which I guessed she'd stowed her cigarettes and lighter that I volunteered to get her an ashtray. It took a bit of searching, but I finally found one on the porch. It was handmade: a shallow bowl of mosaic tile grouted together not very skilfully with an old silver dollar stuck in the middle.

Delia smiled when I handed it to her. "Kevin made this when he was a kid," she said. "Amazing he didn't pursue a career in fine art." She pulled out a cigarette, lit up, and dragged gratefully. "God, it's been a lousy week."

Her voice cracked like an adolescent boy's, and Noah cast her an anxious glance. "We'd better get this over with," he said. "Delia and the others were going to put Chris's graduation portrait from law school in the funeral program, but now they've decided they'd like to have a photo of all of them."

"Of the Winners' Circle," I said.

Delia nodded. "The problem is we can't find a good one. Everybody's always been too busy to put things in albums, and of course we thought we had forever." She ran a hand over her eyes. "Noah remembered that Mrs. Hynd put our summer pictures in her albums. Can we dig around a little and see what we come up with?"

The albums were stored in a bookcase in my bedroom. I led the Wainbergs in and flicked on the light. "Dig away," I said, then I went back to check on the girls.

Interest in Monopoly was waning. The board bristled with hotels, and from the stacks of neatly ordered bills and properties in front of Isobel, her victory seemed imminent. Taylor had already folded. Gracie threw the dice with great sang-froid and whooped when she landed on a heavily built up Park Place. "That's it for me," she said. "I'm outta here."

"Good," Taylor said. "Because the rain has stopped and this is getting boring. Let's get back into our wet clothes and go out and run through puddles." She looked uneasily at her friends. "Is running through puddles immature?"

Gracie shrugged. "Not if it's fun."

When the Wainbergs came back, I was glad the girls weren't in the room. Delia was clutching a photo album, and her eyes and the tip of her nose were red from crying.

"You found something," I said.

Delia placed the album on the table and opened it to a large black-and-white photo. "Our first summer at Lawyers' Bay. We used to camp out on the beach, and when it rained we'd grab our sleeping bags and head for Hynds' cottage."

I picked up my glasses so I could get a closer look. All the members of the Winners' Circle were there: Delia, Kevin, Chris, Blake, and, in the middle, Zack Shreve. They were up to their waists in water – Zack, too. He'd wheeled out so far that the lower part of his chair was submerged. Squinting into the sun, their faces suffused with joy, they were incredibly appealing.

The girls drifted back in and draped themselves around our chairs to look at the photograph. Isobel Wainberg looked at her mother through lowered lashes. "You were beautiful, Mum," she breathed.

"Everybody was beautiful then," Delia said. She shook her head as if to bring herself back to the present. "Beautiful and smart. Why weren't we smart enough to know that it was too good to last?" Without explanation she pushed open the screen door and walked away.

Isobel's eyes didn't stray from the picture. "Mum looks so different," she said.

"She was different," Noah said simply.

"What happened?" Isobel asked.

Noah looked puzzled. "I don't know. It was like dominoes. One thing went wrong, then everything went wrong."

Isobel's gaze was piercing. "What was the first thing?"

Noah bent over the album. His big hands were not made for delicate work, and there was something poignant about the care with which he removed the photo from its plastic sheath. "There's no use talking about it, Izzy. Talk never changes anything." He brightened. "Look, I'm supposed to drive this picture into town to get it enlarged. There's a pizza place near the 50 Minute Photo. Why don't we grab us a pie?"

Taylor dug her fingers into my arm. "Please?"

"Okay," I said. I picked up my purse. "Why don't you go crazy and hit the Dairy Queen, too?"

That night, Leah and Angus decided they needed some quality time. They rented videos and retreated to the room over the boathouse. That left the cottage free for a sleepover, so Taylor and I invited Gracie and Isobel to stay the night. I'd driven into town with Noah and the girls. He had done his best at the pizza joint, but despite the food and the girls' exuberance, Noah had been distracted. It occurred to me that he and Delia could use a little quality time too.

It had been a long day, but deep-dish all-dressed pizza and Peanut Buster Parfaits had refuelled the girls. As soon as we got back, they leaped out of the car and raced over to Falconers' to pick up CDs and Gracie's stash of gift-with-purchase makeup. They were back in a flash, cranking up the music and slathering on the makeup that transformed them from beautiful sunburned children into voguing young women with purple eye shadow and edge. It was a painful portent of things to come, and I lasted less than ten minutes before I withdrew to my bedroom.

Harriet Hynd's photo albums were arranged chronologically. My fingers lingered over several of them, but I settled on the summer of 1973, the year my first child, Mieka, was born. Harriet had arranged the photographs with an archivist's precision. Beneath each picture, the particulars of the subject and the occasion were described in her small neat hand. In truth, the pictures didn't require text. Photos like them could have been found in albums in tens of thousands of Canadian homes. A man with shoulder-length hair and a beard grinned as he fired up a Hibachi; a woman wearing a peasant dress and a silver-and-turquoise necklace held up a birthday cake for the camera. A young boy – clearly Kevin – sat surrounded by birthday booty: a pile of action figures for his superhero collection. Moments in time, as ordinary as they were irrecoverable.

In the living room, Taylor and her friends danced and dreamed to the music of their own time. My camera was slung over the doorknob. I put down Harriet's album, picked up the faithful Kodak, and headed into the living room. The girls of summer deserved to be immortalized.

The night of Chris Altieri's wake, the beautiful cars started arriving just after suppertime. The sun slanted in the sky, picking up the metallic sheen of BMWs, Porsches, Jaguars, and Mercedeses as they purred through the gates to Lawyers' Bay. The event was being held at Zack Shreve's home. It was a shrewd choice for a wake. With its large uncluttered spaces painted in cool monochromatic greys, it militated against an overheating of emotion. The furniture in the house was simple and expensive, the art spare, original, and arresting – abstracts in rust and silver. Both furnishings and art had the patina of unobjectionable good taste that only a fine decorator with a blank cheque can bring to a living space. The only personal touches were the piano – a concert-sized Steinway – and, oddly, a collection of moths mounted in shadow boxes on the wall.

The piano dominated the room and Zack was seated at it, playing, when we arrived. The music was light and unobtrusive, yet it kept everyone in the room aware of the pianist's presence. Seemingly, Zack's skill at playing a crowd equalled his skill at the Steinway. When he caught me watching him, Zack winked conspiratorially, and I remembered a lawyer friend's telling anecdote about an encounter she'd had with him. She was appearing opposite him in court, and when his case began to go badly, he hunched his shoulders and drew back into himself, in her words "defying the jury to kick the cripple." The tactic paid off. Zack won his case, and the next morning he'd sent my friend a box of the Bernard Callebaut truffles she favoured and a copy of *Richard III*.

No doubt about it, Zachary Shreve was a man who knew how to control events. As he moved effortlessly through the tunes in the Rodgers and Hart songbook, I wondered what outcome he was seeking from this party. As it always was at Lawyers' Bay, the *mise en scène* was flawless. A brief and intense shower late in the afternoon had cooled the air and left a lingering smell of wet wood. The dinner was planked salmon, and when guests arrived, the barbecues were smoking. In the meantime there were delights: plates of baguettes and thinly sliced black bread to accompany bowls of feta cheese splashed with olive oil and sprinkled with fresh oregano and dried red peppers, marinated artichoke hearts, tangy radishes, crisp and rolled in butter and salt, olives seemingly from every port on the Mediterranean. It was a feast fit for a king, and there was no doubt that Zack Shreve was presiding.

He announced dinner, directed us towards our places at the tables that had been set on the lawn, then moved among us as we talked of the usual things people talk of at barbecues: the triumphs, tragedies, and love lives of ourselves and others, then, as the wine flowed, the meaning of it all.

After we'd finished eating, Zack summoned us back into the house where the caterers poured brandy and people steeled themselves for the painful task of remembering the man who wasn't there. When we all had a glass in hand, Blake Falconer offered a simple toast; then, as we raised our glasses and murmured Chris's name, Zack began to play a heart-stoppingly poignant song. It, too, was Rodgers and Hart, and it was about a man who brought the sun but didn't stick around to enjoy it. The title was "He Was Too Good to Me," and Zack played with shimmering intimacy. When the last note died, the room was silent. Finally, a blonde with a deep fake-and-bake tan, and the unfocused eyes of a woman who had drunk well if not wisely, cuffed Zack on the arm. "How can you be such a bastard in the courtroom and play piano like that?" she asked.

Zack picked up his snifter, drained it, and smiled. "You know what they say about Miles Davis. He played the way he'd have liked to be."

The woman splayed her hands on the piano and leaned towards Zack. "We've had enough show tunes," she said. "I have a request."

"I aim to please," Zack said smoothly. "What'll it be?"

"Anything by Paul Anka," the woman said.

Zack's smile grew deadly. "So many possibilities," he said. "Since your name is Kim, 'Diana' doesn't work. 'Puppy Love'? Hardly. With respect, I believe we'd both agree that you've wagged good-bye to your puppy days. I personally have been present at the kickoff of three of your marriages, so the sheen of 'I Went to Your Wedding' has grown a little tarnished. How about that old Frank Sinatra showstopper 'My Way'?"

Kim pouted. "I hate that song." Leaning over the piano, heedless of the breasts spilling out of her silk halter-top, she was visited by inspiration. "Play 'Havin' My Baby.'"

Zack bowed to her. "A provocative choice, madam," he said. "But your wish is my command." He placed his fingers on the keys and played the opening bars of "Havin' My Baby." After a moment of astonished silence, people began to sing along, tentatively at first, then as liquor released inhibitions, lustily. Kim's choice was cruelly ironic, but it did the job.

"Havin' My Baby" was as remote from Noel Coward as it was possible to be, but as one who understood "the potency of cheap music," Coward would have recognized the phenomenon taking place in that room. An old and cheaply sentimental song was melting the ice of grief and releasing real emotion. When the music was done, people began – finally – to talk about what they had lost. Nowhere in their remembrances was there a hint of the spectral sadness I'd seen in the man in the gazebo. Their Christopher Altieri was a man of joy and shuddering energy, warm, thoughtful, funny, brilliant. As I picked up my coffee cup, I found myself wishing that I had known him.

The funeral was at three o'clock Saturday afternoon, but I drove into the city just after breakfast. I was alone. Saturdays were the Point Store's busiest days. It would have been difficult for Leah and Angus to get away, and there was no particular reason why they should. Fate had spun Angus into the vortex of Chris Altieri's death, but my son had not been a part of Chris's life. Taylor had stayed behind, too. Rose was bringing Gracie and Isobel into the city, but Taylor had already been present at too many funerals in her young life, and I was relieved when Leah suggested she could spend the day helping out at the store.

It was good to be alone. I needed to get away from everything and everybody. In the past week, the name of an old TV quiz show called *Who Do You Trust?* had nagged at me. I was growing genuinely fond of my neighbours at Lawyers' Bay. Despite what must have been a devastating shock, they had made every effort to be kind to my family and me. They had been Kevin Hynd's friends for twenty-five years. He trusted them, and I trusted Kevin. But try as I might, I couldn't shake off Alex's warning to tread lightly among these people. Nor could I dismiss the questions I had about Alex himself. Why had he spent so much time at Lawyers' Bay the previous winter? And what was the nature of his relationship with Lily Falconer?

The grass in front of my house on Regina Avenue was too long, the hanging baskets were parched, and the flower beds needed weeding. That said, when I opened my front door I felt a burden lift. It was good to be back on solid ground. I riffled through the mail my neighbour had piled in the basket on the hall table. There was nothing spectacular: magazines, bills, an invitation to a croquet party, and a postcard from Kevin with a picture of the Jokhang Temple in Lhasa and a note: "The Tibetans used to believe this country was connected to heaven by a rope. Today the clouds are low and the mountains seem to scrape the sky. Heaven feels close." Suspecting that in the days ahead I might need a reminder that heaven was close, I dropped the postcard into my bag.

After I'd soaked the hanging baskets and turned the sprinklers on the flower beds, I called the lawn service I'd hired for the summer. Their phone had been disconnected. I started calling Angus's friends, found someone with a younger brother who was desperate for money, and hired him sight unseen. Having put my house in order, I went upstairs to troll my closet for a dress suitable for a funeral.

I read once that Pat Nixon never hit the sack without first pressing and repairing every outfit she'd worn during the day. The image of her sewing on a button while Dick scowled and lusted had stuck with me, but I was never impressed enough to emulate her. That morning I wished I had. The only lightweight black dress I owned looked as if I'd slept in it. I hauled out the ironing board, plugged in the steam iron, and began.

Fired by the axiom that when you feel bad you should look good, I had called from the lake and made an appointment to have my hair cut. It had been a rough week and I wanted to get away from everything, to be submerged, if only for two hours, in the warm bath of a female culture where the largest questions were whether my eyebrows should be waxed or if my roots needed touching up.

Five minutes after I walked through the doors of Head to Toe, I knew that the answer to both questions was yes, but help was at hand. Business was brisk that Saturday morning – an entire bridal party, including, by some cosmic joke, not only the bride's mother, but also the woman who had replaced her as the main squeeze of the bride's father. My hair-stylist, Chantelle, and I agreed the situation had definite French-farce potential. After my roots were covered, I chose the newest of the glossy magazines, settled into my chair, and waited for the pleasures of a drama in which I would play no role whatsoever.

As always, I left Head to Toe grateful that I was part of the female mystery. Chantelle had decided I needed to go shorter and lighter, and the results were pleasing. I'd pored over all the recipes in the glossy magazine and reached the Zen conclusion that henceforth I would read recipes for the pleasure they brought me in the moment rather than for any hope of reaching future perfection. And – icing on my metaphorical cake – the bride's mother and her replacement had come face to face and ended

up trading stories about what a cheap son of a bitch
the bride's father was. Molière would have been
licking his chops.

The good times continued. When I went home
to change, my neighbour Lynn Chapman was
waiting at my front door, offering an apology, an
explanation, and an invitation to lunch. Lynn and
her family had just come back from a holiday in
Quebec. They hadn't realized my lawn service had
gone belly up, but they had now placed themselves
on alert, and if I was interested in a tuna-salad sandwich and a glass of iced tea, they would continue
to apologize until I forgave them for letting my
grass reach a state where it required life-support.

After I'd dressed, my freshly ironed dress revealed
upper arms that weren't bad for a woman of fifty-
five. As I drove over to the cathedral for the funeral,
I thought it was possible I'd make it to the end of
the day.

I was early, but parking was already a problem.
The sky was cloudless and the temperature soaring
– a perfect day to get out of the city – but half an
hour before the funeral Mass, the streets around the
cathedral were choked. The first parking spot I
found was four blocks away. By the time I climbed
the steps to Holy Rosary, my newly blond roots
were dark with sweat, and I was grateful to step

inside and let the cool wash over me. I found a spot at the end of a pew halfway up the aisle. I knelt, said a prayer, then sat back and looked around.

Regina is a city of 185,000, but lives intersect, and many of the faces in Holy Rosary were familiar to me. When I spotted a colleague from the university, or a friend from politics or the media, we exchanged the small, awkward smiles people exchange on such occasions, then turned back to our programs as if somehow in that brief obituary and description of the order of service, we could discover the reason we were sitting in a shadowy church on a brilliant July afternoon mourning a man who had chosen death over a seemingly gilded life.

As always at funerals, there were surprises, people whose connection with the deceased was not immediately apparent. Given his puzzling links with the residents of Lawyers' Bay, Alex Kequahtooway's presence wasn't exactly a shocker, but as I glanced around the congregation I spotted three of Alex's colleagues from the Regina force. In the normal run of things, the relationship between the police force and the legal community was not chummy, but Chris Altieri's specialty had been family law, and it seemed no one was immune to domestic problems.

When my friend Detective Robert Hallam came up the aisle, I touched his arm, and he stopped to talk. His pleasure at seeing me warmed my heart. Married late and happily, Robert Hallam was the most uxorious of men. His wife, Rosalie, had been the administrative assistant in the political-science department in which I taught, and, in Robert's books, anyone of whom his Rosalie approved was aces.

As always, Robert was a tonsorial and sartorial delight. His steel-grey crewcut and moustache were precision-trimmed. His lightweight beige jacket and slacks were without wrinkle, and the Windsor knot in his coffee-and-cream tie was impeccable. He extended his hand. "How are you, Joanne? I never see you, now that Rosalie's retired, and you and Alex are . . ." He flushed with embarrassment.

"No longer seeing one another," I finished his sentence. "It's all right, Robert. I'm over it."

His face softened with concern. "All the same, it can't be easy for you being in the same room as her, even if it is at a funeral."

I met his eyes. "You've lost me," I said. "Being in the same room as whom?"

Robert did a quick shoulder check to see who was in hearing distance. Many were. Experienced cop that he was, Robert dropped his voice. "The woman the inspector has . . . become intimate with," he whispered. He peered at me anxiously. "You must have known she'd be here today."

It took me a moment to absorb the information. I'd never known the identity of the woman with whom Alex had become involved, and the knowledge that she was somewhere in the cathedral made my heart pound. I struggled to appear calm. "I haven't seen her yet," I said.

"Well, Mrs. Lily Falconer is outside, dressed to the nines, bold as brass, waiting to make the grand entrance with her husband and the other big shots." Robert's tone was acid.

My mind shattered in a dozen directions. Lily Falconer was Alex's lover. It all made sense: her casual reference to Alex by his first name the day after the murder; the number of times the silver Audi had pulled into the Falconers' driveway; Alex's confidence that he was well acquainted with the people at Lawyers' Bay. Remembering how harrowed Alex had looked when he'd interviewed me, I experienced a flash of mean-spirited gratification. If he and Lily Falconer were having an affair, it wasn't bringing him much pleasure.

"Anyway, I think he's crazy." Robert was irate, and in the heat of the moment he abandoned his stage whisper. "No two ways about it, Lily Falconer is a looker, but you're no slouch, Joanne, and you're not married to a millionaire lawyer who could make the inspector's life hell." The message had been delivered loud and clear, and Robert's expression was sheepish as he gazed around to gauge the number of people who had been in earshot. "I'd better get back to work," he said.

"Wait," I said. "Robert, why are you here today? Is there something suspicious about Chris Altieri's death?"

Robert flicked a piece of lint off his jacket. "Where there's smoke there's fire. That's all I can say, Joanne. That, and remember your old friends. I know Rosalie would love it if you came by the house sometime. She's decorated up a storm. She's painted our bedroom something called wasabi green."

"Very trendy," I said. "Do you like it?"

"I never thought I'd sleep in a room the colour of Japanese horseradish," he said. "But Rosalie said it would grow on me, and she was right. Every day I like that wasabi green a little more."

There are times when the truth sets you free and there are times when it just makes you feel like shit. Robert's revelation fell into the second category. I had been angry and hurt when my relationship with Alex ended, but I had never doubted the fact that when we had been happy, his commitment to me had been as deep as mine to him. It seemed I'd been wrong.

My eyes stung. Luckily, a funeral is one of the few places where a woman can cry without drawing attention to herself. I was in the process of having a quiet weep when someone slid into the place next to me on the pew. I dabbed at my eyes, stuck my hanky in my purse, and cursed my luck. Still teary, I opened my funeral program. The photo Delia had taken from Harriet Hynd's album had been printed on good-quality bond and included as an insert. There was no text explaining why it was there. None was needed. Everyone knew the identity of those five young people on the cusp of their stellar lives. But the cosmos had shifted for them. The shining future had brought betrayal, bitterness, brokenness, and violent death. They, too, had discovered that we stand on shifting sand.

The first thing I noticed about the young woman who sat down next to me was the spray of creamy lilies in her hand. They were as simple and exquisite as she herself was. She was dressed expensively in a silk sheath woven with a pattern of birds and flowers and designed to underscore the perfection of her arms and legs. As soon I saw her profile, I recognized her. Her name was Patsy Choi. Her hair was shorter and more chic than it had been three years earlier when she was at the centre of one of our nation's most bitterly fought and divisive lawsuits,

but she had been a girl then, just fourteen. As the
small string orchestra played the opening notes of
the processional, she stiffened. Not that long ago,
she had been a musician herself, a promising violinist. The promise had been cut short when, after
an argument about practising, her uncle and
guardian smashed her fingers to a pulp.

Christopher Altieri had been her lawyer, and
after a protracted trial in which battalions of expert
witnesses sought to discredit or destroy the principals and one another, Patsy Choi had been awarded
a seven-figure judgement. As we stood to greet the
funeral party, Patsy placed the lilies on the pew,
picked up the hymnal, and began to sing. Her hands
were mutilated but functional. Perhaps the same
could now be said of her life, and as I glanced
around the cathedral, I wondered how many of
those who'd come to celebrate Christopher Altieri's
time on this earth had found it easier to bear their
own crosses because of him.

The three remaining partners of Falconer Shreve
made their entrance together. Blake carried an
earthenware urn whose purpose was all too evident.
Behind the partners, like an afterthought, Noah and
Lily walked with their daughters. The priests and the
clerical party made their way up the aisle, and the
Mass for the dead began.

The incense was lit, reminding us of the moment of Christopher Altieri's baptism; the words of comfort were offered and people sat back lulled by a liturgy that either soothed or bored them. Only when Zack Shreve pushed his chair to a spot in front of the chancel steps did the air become charged. The priest, whose speech carried the soft lilt of the West Indies, had used a microphone, but Zack had an actor's voice, deep and sonorous. Kevin told me that in a courtroom Zack used his voice like an instrument, whispering, booming, dripping with venom as the occasion demanded. That day, Zack chose to draw the huge and disparate crowd into a circle of intimacy with him at the centre.

His words cut deep. "Life is precarious," he said. "The only certainty is that we are mysteries even to one another. All of us loved Chris Altieri. None of us could save him. Chris had a favourite piece of music. It's called *Lux Aeterna*, which for those of you who have forgotten means Eternal Light. That, of course, is what Chris was to us."

From the first notes, the piece was – no other word for it – transcendent, a work of such radiant beauty that it seemed to bathe us all in the perpetual light of its Latin title. The text was drawn from many sources, sacred and secular; the words were, by turns, lyric, contemplative, exultant. I turned my mind off and let the music wash over me. When the choir concluded with an exuberant "Alleluia," I felt my heart lift. Beside me, Patsy Choi's lips curved with joy – the music had touched her too. As I knelt to say a final prayer, I wondered whether *Lux Aeterna* had worked for Chris – whether in the last months of his life he had found a measure of peace in this ethereal music.

Patsy Choi slipped away before the recessional. Understandably, she was no fan of crowds. Neither was I, but I was in no hurry to leave the cathedral, and I was not anxious to face Lily Falconer, so I stayed behind, and as the mourners trailed out I walked to one of the side aisles to look at the building's famous stained-glass windows.

I was pondering what was going on behind the sorrowing face of the Queen of Virgins when I sensed that I wasn't alone. Once again, someone had joined me, but this time I knew my companion. Anne Millar had been a student of mine. "I have to talk to you, Joanne," she said. "There's something terribly wrong at Falconer Shreve."

CHAPTER 4

When she'd been a seminar leader for the Political Science 100 class I taught, Anne Millar had been a plump, quietly pretty girl who wore no-name jeans and baggy sweaters and eschewed makeup as a political statement. Since then, she'd graduated from law school and landed a job with our city's oldest and most prestigious law firm. Apparently, success had caused her to revisit both her philosophy and her wardrobe. With her shoulder-length blond hair, black miniskirted power suit, and strappy stilettos, she was now the epitome of courtroom chic – a woman to be reckoned with. From the set of her jaw and the tension in her body that afternoon, it was also clear that she had an agenda.

"If there's something wrong at Falconer Shreve, you should talk to one of the partners," I said.

Anne's gaze was withering. "Those are the last people I'd talk to about this," she said.

An old woman smelling of mothballs and piety joined us and gazed with rheumy, loving eyes at the stained-glass portrait of Our Lady. When Anne spotted the old woman, she clamped my elbow and steered me to the next window: Mary, Comforter of the Afflicted. Anne apparently was not in need of comfort. Without giving Mary even the most cursory of glances, Anne began her story. "Chris Altieri left a message on my machine the night he died. He said he had to talk to me." She raised an eyebrow. "He said he had to atone."

My mind jumped to the first and most obvious possibility: Anne had been the woman with whom Chris had been involved, the lover he had forced to seek an abortion. "Maybe you should start at the beginning," I said.

"There is no beginning," she said. "I was away for the long weekend and I didn't get back till after midnight, so I didn't pick up the message till Tuesday morning. By then, of course, it was too late."

Anne's eyes darted around the cathedral. A few people had lingered to pray. Others were staying behind to take in the famous windows of Holy Rosary.

"This isn't a good place to talk," she said.

"No," I agreed, "it isn't."

"Then let's get out of here. I live at the Balfour. It's five minutes away and air-conditioned."

Hot and sick at heart, I was an easy sell. "Let's go," I said.

I didn't manage a clean getaway. As I walked down 13th Avenue to my car, I heard Zack Shreve behind me.

"Hey," he said. "You can't blow off the reception. I promised to pour."

"You'll have to show me your technique another time," I said. "I've decided just to drive straight back to the lake."

He looked at me hard. "That's a lie," he said pleasantly.

I flushed. "Why would I lie?"

"I don't know," he said. "Why would you?" He shrugged and smiled. "You're a woman of mystery," he said, and he wheeled away.

On a day when the world seemed an increasingly uncertain place, the solid bulk of the apartments that had become the Balfour Condominiums was reassuring. Sturdily built and handsome, the Balfour had anchored the corner of Victoria Avenue and Lorne Street for generations. Once the preserve of lifelong bachelors with ascots and ladies with mauve-tinted hair, the Balfour had been discovered by the young and affluent, people willing to pay a good chunk of change for a central location, classic lines, and the chance to do a serious reno.

Anne Millar had apparently decided against knocking down walls and installing stainless-steel appliances. Her apartment had the antique charm of a carefully preserved dowager: floors covered with the boundless richness of Persian carpets; walls hung with lush landscapes by long-dead Victorians; massive ornate furniture that glowed with the patina of age.

Anne was a distracted but efficient hostess. She filled a silver bucket and placed it on a tray with gin, tonic, two heavy monogrammed glasses, and two ecru linen napkins, also monogrammed. We sat at a round breakfast table that looked out on Victoria Park. Anne poured the drinks, handed me mine, and took a large sip from hers.

"This could get to be a habit very easily," she said.

"Luckily, we don't bury a good man every day," I said.

Anne eyed the condensation on her glass. "I'm not sure Chris Altieri was such a good man," she said.

She walked over to a side table and touched the button on her answering machine. Chris Altieri's voice, nervous and tentative, filled the room. "I need to atone," he said. "There are a lot of people I have to talk to, but I thought I'd start with you. Name the time and place and I'll be there." His laugh was nervous. "And make it soon, please. I'm losing my courage."

I felt a pang. The last time I'd seen Chris Altieri, I told him nothing was unforgiveable. Apparently, he'd been listening.

Anne held out her hands, palms up, in a gesture of frustration. "What do you make of that?"

I was still operating from the script in which she and Chris had been lovers. "It must at least give you some kind of comfort," I said.

She looked genuinely surprised. "Why would it give me comfort?"

"Obviously you two had differences," I said. "It must be a relief to know that he wanted to reconcile them."

Anne leaned across the table and locked eyes with mine. "Joanne, I barely knew Christopher Altieri. I went to him because I was apprehensive about what had happened to a friend who'd worked for Falconer Shreve and left abruptly. I'd met Chris a couple of times at parties, and he'd always seemed like a pretty decent guy."

"But he wasn't decent to you."

"No," Anne said. "When I asked him for reassurance that all was well with my friend, he was evasive. He promised to look into things and get back to me, but he never did. And he never returned my calls. I think the night he died, he'd decided to tell the truth."

"And you think there's some connection between Chris's death and what happened to your friend."

Anne picked up her napkin and folded it carefully into the smallest possible square. "I don't even know if anything *did* happen to her. She may have simply decided to move on and not look back. That's what everyone keeps telling me."

"But you don't believe them."

"I don't know," she said. "She didn't strike me as the kind of person who would leave without saying goodbye, but people surprise us all the time, don't they?"

I looked out the window. Across the street in the park, lovers were strolling hand in hand and children were fighting over swings. Their sunny world was seductive. If I were to agree with Anne Millar that people were unpredictable, finish my drink, and thank her for her hospitality, I could be part of that sunny world in five minutes.

The temptation was real, but so was the evidence that the universe was not unfolding as it should. A man I was certain cared for me had been unfaithful with the wife of a Falconer Shreve partner, a Falconer Shreve partner who seemed to be finding his way back from despair had committed suicide, and now a young lawyer at Falconer Shreve had left under unsettling circumstances. I turned to Anne Millar. "Tell me about your friend," I said.

The day's events had clearly rattled Anne, but she didn't allow emotion to distort her narrative. She told her story well, without digression or unnecessary detail.

"Her name was Clare Mackey," Anne began. Neither of us responded to the fact that she referred to Clare in the past tense. "We ran together," Anne continued. "It started out casually enough – we both had the same route in the mornings, down Lorne, into the park, and around the lake."

"That's my route, too," I said. "At least the lake part."

"Six-thirty in the summer, seven in the winter," Anne said. "Are you earlier or later?"

"Earlier," I said.

Anne sighed. "And we thought we were virtuous."

"I have a virtuous dog," I said.

The comment earned me a smile. "Anyway," Anne said, "Clare and I started running together. You know how informal those things are. We'd just meet up, do a few stretches, and start. We discovered early on that we were both lawyers. Every so often one of us would have a breakfast meeting, and we agreed to let the other know by e-mail so nobody had to hang around." Anne's face clouded. "Last November 11, Clare didn't show up. It was a holiday; I thought maybe she'd decided to sleep in. I waited for a few minutes, but it looked like rain, so I got in my run, came back here, and checked my e-mail. There was no message.

"That night we had an ice storm, so the next morning I ran at the Y. Same thing the next day, but before I left home I e-mailed Clare asking if she wanted to join me. She didn't show up, and she didn't respond to my note. The third day the streets were clear, so I waited for her at the corner of Lorne and Victoria. Another no-show. When I got home, I e-mailed her and asked if she was okay." Anne took a small sip of her drink. "She answered right away. Clare's e-mail name was 'roadrunner.' I was so relieved to see it pop up on my screen. Her note

said that she was in Vancouver. She'd flown out for
an interview with an all-female law firm there – her
dream. She said she'd let me know if she got the job.
A couple of days later she e-mailed to say everything had worked out. The new firm had liked her,
she'd liked them, and she was going to start immediately. I sent congratulations and asked her to stay
in touch."

"But Clare didn't stay in touch," I said.

"No." Anne's eyes were troubled. "To be honest,
there was no particular reason why she should have.
I hope I haven't misrepresented our relationship,
Joanne. We were just friendly acquaintances. Clare
and I ran together, but we didn't chat a lot. We were
both pretty internal people. I think we both saw
running as a good way to get centred for the day."

"Then what's the problem?" I asked. "The way
you've explained the situation, everything sounds
perfectly normal."

Anne clenched her fists in frustration. "I know
it does. It just doesn't ring true – at least not to me.
Clare wasn't impulsive. She was methodical. She
saw things through. No matter how good the job
at the law firm in Vancouver was, she wouldn't have
walked away from Falconer Shreve without clear-
ing off her files."

"You think something happened at Falconer Shreve to make her want to leave?"

"I don't know. All I know is that nothing adds up. A few weeks before she moved away, Clare asked me about vacancies here at the Balfour – she was interested in buying a condo, 'putting down roots,' to use her term. If anything went wrong at Falconer Shreve, it must have been very sudden and very serious."

I felt a chill. "And you went to Chris Altieri to ask if he knew why Clare had left so abruptly."

"Yes. And he was ready with an answer. He corroborated all the information in the e-mail. He said Falconer Shreve had been sorry to lose Clare, but she'd been offered her dream job, so they let her go. He also said the partners found it easier to make the decision because they knew they wouldn't have any trouble replacing Clare."

"At least that part is true," I said. "Falconer Shreve is a hot ticket. Any young lawyer with an ounce of ambition would give her eye teeth to work there."

"Chris pointed that out, too, and I bought his explanation. We were quite matey. Then just as I was leaving I asked Chris if he could give me the name of the firm Clare was working for. He became flustered. He said he couldn't remember the name, but if I left him my card, he'd send me the information. He was so anxious to get me out of the office he almost pushed me out the door."

"And he never got in touch."

"No, so I started looking elsewhere for information."

"You were that concerned."

"Concerned and, to be honest, pissed off. I don't like being stonewalled. At any rate, I started asking around. The legal community here is a pretty small one, so it wasn't hard to find people who'd had some contact with Clare. As it turned out, she'd moved to Regina only last spring."

"And she left Falconer Shreve in November."

Anne's nod was emphatic. "The timing is all wrong, isn't it? How could she move here in April, be happy enough to consider settling permanently in September, and then just leave?"

"I don't know," I said, but I felt my nerve ends tingle.

"It didn't make sense to me either," Anne said. "And then, towards the end of November, I got an electronic card from Clare, thanking me for being such a good friend."

"And that didn't reassure you?"

"It made me even more anxious. None of the women I know would dream of sending an e-card thanking another woman for her friendship, but I went along with the charade. I replied, thanking Clare for the card, but I also asked a question only Clare could answer."

"You suspected someone other than Clare was using her e-mail address," I said.

Anne's eyes met mine. "I knew it," she said simply. "But I decided before I went to the police to test my theory one more time. Coming up with a question that required intimate knowledge was difficult. Clare and I hadn't exchanged confidences. Then I remembered that she'd teased me about the laces on my running shoes. They're Strawberry Shortcake laces." Anne coloured. "There were these dolls in the early eighties . . ."

"I remember them," I said. "My daughter Mieka was a fan."

Anne's smile was wan. "Anyway, I e-mailed Clare a note asking her to describe my shoelaces. The e-mail program I use lets me know when my messages have been read, so I know someone opened the e-mail, but there was no response. That's when I went to the police."

"And the police didn't investigate?"

"They said they did." Anne bit off the words.

"But you didn't believe them."

"I believe they went through the motions. The

kindest construction is that the detective they sent to investigate was simply out-manoeuvred by the partners at Falconer Shreve. According to the detective I spoke to, events unfolded exactly as Clare's first note to me said they had. She received the Vancouver offer out of the blue – it was everything she'd ever wanted, so she went for it. Falconer Shreve accepted her resignation reluctantly, but they didn't want to stand in the way of a woman's chance at her 'dream job.'" Anne peered at me closely. "The detective used that phrase, too, Joanne. They were all reading from the same script."

"And you let the matter drop?"

"I was advised to . . ."

"By whom?"

"By the detective. He said I should drop the case, that people are complex and that sometimes their behaviour is inexplicable."

"Sounds condescending," I said.

"The words do," Anne said. "But if you could have seen his face . . ." She shook her head, as if to clear the memory. "He seemed to be wrestling with something. At the time I thought his superiors had told him to put a lid on the case, so I tried to psych him out. I told him if the police weren't going to find Clare Mackey, I would."

"Did he try to stop you?"

"No. His response was quite bizarre. For the longest time he just stared at me. Finally, he said, 'Sometimes when the pressures get to be too much, people walk away.' You know, Joanne, I don't think he was talking about Clare at all. I think he was talking about himself."

"It sounds as if he should be reported. Do you remember his name?"

"It was a hard one to forget. He was aboriginal. His name was Alex Kequahtooway."

I tried to keep my voice steady. "I don't suppose you remember exactly when you talked to him."

"Oh, but I do," Anne said. "It was my birthday. November 30."

I looked down at my hands. They were trembling as if they belonged to a very old lady or a very sick one. November 30 was the date on which Alex had ended our three-year relationship.

I'd planned to drive straight back to the lake, but my conversation with Anne Millar had been a stunner, so I drove home instead. The story of Clare Mackey had been deeply unsettling; it had also opened a Pandora's box that I'd hoped I'd finally managed to nail shut. I needed time to absorb Anne's story, but I also needed time to regroup.

My breakup with Alex had been, as these things

often are, both a shock and a relief. We had never lived together, but we had created a life together that I thought had fulfilled us both. Unmarried, Alex had a nephew, Eli, who was the same age as Angus, and after a few false starts our families had blended seamlessly. Our pleasures were domestic: cross-country skiing, watching videos, going to Roughrider games or the symphony, being together. At our best, we stretched one another's spirits, and even at our worst, we had been passionate.

Our relationship was not ideal. The fact that I was ten years older than he had never been an issue; the fact that I was white and Alex was aboriginal had been a wound that never healed. Alex was one of the gentlest human beings I'd ever known; he was also one of the angriest, and the rage never left him. For long periods we would be happy, but just when I believed the anger had been quenched, it would flare up in a blaze that consumed us both. Alex would wall himself off and become, in one of the buzzwords of our day, emotionally unavailable.

In the months before our breakup, the walls never seemed to come down. Nothing I did or said could dent his armour of anger. When he told me we were through, I was relieved but I was also bewildered. I genuinely didn't understand what had gone wrong. Anne's portrait of Alex's state of mind on the day we broke up offered a flash of insight, but it also raised questions far too vexing for a hot summer afternoon. What was the source of the pressures Alex had been experiencing? He was a man who believed in the value of police work, yet he had blown off Anne Millar, dismissed her very real concerns as if they were less than nothing. He had also dismissed me. Tempting as it was to blame Lily Falconer for everything that had gone wrong, I couldn't convince myself that Alex's attraction for her could change the man he was.

It was a relief to peel off my funeral clothes and put on a sundress and sandals. In a perfect world, changing clothes would have transformed my mood, but even the summery lightness of a cotton dress and bare legs didn't raise my spirits. I wasn't surprised. This was not shaping up to be a summer of easy solutions.

Angus had asked me to bring back some of his CDs. When I went into the family room to get them, I noticed my laptop, still in its carrying case, propped against the bookshelf. I'd promised myself I wouldn't take a computer to the lake, that this summer I would recreate the innocence of the pre-information-technology world at the pristine beach and sparkling water known as Lawyers' Bay. But now isolation was no longer an option – I needed to be connected to the world that lay beyond our privileged half-moon of lakefront cottages. I picked up the laptop, slung the strap over my shoulder, and headed for Paradise Lost.

My radio was tuned to a community-station show that featured up-and-coming young artists. As I turned off the highway onto the road that wound through the Qu'Appelle Valley to the lake, the twenty-something deejay announced that the next selection was by a group called the nancy ray-guns. The name of the song was "Windigo," and the deejay said it was the tale of a giant stone shape-changer who fed on human flesh. Perfect drive-home music.

When I stopped at the Point Store to pick up Taylor, everything was reassuringly ordinary. The old men of Coffee Row were sitting under the cottonwood trees spinning tales, and the store was bustling. It was six o'clock on a hot Saturday evening in July, and wieners, potato chips, hot-dog buns, and mosquito coils were at a premium. Leah was in the front of the store at the till, and Taylor was beside her, bagging groceries.

My younger daughter trumpeted her joy the moment she spotted me. "This has been the best day," she said. "I got to do everything, and Mr. Gardiner showed Angus how to work the meat grinder and he let me hand him the raw meat."

Leah raked a hand through her blond bob. "The fun never ends," she said.

"Had enough?" I asked.

"Actually it is kind of neat," Leah said. "And as my Aunt Slava would say, 'That Taylor – she must have been sent by God.'"

"Nice to know God has his eye on the Point Store," I said. "So, T, are you ready to come back to the cottage and have dinner?"

Taylor gave Leah a sidelong glance. "Is it okay if I go?"

"Absolutely," Leah said. "The store closes at six-thirty sharp."

"Six-thirty on a Saturday night?" I said. "That surprises me. I would have thought there'd be a lot of last-minute business."

"Not for us," Leah said. "Stan Gardiner says if people don't have what they need by six-thirty, they can't have needed it very much."

"Very sensible perspective," I said.

"Sensible and enlightened," my son yelled from behind the meat counter. "Leah and I have a bar-becue to go to."

I walked back and checked out the meat cooler. "Anything you can recommend for Taylor and me?"

"There's one last piece of beef tenderloin," Angus said thoughtfully. "High-end stuff, but just before you came, Stan told me to sell it for what I could get. He doesn't believe in keeping meat too long, and he says you ruin meat when you freeze it."

Taylor and I dined elegantly that night. Beef tenderloin, tiny carrots, fresh peas, and fried bannock, a treat from Rose. After dinner, we took Willie for a walk along the beach. The sun smouldered against the horizon. We were, in that most poetic of phrases, in the gloaming. For years, I'd loved this time of day when the half-light signalled that the passions and frets of a day with kids had burned themselves out and that it was time to indulge in private thoughts. But that night the prospect of being alone with my private thoughts had little appeal.

Chris Altieri's cottage was in darkness and we hurried past it, but piano music drifted through the open windows at Zack Shreve's. Tonight, he was playing one of my favourites, Johnny Mercer's "I Remember You." The setting sun made a path of light across the silent lake. It was a night for memories, and as we walked along the horseshoe I found

myself wondering whether the people inside the
cottages were cherishing their memories or wrestling
with them.

Taylor had been uncharacteristically quiet on
our walk, and she'd been watching me carefully.
"You're not having a good time at the cottage, are
you?" she asked.

"It's been a rough week, Taylor."

"Isobel says her mum never stops crying."

"Mrs. Wainberg and Mr. Altieri were good
friends," I said.

"But he was friends with Mrs. Falconer, too, and
Gracie says her mother hasn't cried at all."

"People react differently," I said.

Taylor stopped to shake a pebble out of her sandal.
"Gracie says her mum and dad fight every night."

"That's not good," I said.

"I wouldn't want people fighting at our house
every night," Taylor said.

"Neither would I." I read the worry on her face.
"You know what I'm in the mood for?" I asked.

"What?"

"Crazy eights," I said. "Are you feeling lucky?"

Taylor grinned. "I wasn't, but I am now."

Our card game was raucous and diverting. When
I tucked Taylor in, she'd lost her careworn look and
was planning the next morning's agenda. I was less

keen about seizing the day. Even the prospect of enduring the next few hours was daunting. As far as I could see, my options had narrowed to a classic example of Hobson's choice: go to bed, stare at the ceiling, and brood about the events of the afternoon, or stay awake, stare at the wall, and brood. The knock at the door was a relief.

Delia Wainberg's hair was wet and curly, as if she'd just come from a swim or a shower, and she was wearing navy shorts and a white T-shirt. She looked like the kid sister of the haggard, urbane lawyer who strode up the aisle at the funeral Mass.

"Too late for a visit?" she asked.

"Not from you," I said.

Delia followed me inside, then gestured towards the back porch. "Mind if we play through?"

The silver-dollar ashtray was in the dish drainer beside the sink. I picked it up and handed it to Delia.

"Thanks," she said. She walked onto the porch, collapsed into the nearest chair, and lit up. "I'm supposed to find out why you blew off the reception today."

"I ran into an ex-student of mine."

"I said it was probably something like that." Delia shrugged. "Anyway, you didn't miss anything – my face is stiff from being stoic. What kind of sadist invented the post-funeral party anyway?"

"The theory is that the reception gives the bereaved a chance to connect with the living again."

"Even if that's the last thing the bereaved want to do?"

"Especially if that's the last thing the bereaved want to do," I said.

"I guess I see some logic there," she said. "Enough chit-chat. I've been sent to extend an invitation you can't refuse."

"Go for it."

"We're taking what remains of Chris out on the lake tomorrow morning." She drew deeply on her cigarette. "His last boat ride, and the consensus is that you should come along."

"I take it you didn't lead the march to the consensus."

"No, I think it's a stupid idea."

"I agree. You did your duty. Just report back that I said no."

"It's not that simple." Delia extended a leg and wiggled her foot. She was wearing flip-flops with daisies. Frivolous footwear for a woman on a serious mission. "Anyway, you probably should say yes. Kevin wants you to come."

"You got in touch with Kevin?"

"Lily did." Delia arched an eyebrow. "According to her, Kevin would like you to go in his stead."

"That doesn't make sense either," I said. "Kevin and I are friends, but we're not . . ."

"You're not lovers," she crowed. "I knew it. The others all thought you were — that Kevin had sent you up here this summer to try you out — see how well you fit in with us."

"That's bizarre," I said. "Delia, Kevin walked away from Falconer Shreve because he wanted something else. He's hardly going to wander all over Tibet so that his ex-partners can check out his new girlfriend."

"Thanks for the reminder." Delia's eyes glittered. "You're right, of course. Kevin stopped caring about what we thought a long time ago. As far as he's concerned the Winners' Circle is dead and Falconer Shreve is just another shitty law firm."

Delia's face was grey. It seemed unconscionable to add to her burden. "I'll be there tomorrow morning," I said.

Delia slumped with relief. "I owe you," she said, crushing out her cigarette.

"It's the least I can do," I said. "You've all been kind to us, and Kevin may not be a lover but he is a friend."

"Sometimes that's better," Delia said. "Less wear and tear on the heart." She stood, removed a fresh cigarette from her pack, and gave me a small smile.

"So I'll see you at the dock at five? Early, I know, but we wanted to get out on the water before the invasion of the Jet Skis."

"Five is fine," I said. "Delia, can I ask you something?"

She tensed. Her fingers still rested on the handle of the screen door, but her voice went unexpectedly hard. "If it's about the rumour that Chris's death wasn't an accident, forget about it. I refuse to give headspace to that theory."

"No, it's something else," I said. "Can you tell me about Clare Mackey?"

I was watching Delia carefully for a reaction. What I got wasn't subtle. She shuddered as if she'd touched something loathsome. "If you know someone who's thinking of hiring her, tell them to forget it."

"She didn't work out at Falconer Shreve?"

"*Au contraire*. She worked out fine – quite the rising star – then she just took off, leaving her files in an absolute mess."

"Disorganized?"

"Oh, they were beautifully organized. They were also incomplete. A lot of lawyers, me included, carry information about cases around in their head. Sometimes it's just safer that way. But if circumstances change, and you know you're not going to be handling a particular file, you have a duty to your clients and to your colleagues to make sure somebody knows what you know. Little Clare must have been absent the day they covered that particular obligation in ethics class. When she got that job offer in Victoria, she just took off."

"I thought she went to Vancouver."

"Somewhere on the left coast, I don't know. All I know is she skipped off and took a lot of essential information with her." Her face clouded at the memory. "It still makes me furious. Clare wasn't a novice. She knew someone would have to pick up the slack, go over ground she'd already covered. She also knew that, unless you had specialized knowledge, it would be tough sledding. Clare does corporate work. She also has a commerce degree with a specialty in forensic accounting –"

"Accounting analysis," I said.

"With enough precision to make the results stick in a courtroom. Forensic accountants offer a lot of litigation support, quantifying economic damages – the economic loss involved in a breach of contract or the loss of future earnings. I guess when Clare was playing second fiddle to the litigators she got the hots for the law – I used to nod off in corporate law, but some lawyers love it, and of course, with corporate clients, the money's good. Anyway, to give Clare her due, she was a whiz."

"But she left her clients and her colleagues in a mess," I said.

"Oh boy, did she ever. There was one particular case — I still get the shivers when I think about it. It was so complicated and we were working against the clock. None of us had pulled that many all-nighters since law school."

"Why didn't you just get in touch with her? Surely she had an obligation to her clients to tell you what she knew."

"Lily tried. Clare clammed up, said there were numbers she simply didn't remember and didn't feel comfortable estimating. Which was bullshit. We didn't need her to give us the numbers; we needed her to give us the information she'd used to arrive at the numbers."

"And she refused?"

"Apparently. And if she ever shows that sweet little heart-shaped face around here again, I will personally punch out her lights." Delia struck a match and touched the end of her cigarette. "Do you know I'd quit this for ten whole days before Clare left? But as soon as I saw that mountain of work she'd left behind I bummed a smoke from one of our clerks, and I was back to square one."

"I understand Clare left on Remembrance Day," I said.

Delia exhaled slowly. "You'd have to ask Lily, but considering all the memories little Clare left behind, Remembrance Day would have a certain resonance, wouldn't it?"

CHAPTER 5

When I hit fifty, I vowed to keep physical and mental inflexibility at bay through the practice of yoga. Given my lackadaisical approach, it seemed unlikely that I would ever reach the highest happiness of nirvana, but there was one yoga posture I was faithful to. When my body or my children told me it was time to chill out, I would close the door, dim the lights, roll out my mat, and assume the shava-asana or corpse pose: head centred, body and palms on the floor, mind focused on my breathing. Shava-asana had never failed me, but that night even the corpse position couldn't deliver me from the torment of monkey thoughts.

Nothing about Clare Mackey's sudden relocation to Vancouver rang true, and there was more. Clare wasn't the only one who had been missing in action on that icy Remembrance Day. Alex Kequahtooway had been a no-show too. November 11 was Taylor's birthday, and we'd had big plans: a trip to the Science Centre with nine of her closest friends, then back to our house for cake, ice cream, and presents. We'd arranged to leave our house at two in the afternoon. When Alex hadn't arrived by ten past, I called his office, his home, and his cell. There was no answer. By two-thirty, the kids were bouncing off the walls, and I pressed Angus into service to drive the group Alex was going to take. The rest of the afternoon had been a nightmare – trying to keep the mood light while I watched the door of the Science Centre and waited for my cell to ring. Neither Alex nor the phone call of explanation ever came.

When – finally – I managed to reach Alex the next day, he was distant, and his apology was hollow. We quarrelled – or rather I quarrelled, and he listened. Clearly, his mind was elsewhere. Two weeks later I discovered what had captured his attention. There was another woman, and I found out about her existence through the oldest of B-movie clichés. Alex stopped by the house, and the perfume I smelled on his jacket was not my brand. When I asked him about the scent, he didn't bother to lie – in fact, he embraced my accusation that he had been with someone else. Seemingly grateful that

I had lifted a burden from his shoulders, he said goodbye. It was the evening of November 30. Earlier that day, he had advised Anne Millar that sometimes in life it was best just to walk away. Apparently he had been so impressed with his counsel that he'd decided to follow it himself.

It had been eight months since Alex severed our relationship, but remembering the breakup still made my face burn and my skin crawl. That morning I was relieved when my bedroom began to fill with pre-dawn birdsong and the knowledge that it was time to get up. Riding out to the middle of the lake to scatter a man's ashes wasn't at the top of my list of cottage pleasures, but anything was better than lying in the dark, lashing myself with memory. I swung my legs out of bed, and as my feet hit the floor I came as close to an epiphany as a woman can before she's had her first cup of coffee. I didn't have to lie in the dark, passively accepting every jolt and bombshell the fates sent my way. On my seventh birthday, my grandmother had given me an autograph book. She had handed along her own wisdom on the first page. "Don't be a doormat all your life," she had written. "Learn to give and to take and you'll be happy." Almost fifty years later, I knew it was time to listen to Nana.

I took my laptop into the kitchen, made coffee,

sat down at the kitchen table, and sent a note to Anne Millar, giving her a précis of my conversation with Delia Wainberg and telling her that alarm bells were going off for me, too. I asked if she had the names of anyone Clare Mackey had been close to; then, proving that epiphanies beget epiphanies, I asked where Clare had gone to law school. If she practised in Saskatchewan, chances were that she'd gone to the university in Saskatoon. Clever students often keep in touch with their mentors, and I had friends on the law faculty there. It was a long shot, but there was a decided shortage of sure things.

After I'd sent the message to Anne, I glanced at the phone. Alex had told me to call if anything came up. The past twenty-four hours had brought plenty of revelations, but if I was going to confront him with questions about his relationship with Lily Falconer and his refusal to become involved in Clare Mackey's disappearance, I needed more information. I looked at my watch: it was four-thirty. I let Willie out briefly with a promise of more to come later, showered, dressed, checked on Taylor, whispered to Leah that I'd be back in an hour, then feeling less like a doormat than I had in a long time, I walked down to the dock.

The others were there already, waiting. They could have been mistaken for the most carefree of vacationers: the sun was just rising over the horizon, bringing enough breeze to give the waves a chop. Zack Shreve's Chris-Craft was beside the dock and he was already in the cockpit behind the steering wheel. Lily and Blake Falconer were sitting aft – as far away from one another as it was possible to be. The Wainbergs were standing at the end of the dock, Delia with her inevitable cigarette, and Noah behind her, kneading her shoulders with his big, gentle hands.

When he saw me, Zack waved and pointed to the seat next to his. Relieved I didn't have to sit next to Lily, I took my place. Delia and Noah came aboard, sliding into the space between Lily and Blake.

Zack did a shoulder check. "Looks like we're all here."

"Where's Chris?" Delia said. The question was blackly humorous, and everyone smiled.

"Exactly where he's supposed to be," Zack said, "in a box in the storage area." Then he gunned the motor and backed the boat smoothly away from the dock into the open water. No one spoke as we headed for the lake's centre. When we'd reached the middle, Zack cut the motor. Except for the screech of the gulls and the slap of the waves against the launch's hull, the world was silent. I cast my eyes around the shoreline, getting my bearings. Until that moment, the cottages on the far shore had been dabs on a pointillist's canvas, strokes in a vista created for our pleasure. Now they leaped into dimensional life with boathouses, rafts, floats, and docks of their own. When I looked back at Lawyers' Bay, the handsome summer homes seemed to have no more substance than a stage designer's balsawood mock-up of a set, too fragile by far to support the weight of Chris Altieri's tragic death.

Zack interrupted my musings by tapping me on the arm and gesturing towards the storage area under the bow. "Why don't you do the honours?" he asked.

I leaned forward, opened the latch, and pulled out a cardboard box. Zack took it from me and without ceremony threw a handful of ashes into the water, then passed the box back to Blake. The sequence was so devoid of emotion that it seemed brutal, but when I looked over at Zack, his eyes were moist. In turn, each of the partners and their spouses threw ashes into the water. Lily was the last, and as she took the open box a breeze came up and blew some of the ashes against her. Her reaction was swift: she hurled the cardboard box into the lake, then scooped water and began scrubbing furiously at the ashes on her shirt. I remembered a doctor I knew advising against scattering ceremonies, explaining that human ashes are so dense they stick to skin and embed themselves under nails.

Zack chortled. "Chris seems to be finding it hard to leave you, Lily," he said. I was no fan of Lily's, but I didn't believe in kicking someone when they were down, and at that moment, Lily Falconer was definitely down. She looked ill: her skin had a greenish tinge, and her eyes were as blank as those of the woman in the wood carving at the base of the gazebo.

Her husband leaned forward and put his mouth next to Zack's ear. "Shut up and get us out of here," he said.

Zack gave him a mock salute and gunned the motor. The surge of power lifted the boat out of the water and within seconds we were kicking up spray, pounding towards the shore that lay across from Lawyers' Bay. The rafts and water-ski ramps seemed to jump at us, but Zack didn't change course.

I grabbed his arm. "Are you trying to kill us all?"

His lustrous green eyes danced with malice. "Would that be such a loss?" he asked.

I tightened my grip. "For me, yes, it would be," I said.

He gave me a small smile. "In that case . . ."

He turned the wheel sharply and the landscape changed – the shore that had loomed so ominously vanished, replaced by open water. We were safe. For the next fifteen minutes we sped around the circumference of the lake. When finally we came to Lawyers' Bay, Zack's fury seemed to have spent itself. He cut the engine and the launch drifted in. We climbed out and waited as Zack slid onto the lift that moved him from the launch to the dock.

After the boat was safely moored, Blake ran a hand through his scrub-brush hair. "So what's the preferred activity after you scatter a friend's ashes?"

Zack shrugged. "Linking hands and singing 'Kumbaya'?"

"How about getting back to work?" Lily said. "The firm still has bills to pay." Her colour had come back and she seemed in command of herself. "I'm going into the city. Chris has files that need attention. We don't have anybody in family law with enough experience. We need to find someone fast."

Delia frowned. "Do you think we have to hire someone this soon?"

"Chris's clients will think so," Lily said dryly. "And we've already had letters of inquiry and resumés from lawyers who are anxious to join the Falconer Shreve team."

"Scavengers circling the fresh carcass," Zack said. "Clearly Falconer Shreve material."

Blake shook his head. "Well, now that we've established the criteria —"

Delia cut him off angrily. "Those aren't our criteria. We're better than that."

Zack's smile was almost pitying. "With all due respect, Delia, that was then and this is now."

"We can be good again," Delia said. "We only have to find someone with that lust for justice we used to have."

"We don't want any young hotshots who think they have to right every wrong," Blake said wearily. "We just need someone to replace Chris."

"Chris is irreplaceable," Delia said.

Her husband took her hand. "No one's irreplaceable," Noah said softly. "Let's go back to the house. You had a bad night. You could use a little sleep."

Blake was thoughtful as he watched the Wainbergs walk towards their cottage. "Maybe with Chris gone, they'll have a chance," he said.

"Maybe we'll all have a chance," Lily said. She reached out and touched her husband's cheek. It was a small gesture, but the effect was electric. He turned and looked in her eyes.

"I'll come into town with you," he said. "An office can be a lonely place on Sunday afternoon."

Since the day I'd met Blake and Lily, I'd wondered what kept them together; I wasn't wondering any more. Clearly, Lily's involvement with Alex hadn't diminished the marital passion of the Falconers. The sexual charge that flowed between them as they stood together on the dock could have powered the CN Tower.

Not a creature was stirring when I got back to our cottage, but when I checked on Taylor, she rolled over and mumbled about breakfast. Peace would be short-lived. I smoothed her sheet and went back to my bedroom to check my e-mail. Anne Millar hadn't lied about being an early riser. She'd already answered my note, and what she said was promising. Clare had graduated from the University of Saskatchewan College of Law. Anne remembered her mentioning two professors who had been particularly helpful. Clare hadn't named them, but she had said that both professors were women. That narrowed the field. It also gave me an in.

My friend Holly Knott taught family law at the University of Saskatchewan. She was smart and she was a feminist, exactly the kind of professor to whom a bright young female student might gravitate. I typed in Holly's address and wrote a note explaining that I was spending the summer at a friend's cottage on Lawyers' Bay, that Clare Mackey's name had come up, and I wondered if Holly remembered her. Just as I was finishing off, Taylor drifted in to my bedroom, draped her arms around my neck, and stared at the screen. "Who's Clare Mackey?" she asked.

"That's what I'm trying to find out," I said.

It was Sunday – pancake day – and when we went into the kitchen Leah and Angus, well aware of family tradition, were there in T-shirts and match-ing polar-bear boxer shorts mixing batter.

I poured myself coffee. "Gold stars all around," I said.

"Two for me," Angus said. "I took Willie for his walk."

Leah wiped her brow with the back of a floury hand. "One star for you," she corrected. "You were here all of thirty seconds before Jo and Taylor showed up. So far all you've done is grunt 'Make way for a man who needs his engines stoked.'"

As I leaned across her to turn on the griddle, I patted Leah's shoulder. "Thanks for not dumping the batter over his head."

"It would have meant starting again from scratch," Leah said. She narrowed her eyes. "Why don't you sit down and let the hungry man serve you some pancakes? You look like you could use a little sustenance. In fact, you look like you need a holiday from your holiday."

After we'd eaten, I checked my e-mail. I'd sent my note to Holly Knott's university address so I was surprised to see her name in my inbox. As it turned out, she was at work. She was off to Crete the next day, so she was spending Sunday in her office finishing an article. She suggested that I give her a call to talk about Clare. The tone of her note was brisk except for the last line. "It'll be good to hear your voice," she wrote. "It's been too long."

Something about the words "it's been too long" tugged at me. It had been too long since I'd seen Holly. It had also been too long since I'd talked to someone with whom I could let down my defences. My daughter Mieka and her family lived in Saskatoon. A visit with them might prove to be just the holiday from my holiday I needed.

I called Mieka and Holly. Both were enthusiastic about a visit. Holly said she'd see me at three o'clock that afternoon at the university, and Mieka had already planned our dinner menu by the time I hung up.

Taylor was sitting cross-legged on her bed knitting when I walked in. "Hey, are you up for an adventure?" I asked.

"Sure," she said. "What is it?"

"I thought we might drive up to Saskatoon to see Mieka and Greg and the little girls."

"Today?"

"Right now. Throw some stuff in your back-pack and we'll hit the road. If we get moving, we can make it in time for lunch."

"And after supper, when it's not too hot, we can take Maddy and Lena to the merry-go-round in Kinsmen Park and Maddy can ride the unicorn and I can hold Lena on the yellow pig."

"I used to hold you on the yellow pig," I said.

"When I was young," Taylor said.

A half-eaten apple peeked out from under Taylor's pillow. I picked it up and held it in the air. "Right," I said. "When you were young."

The moment I walked into the backyard of the house on 9th Street, I knew the trip had been worthwhile. Mieka and her girls were sitting on an old quilt under the shade of the elm tree. My seven-month-old granddaughter, Lena, was on Mieka's lap, her Woody Woodpecker thatch of black hair on end, her bright brown eyes focused on her sister, Maddy, who was singing a song about five little rabbits.

For a beat, I stayed silent, revelling in the sun-dappled Mary Cassat lyricism of the scene. But Taylor was not partial to scenes in which she played no part. "We're here, guys," she said, and tranquillity gave way to an exuberant jumble of hugs and greetings and confusion.

"Is it always this idyllic?" I asked Mieka.

"Sunshine and lollipops, twenty-four/seven. Never a tear, never a tantrum. That's our motto here at the Kilbourn-Harris home. How's Lawyers' Bay?"

I looked at the fresh yellow paint on Mieka's clapboard house, the frilled red and white petunias in the window boxes, the sand spilling out of the tire by the fence, and the little-girl bathing suits and rinsed-off Ziploc bags pegged to the clothesline.

"Not as nice as this," I said.

Mieka took my hand in hers. "Is the accident still weighing heavily on you?"

"Among other things," I said.

"What other things?" Mieka asked.

I squeezed her hand. "Things you and I are going to need two long spoons and a quart of Haagen-Dazs to talk about," I said.

In midsummer, most university campuses manage to look almost as good as the photograph on the front of their calendar, and the Tyndall-stone buildings and big prairie sky gave the University of Saskatchewan a special glow. It was a Sunday, but there were still enough tanned and leggy students tossing footballs and ambling past flower beds towards the libraries to create a Kodak moment.

As she was about everything, Holly had been precise about the time of our meeting. When I parked in front of the law college and checked my watch, I discovered I was ten minutes early. Rather than take the elevator, I hoofed it up the three flights of stairs to her floor; then with more time to kill, I wandered into a small student lounge, found the ubiquitous soft-drink machine, and bought a bottle of water. I sipped it as I checked out the walls of the lounge. They were lined with photos of recent graduating classes. It took me less than a minute to find Clare Mackey's photograph.

Delia Wainberg had threatened that, if she ever saw Clare Mackey again, she would punch Clare's heart-shaped face. Clare's face was indeed heart-shaped, and at first glance she did seem chocolate-box pretty: honey-coloured hair with a gentle curl, and a nose with a becoming upward tilt. But her blue eyes were penetrating, and there was a firmness in the set of her mouth that stamped her as a woman who knew her value. She would, I sensed, be a formidable opponent. I finished my water, and then obeying an impulse I leaned over and spoke to Clare Mackey's photograph. "I'm going to find you," I said. My moment of high drama over, I pitched my bottle into the recycle bin and walked down the hall to the office of my old friend. I was right on time.

Holly Knott was Saskatchewan-born and -bred, but there was something ineffably French about her style. She was in her late forties but her look was timelessly chic: the lines of her shiny black bob were ruler-straight, her makeup was skilfully muted, and the lipstick-red scarf knotted casually around her shoulders was a precise match for the colour of the polish on her nails. When she stood to greet me, she moved with the athleticism of the lifelong tennis player.

"Jo, this *is* kismet. One more day, and I would have missed you, and that would not have pleased me." For a small woman, the timbre of her voice was surprisingly rich. She motioned me to the chair on the student side of the desk. "Make yourself comfortable. I can't offer anything that doesn't come out of a machine, but if you'd like a soft drink . . ."

"I'm fine," I said. "And I know you're busy, so I won't take much of your time."

"You wanted to talk about Clare Mackey." Holly slid into her own chair. "On the phone you said you needed to know what kind of person she is. Obviously, since your call I've been trying to come up with a sensible answer. I'll have to confess I didn't know her well. She wasn't a woman who invited intimacy. She was a very good student – older than most of the others and serious about her work. She was an accountant before she started law school, and she had an accountant's approach to her studies: precise, painstaking, diligent. She did her home-work. Her cases and notes for study were the gold standard. She prepared everything meticulously. She didn't like surprises, a significant trait in a lawyer, and even as a student she was thoroughly profes-sional." Holly smiled. "Do you need more?"

"No," I said. "That's enough. It doesn't fit."

Holly's eyes widened. "What doesn't fit? Jo, on the phone you were vague about your reasons for wanting to talk about Clare, but I assumed they were professional."

"In a way, I guess they are," I said. "There are some questions about the way in which she left her last job."

"At Falconer Shreve," Holly said.

"So Clare did stay in touch with you."

"Minimally. When she was approached by Falconer Shreve, I supplied a reference for her. She sent me a thank-you note when she got the job." Holly picked up a chunk of quartz resting on top of a stack of journal articles. She turned the rock until the sun from her office window bounced off the quartz, igniting pinpricks of fire on its surface.

She stared at it meditatively. "And then, of course, at Christmas there was a card."

I felt my pulse quicken. "You heard from Clare this past Christmas?"

Holly frowned. "In my books it wouldn't qualify as hearing from her. She sent an electronic card – pretty enough, snow falling on a cabin – but I remember thinking it was uncharacteristic."

"She isn't the type of woman to send e-cards?"

"She isn't the type of woman to send cards at all." Holly narrowed her eyes. "Jo, what's this all about?"

"There was something *odd* about the way Clare left Falconer Shreve," I said. "Apparently she was content enough with her job and her life to talk about buying a condominium. Then out of the blue she just took off."

"Without telling her firm?"

"No. I gather she told them she was leaving, but she didn't give them notice. She just took off and let her colleagues deal with the mess."

"She would never do that. Never. Never. Never." Holly slammed the quartz down on her desk, then she smiled sheepishly. "Sorry about the dramatics. Old litigation lawyers are incurable."

"You've convinced me," I said. "But the fact is, Clare Mackey did leave Falconer Shreve."

"Without an explanation?"

"No, there was an explanation. She'd found her dream job in Vancouver."

"Bullshit. Clare's not a liar, Jo, but if that's her story, she might have been covering up a problem that had developed at Falconer Shreve."

"The problem must have come up pretty suddenly," I said. "I talked to a young woman Clare ran with every morning. The woman's name is Anne Millar, and she says Clare was talking about putting down roots in Regina."

"Maybe the person Clare planned to put down roots with had a change of heart." Holly reached over and picked up her cordless phone. "And maybe you and I should stop speculating and just pick up the phone and ask Clare."

"That would be logical," I said. "But unfortunately no one seems to know where she is."

Holly's face darkened. "But that's nonsense. Falconer Shreve would have a contact number and Clare must have had friends."

"So far, Anne Millar seems to be the only friend who's been concerned enough to ask any questions. When Clare didn't show up at their regular running time, Anne went to Falconer Shreve and talked to one of the partners. He was the one who told her the dream-job story, but when Anne pressed him for specifics he – to use her word – 'stonewalled.'"

"Which partner did she talk to?"

"Christopher Altieri."

Holly winced. "I still can't believe he's gone. I was a year behind him in law school. He was one of the few truly moral human beings I've ever known. People always said he was the conscience of Falconer Shreve." She straightened her shoulders and breathed deeply, the former litigation lawyer getting her second wind. "At any rate, Chris's innate decency aside, he didn't have anything to gain by stonewalling. If the situation is as you described it, Clare was the one who walked away. Falconer Shreve was the injured party."

"That's certainly how Delia Wainberg sees it," I said. "When I broached the subject with her, she was still seething."

"Why am I not surprised?" Holly said. "Delia was always a pistol, and her loyalties were primal. She *would* see what Clare did as betrayal."

"But you don't?"

She shrugged. "I don't know the whole story."

"Neither do I. That's why I came to you."

"And I was no help," she said. "But I *can* point you to some possibilities." She walked to her bookshelves, knelt, and began checking the spines on a number of green leatherette yearbooks. She pulled one out and flipped through until she found what she was looking for. "Clare's graduating year," she said. "One of the women in her Moot Team will know where Clare is. They were exceptionally tight."

"What's a Moot Team?"

Holly chuckled. "The students say they're the law-school equivalent of varsity football, but with more bloodshed. Really, they're just mock courts. Someone comes up with a hypothetical legal dilemma, and the teams come up with arguments and make submissions the way they would in a real court. The competition can get pretty cutthroat." She handed me the yearbook. "Anyway, here are the Moot Teams. You'll notice that Clare's group takes the entire venture very seriously."

Most of the students had opted to be captured in a moment of goofy high spirits: mugging for the camera or striking over-the-top formal poses. In one grouping, a petite female lounged Cleopatra-style on the outstretched arms of her three strapping partners. Clare's group, all women, wore matching open-necked white blouses, smartly tailored dark suits, and the tight smiles of students who knew this photo was one more hoop they had to jump through before they could get on with the serious business of their lives.

Holly handed me the yearbook. The women's names were listed under the photo: Sandra Mikalonis, Maggie Niewinski, Clare Mackey, Linda Thauberger. "I'll e-mail the head administrator at the College of Law and tell her it's okay for you to get the contact information. And Jo, when you find out what's going on with Clare, let me know. If she's backed herself into a corner somehow, I may be able to show her the way out."

It was my cue to leave, but I didn't pick it up. I stood in the doorway. "Holly, how well did you know the members of the Winners' Circle?"

"Not as well as I wanted to," she said, and her voice was wistful. "None of us knew them as well as we wanted to. Law school is a funny place – despite the august trappings, it's like high school in many ways, cliquey. There are the jocks and the beautiful people and the brainiacs and the spoiled rich kids and the leftovers who band together because nobody else wants them. And, just the way they do in high school, everyone knows exactly who fits where. Everyone at this law school knew

about the Winners' Circle, and we all envied them."
Holly glanced at her watch. "If you have a moment,
I can show you the way they were when I knew
them first."

"I have a moment," I said.

Holly led me down the hall, past more photos of
graduating classes, and opened the door to a class-
room. The air in the room was stale with the smell
of a closed-up room in summer. There were cari-
catures on the wall, likenesses of justices whose
names I recognized from the long-ago newspaper
stories. And there were yet more photos – older
ones. Holly steered me towards the back. "There I
am," she said.

"You haven't changed much," I said. "Still a
looker, as my friend Howard Dowhanuik would say."

"Thank you. On the day before I fly off to an
island where I plan to wear a bikini, albeit a modest
one, I appreciate that." Holly moved to the framed
class photograph next to hers. "And here they are,"
she said. "The members of the Winners' Circle.
There's Chris. He was so beautiful – in every way."
She shook her head. "There weren't many women
in our class, and all of us would have been livid at
being objectified as sexual objects, but we had a
lot of fun speculating about the men in the
Winners' Circle."

"Who would be the best lover?" I said. "That kind of thing?"

"We were much more cerebral than that," Holly said. "We had a theory that you could discern a great deal about a woman by the man she most admired in the Winners' Circle. Chris was for the altruists. Blake Falconer was for the party girls. Your friend Kevin Hynd was for the rebels."

"How about Zack Shreve?"

"The Prince of Darkness. We always figured he was for women who longed to get up close and personal with a chainsaw. But he certainly had his partisans."

I laughed. "Where did Delia fit in?"

"One of the gang."

"Any theories about which member of the Winners' Circle she most admired?"

"No need for theories. It was Chris Altieri. They were both idealistic – passionate about changing the world, big into human rights. A lot of people thought they'd end up together."

"But they didn't?"

"Nope. Delia ended up with one of the left-overs." Holly pointed a perfectly manicured nail at the last picture on the page. "Good old Noah."

"Noah Wainberg is a lawyer?"

"He has a law degree."

"I thought he was a sort of handyman."

"Well, that's pretty much what lawyers are."

"Is that what you tell your students?"

She smiled. "Not until they're in third year. By third year, they've pretty well lost their illusions."

"The members of the Winners' Circle have certainly lost their illusions," I said.

"So I've heard," Holly said. "And it really makes me sad. When they were here at the college, they were dazzling. They used to talk about their 'lust for justice.'"

"Delia still does," I said.

"Good for her," Holly said. "Who knows? Maybe Falconer Shreve can reclaim its magic. I always wondered about exactly what went wrong there . . . not that there was a dearth of rumours."

"What kind of rumours?"

"None worth repeating." Holly's pretty mouth had hardened into a line. "People I trusted said they had some kind of money problem. Whatever happened, it was a crucible for Falconer Shreve. Before it happened they were one kind of firm; after it happened they were another. They took cases they wouldn't have taken before, cut corners the old Winners' Circle never would have dreamed of cutting. Nothing to get them in front of the Law

Society, of course, but they started operating in the grey area."

"The worm was in the bud," I said.

Holly raised an eyebrow. "I'd never thought of it that way," she said. "But yes, they had been corrupted."

After that, there didn't seem to be much to say, except goodbye. Holly walked me to the stairs. "Thanks for squeezing me in today," I said. "I know you were pressed for time."

"It was the least I could do. Clare's a decent person. If Falconer Shreve railroaded her, she deserves justice. She was a student of the College of Law, and our motto is *Fiat Justitia*."

"Let justice be done," I said.

Holly nodded. "Right," she said. "And those should not be empty words."

CHAPTER 6

It was drizzling by the time I got to my parking spot in front of the College of Law. I was as tired as I could ever remember being, and when I checked the skies, I was relieved to see that the clouds rolling in were the colour of asphalt. God in Her infinite wisdom had heard my prayers. A gully-washer was on the way, and that meant a reprieve from my date with the yellow pig on the merry-go-round at Kinsmen Park.

The blessings continued. Mieka made my favourite creamy Spanish gazpacho with sourdough bread for dinner, and after we'd finished eating we sat by the big window in the kitchen watching the storm and listening to Taylor read from a book she'd found in Maddy's room about Inuksuit, the rock figures the Inuit build to mark the Arctic landscape.

Taylor was passionate about process. She liked to know how to make things – origami, compost, lasagna from scratch – and the book's instructions about how to pile stones to create landscape intrigued her. She was, however, puzzled by the fact that a book so obviously intended for adults had found its way into Maddy's library. When she asked, Mieka was matter-of-fact.

"A father's logic," she said. "Maddy's favourite book this summer is *Hide and Sneak*, and there's an Inukshuk in it. So Maddy's father bought her a book that tells her more than anyone needs to know about Inuksuit."

"History repeating itself," I said. "When Mieka was Maddy's age, she stacked six blocks on top of one another, and her dad came home with a book on the world's greatest architects."

Taylor turned to Mieka. "So how come you didn't grow up to be an architect?"

Mieka shrugged. "I discovered the Easy-Bake Oven," she said.

When the lights flickered and the power went out, Mieka lit candles to ward off the gloom. I held Lena a little closer, and Taylor taught Maddy how to tell the distance of a strike by counting off the time between a lightning flash and a thunderclap. It wasn't long before my eyes grew heavy, and when

Maddy decided it was story time, she didn't have to coax me to crawl into bed with her and read. We unearthed a flashlight, burrowed under the covers, and started on the pile of books beside her bed. Somewhere between *Hide and Sneak* and *A Promise Is a Promise*, I fell asleep. When I awoke, the room was dark and quiet, and my granddaughter's small fingertips were resting on the pulse in my neck. I turned so I could see the other twin bed in the room. Taylor was in it, breathing rhythmically. I watched as she stirred, then settled in. A sense of peace, unfamiliar as it was welcome, washed over me, and I rolled over and drifted into a deep and dreamless sleep that lasted until morning.

During the next twenty-four hours I kicked back and let the domestic rituals of a happy household carry me along. When we woke up, Taylor and I took the girls outside so Mieka could catch some extra sleep. The horizon was bright, and Taylor dried the front steps off with an old beach towel so the four of us could sit on the top step in our nighties, watching 9th Street spring into the accelerated rhythms of Monday-morning life. Mieka's catering business was closed on Mondays, so when she woke up we all gave ourselves over to the sweet laziness of a day off. We took a long and aimless walk, then spent the rest of the morning in the backyard, running through the sprinkler and playing ball. Mieka cranked up James Brown on the CD player, and she and the girls rocked to "Papa's Got a Brand New Bag"; we ate a picnic lunch, and then the little girls and I retreated to my shady bedroom and I napped with a granddaughter in each arm.

When we woke up, we made the long-anticipated trip to Kinsmen Park, where Taylor and my granddaughters squeezed into the seats of the same miniature train and rode the same merry-go-round that Mieka and her brothers had thrilled to during Saskatoon visits when they were kids. There were a few changes – an ear-splitting whistle on the train and two new horses on the merry-go-round, a black stallion with wild green eyes and a zigzag blaze of white on his chest, and a bubblegum-pink pony with curling eyelashes and a lush showgirl mane. Maddy tried out both the newcomers, but the old yellow pig with a handful of freshly painted blue daisies sprinkled like freckles over his snout was still the favourite. As I watched Taylor hold Lena on the pig's broad back and saw my granddaughter's small body sway to the music and the wonder of it all, I gave thanks for summer moments – inconsequential and ephemeral, but capable of warming the bleakest day of deep winter.

Magic time, but Lawyers' Bay was never far from my mind, and Mieka was quick to pounce when my smile grew fixed and my eyes deadened into a five-mile stare. A half-dozen times she asked me to tell her what was wrong, and a half-dozen times I shook her off and changed the subject. That night, after the kids were in bed, she buttonholed me.

"Last chance to tell me what's going on," she said. "I should warn you that I'm not going to let you leave town until you open up."

"Mieka . . ."

"I've been your daughter for thirty-one years, remember? I know you. There's nothing you love more than being with the grandkids, but you breeze in here yesterday, looking like hell, pat the girls on their heads, rip up to the university to see a law professor – no explanation given – then you fall into bed at seven p.m. and sleep for twelve hours."

"It's been a lousy week," I said.

Mieka raised her hand in a halt gesture. "I'm not criticizing you; I'm worrying about you. You've been doing all the right things this weekend, but you keep slipping away from us. I know the accident at Lawyers' Bay must have been a nightmare, but you haven't brought it up once. There has to be something else."

I took her hand in mine. She had her father's hands, long-fingered, slender, and heartbreakingly familiar. The inner walls came tumbling down. Suddenly, the prospect of talking was very appealing. "There is something else," I said.

"Let's get some coffee and go out on the deck where it's cool," Mieka said. "The upstairs windows are open, so we can hear the girls if they need us."

We carried out a tray with coffee things, and Mieka touched a match to a votive candle in a small blue metal box that protected it from the wind. Letters were cut out of the metal, and when the candle was lit, the spaces glowed, spelling out the word *Harmony*. For a few minutes we sat in the comforting half-light, inhaling the heavy sweetness of a July garden and listening to the low voices and bursts of laughter from the guests at a barbecue next door.

Finally, Mieka put down her mug and leaned towards me. "So, what's going on?" she asked.

"I wish I knew," I said. "Nothing fits, Mieka. For starters, despite what the media says, Chris Altieri's 'accident' was no accident. It was a suicide, but I was with Chris the night it happened. He'd been through a rough time. A woman he'd been involved with had an abortion, and he'd been depressed about what had happened. But that night he seemed to turn a corner. When we said good night, he asked if he could come for a run with Willie and me the next morning. Two hours later he was dead."

"Something could have triggered a relapse," Mieka said. "He might have seen a baby or heard a child's voice." She peered at me, checking for a response. "Too melodramatic?"

"No," I said. "He just seemed to have moved past that. And then at the funeral, a former student of mine who's now a lawyer herself said she thought there was something very wrong at Falconer Shreve."

A breeze caught the candle on our table; the letters spelling out *Harmony* flickered, then disappeared. Mieka didn't seem to notice.

"Why was this woman talking to you? Why didn't she go to the police?"

"She did go to the police," I said. "She told them she was concerned about an acquaintance of hers who left Falconer Shreve suddenly and without explanation. The detective she talked to told her that sometimes people just walk away, and she should forget about it."

"That's ridiculous. I hope she reported him or her."

I took a breath. "Mieka, the detective she talked to was Alex."

Mieka shook her head vehemently. "I don't believe that."

"I didn't want to believe it either, but it turns out Alex has a Falconer Shreve connection of his own. The new woman in his life is Lily Falconer, the wife of one of the partners."

My daughter's face tightened. "A married woman – great. What's she like?"

"Enigmatic. Angry. Erotic."

Mieka snorted. "Call me superficial, but I was thinking more along the lines of whether she's drop-dead gorgeous and has a great bod."

"No to the first, yes to the second," I said.

My daughter took a sip of coffee. When she spoke she made no attempt to hide her impatience. "I don't buy it," she said. "You and Alex were happy together. He wouldn't just sniff the air and follow the first woman who put out a scent, no matter how enigmatic, angry, and erotic she was."

"Lily didn't just happen along," I said. "She and Alex have known one another for years. They both grew up on Standing Buffalo."

"Then it could just be a brother-sister thing."

"Like Siegmund and Sieglinde?"

"I don't know who Siegmund and Sieglinde are," Mieka said. "I'm the one who dropped out of university in first year, remember?"

"I remember," I said.

"Till your dying day," Mieka said dryly. "Anyway, Alex wanted out of your relationship. That happens. But the rest of this just doesn't make sense. Alex wouldn't get involved with a married woman. And he wouldn't compromise his job by refusing to talk to someone who came to him with a problem."

I picked up the pack of matches on the table and relit the harmony candle. It was cold comfort. "We're dealing with facts here," I said. "We may not want to believe them, but that doesn't make them less true."

"Poor Mum," Mieka said. "No wonder you looked wiped when you got here. So what are you going to do?"

"Go back to the lake, I guess. See what happens next."

"Not good enough," Mieka said. "Be proactive. Talk to Alex."

"As your Uncle Howard would say, 'I'd rather be pecked to death by a duck.'"

Mieka laughed softly. "Funny, I don't remember your ever going for the duck option. You've always been gutsy about tackling things head-on, and that's what you should do now. Ask Alex why he blew off that lawyer who tried to tell him something was rotten at Falconer Shreve, and ask him, as nicely as possible of course, if the reason he left you was that he was screwing around with this Lily Falconer."

"That'd be a memorable conversation," I said.

"But a productive one." Mieka stood up. "Clear the air. Find out what you can. Make sure the authorities know everything they need to know, then let them handle it. Mum, Greg and the girls and I are coming up to Lawyers' Bay for the entire month of August. You're going to have to be in fighting trim to put up with us till Labour Day." She stretched. "Bedtime for me," she said. "And for you." She lifted my chin and looked at me speculatively. "You know what you need?"

"Do I have a choice about hearing this?"

"The same choice I had when you shared your thoughts about my dropping out of university."

"I'm listening," I said.

"You need a good all-night date. Put Alex behind you and find a new guy. A little romance will give you back your glow."

On the drive back to the lake, Taylor continued to be absorbed in the Inukshuk book Mieka had lent her, so the miles sped past in silence. I had plenty of time to consider my daughter's advice – all of it. Mieka's counsel to confront Alex was solid. Asking him the hard questions would be painful, and I might not like the answers. Still, it would be better to know. It would be good to learn what I could about Clare from the members of the tightly knit Moot Team, too. If one of the women had been in touch with her in the last eight months, the case was closed, but if none of those closest to Clare had heard from her, we were clearly dealing with a matter for the police. *Fiat justitia*: I would do what I could to make certain that justice was done, but once I'd got the ball rolling, I was going to step aside and let Anne Millar and Clare's law-school friends take over. As Mieka had reminded me, August wasn't far away, and I wanted to be in shape for some serious fun.

Mentally, I had crossed every *t* and dotted every *i*, but the sight that greeted me when we pulled up in front of our cottage was fresh proof that when humans make plans, the gods laugh. Noah Wainberg was on his hands and knees on the mat in front of our door. He had a green tool box beside him, and it appeared he was jimmying our lock.

"What's Isobel's dad doing?" Taylor asked.

"Only one way to find out," I said, sliding out of the car and shaking the stiffness out of my legs. "Let's ask him."

Noah turned when he heard us. "Bad news," he said. "You were robbed."

My pulse quickened. "Is everybody okay?"

"Yeah. Nobody was home, but you should probably take a look around. Your son's girlfriend – Leah, isn't it?"

I nodded.

"Well, Leah gave the place the once-over. She didn't think anything was missing except your laptop computer."

"No great loss," I said. "It's vintage, and I haven't really used it in ages. The main thing is that no one was hurt."

"I agree. Material things are replaceable."

Taylor's eyes were wide. "Cats aren't. They better not have taken my cats."

"You're probably safe on that score," I said, but Taylor didn't hear me. She had already raced into the house to check on Bruce and Benny.

"So when did the break-in happen?" I asked Noah.

"Last night. Leah and your son had taken your dog for a run down the beach. When they got back, the front door was open. This is the only cottage here without a security system. Kevin's parents were pretty trusting, and he takes after them. Anyway, the lock I've installed is just temporary. A security company is coming out from the city tomorrow to hook you up."

"That's sort of sad, isn't it?" I said.

Noah wiped the sweat from his brow with the back of his hand. "Sad but inevitable," he said. "Oh, and I was supposed to tell you that Lily's ordered a new laptop for you."

"Everything taken care of," I said.

He smiled lazily. "I can take the lock off the door if you want."

"I didn't mean to sound ungrateful," I said. "I guess I'm just a little shaken. How can there be a robbery in a gated community?"

Noah shrugged. "The water isn't gated. Somebody wants to come up onto the beach in a canoe, I guess they can do what they want."

"It's kind of hard to imagine someone paddling up to steal a laptop," I said. "The images don't quite mesh."

"We live in troubling times," he said.

"That we do," I said. "Look, can I get you a glass of iced tea or something? You're getting the full blast of the sun there."

"Some water would be good. Actually, so would some shade."

I gestured towards the cottage's shadowy recesses. "Let's go inside," I said.

Taylor was curled up on the couch with her cats and Willie. When he spotted me, Willie leaped off the couch and scrambled over to me.

"I'm glad to see you too," I said, rubbing his head. When Noah and I went out to the porch, Willie stuck to me like glue.

"Bouviers are great dogs," Noah said.

"Best dog I ever had," I said. "If you're ever in the market for a loyal if challenged companion, I highly recommend them."

Noah scratched Willie's head. "Delia's frightened of dogs."

"Did she have a bad experience?"

"No. She's scared of a lot of things – dogs, spiders, thunderstorms. But she can present a brief to the Supreme Court without breaking a sweat, and I know of more than one macho lawyer who's looked up at that big bench and fainted dead away."

"Did you ever present a brief to the Supreme Court?"

"I never practised law," Noah said quickly.

"But you graduated from law school," I said. "When I was in Saskatoon I visited an old friend of mine who teaches at the College of Law. We were looking at photos of graduating classes. I hadn't realized you were in the same class as Delia and . . . the others."

"The 'others' being the members of the Winners' Circle," Noah said. "I was never a member of the Circle, but it's been years since I was crushed by

the omission. They've discovered I have my uses."
He tapped his tool box. "I'm the only one around
here who can unplug a toilet."

"My husband was a lawyer," I said. "He always
said that lawyers and plumbers did pretty much the
same thing: remove the blocks that stop the system
from working."

"That's about it. Give me a call if anything makes
you nervous." Noah drained his glass. "Hey, I almost
forgot. That was a nice picture of you in the paper."

"I didn't see it," I said.

"Sorry. How could you?" Noah walked over to
the front door and picked up a rolled copy of the
Leader Post. "Here – page one."

One look at the picture and it was easy to see
why it had made page one. The photograph was of
me and Patsy Choi.

"I didn't see her at the funeral," Noah said. "Do
you know her?"

"Just from the media," I said. "She came in late
and sat beside me."

"She looks good," Noah said.

"She does in person, too," I agreed.

"I wonder what she's like on the inside," Noah
said.

"Pretty fragile, I would imagine."

"Aren't we all?" Noah said. "Now let's take a tour of your house and see if anything besides the laptop is missing."

"You don't have to stay," I said.

Noah nodded. "I know, but there are times when a person shouldn't be alone, and this is one of them."

The place was shipshape. Having assured me that he could be there in two minutes if I needed him, Noah left with Taylor in tow. She'd had a good time in Saskatoon, but being away from the other two members of her triumvirate had been a wrench. After two days of Blue's Clues and the Wiggles, Taylor was hankering for the company of girls who knew how to apply eyeshadow.

Alone, I realized that the break-in had made me anxious for reassurance that all was well with those I loved. A rumbling in my stomach tipped me to the fact that I was also hungry. Clearly, a visit to the Point Store would be just the ticket. Willie was mournful as I started out the door, so I picked up his leash. "You'll have to wait outside, you know," I said. He didn't care.

Leah was busy behind the till when we arrived. She blew me a kiss, and I went back to the meat counter, where Angus was jawing with a customer.

I waited while he finished up, then gave him a hug, asked him to make me a salami sandwich, and filled him in on his sister's news. I was hankering after company, so I took my sandwich outside to pass the time at Coffee Row. The regulars had taken their places at the picnic table, but a card table was empty, so I poured myself a cup of weak coffee, chose a cookie from one of the yellow bags of generic biscuits, and settled in with Willie to eat my salami sandwich and see where the morning took us.

I wasn't the only one who'd brought a dog to Coffee Row that morning. Morris, the dedicated smoker of Player's Plains, had brought along his pet, a big yellow animal with a Buster Keaton face and what looked like a golden lab–mastiff pedigree. She was lying at her master's feet, snoring. It was a tranquil scene: the old men in their John Deere caps sitting in the shade of the cottonwood trees smoking and nodding, and the dog with her head resting on her front paws, jowls spilling to the ground, body vibrating with every rumbling inhalation and exhalation. When Stan Gardiner came down from his flat and took his place at the head of the table, it was clear that the catalyst for some conversation had arrived.

"About time you came down to join your friends," Morris said.

"Instead of sitting in your room watching your Lawrence Welk videos." The speaker, a gnome with big ears and a high, aggrieved voice, picked up the theme. "What kind of thing is that for a man to do?"

"In my opinion, Aubrey, it's about as valuable as sitting down here waiting for the hair in your ears to grow," Stan Gardiner said. "So what's the news across the nation?"

"Endzone's got herself a new trick," said Morris. "Watch this." He waved a piece of bologna in the air. The big yellow dog opened one eye, then the other. Clearly, her master knew how to get her attention. "Endzone, drive the truck," Morris barked.

The dog loped lazily towards a Ford half-ton. The door on the driver's side was open and Endzone jumped into the driver's seat, placed her paws on the steering wheel, and peered around.

"Look at that," Morris marvelled. "Wouldn't you swear she was driving that truck?"

"Apart from the fact that the door to the cab is open and the motor isn't running, I guess I would," Stan Gardiner agreed.

"Exit the truck," Morris yelled. He held out the bologna. Endzone leaped down and snapped up the treat with a single bite. "Did you hear she took off again?" he asked.

"It's in their blood," Aubrey said sagely. "They can't help themselves. Her mother was the same."

"Let's hope she doesn't end up killing two men like her mother did," Stan said. "That was a real tragedy."

I stared at Endzone with new eyes. It was hard to believe this sad-sack Buster Keaton dog had killer genes.

"She may have already started," Morris said. He peeled a slice of bologna from the package and gummed it absent-mindedly. "I'll bet when all is said and done, they'll find out she had something to do with that Chris Altieri's death. If he did commit suicide, which I doubt, I'll bet it was because of her. The nut doesn't fall far from the tree, and if the particular nut we're talking about had stayed closer to the tree, it would have been better for everyone."

Stan dipped a gingersnap in his coffee. "Nuts and trees. Why the hell can't you ever just say what you want to say plain, so that an ordinary human being can understand what you're saying?"

"Because I've been around, and I know the importance of being discreet," Morris said.

"Well, you're just being stupid. Say it plain, man." Stan Gardiner's anger was building.

"All right, here it is plain. If Lily Falconer had stayed closer to her husband and kid, there might not have been a suicide over there at Lawyers' Bay. That Lily is like her mother – a fatal attraction. She can't help the way men buzz around her, like bees around a flower. But two good men died because of Lily's mother, and I wouldn't be surprised if we had a case of history repeating itself here."

My heart was pounding so loudly, I was certain the gents at the next table could hear it, but they had sunk back into meditation. Willie, however, picked up my tension. He strained at the leash. "Stay," I hissed. He looked at me reproachfully, but he stopped pulling. Ears pricked, I listened for the next revelation.

Morris took out a cigarette and offered the pack around. There were no takers. He lit his smoke and sat back. "I owe you an apology, Stan," he said.

"You owe me more than one apology," Stan said crankily.

"Don't push your luck," Morris said. "You're no saint. All the same, I was out of line criticizing your viewing habits. I like Lawrence Welk myself. As for that champagne lady – Alice what's her name – well, she could park her dancing slippers under my bed any time she liked." He laughed his dry, wheezing laugh. "Come on, Endzone," he said. "We've done enough damage here. Time to head back to the house."

Overwhelmed by the enormity of what I'd heard, I watched man and dog make their dusty progress down the road. Morris's words had been plain enough, but I couldn't seem to take them in. I was so engrossed in puzzling out what he'd said that I didn't notice that Leah was standing beside me until she tapped my arm.

"Hey," she said.

"Hey, yourself," I said. "Talk about bad timing. You just missed Endzone, the wonder dog."

"I've caught his act. That dog will do anything for processed meat." Her smile was pained. "I'm glad you're back, Jo. I'm guessing someone's already told you about the break-in."

"Noah was putting a new lock on the door when Taylor and I got back from the city," I said. "He filled me in."

"I feel so awful. Angus does too. But we did lock the door. The lock was just so old – whoever broke in didn't have any trouble forcing it. Was anything else besides the laptop missing?"

"No," I said.

"Weird," she said. "Because that laptop of yours – no offence – but it wasn't worth risking a jail term over. And the place was neat as a pin. We weren't gone long, thirty minutes, tops. Angus says whoever did the job must have been watching the cottage." Leah pushed her chair back. "I'd better get back to work. The store is humming today."

I walked back to the cottage, mulling over the information that had come my way during the last thirty minutes. Despite the gathering heat of the day, I felt a chill. Angus's theory that the laptop thief had been watching our cottage wasn't the most menacing intelligence I'd received, but it was the one most directly connected to my life. For the first time since I'd arrived at Lawyers' Bay, I was apprehensive as I opened my front door. Before I settled in, I went through the house to make sure everything was in order. I was glad Willie was with me. He was a toothless lion, but a stranger wouldn't know that.

I satisfied myself that all was in order, then changed into my bathing suit and picked up my book and a beach towel. I needed the warmth of the sun on my back and I needed not to be alone. But before I could allow myself the luxury of the beach, there were two telephone calls I had to make.

The first was straightforward. Anne Millar deserved a report on my meeting with Holly Knott. I found Anne's business card in my wallet, picked up my cell, and dialled. Anne was in a meeting. Her administrative assistant suggested I leave a message on her voice mail and I did. My message was brief. I said that Holly Knott believed that Clare might have kept in touch with the members of her Moot Team and that Holly had e-mailed the head administrator at the College of Law giving her the go-ahead to release the women's contact information to me.

The second phone call was not so easy. My hands were shaking as I dialled Alex's number at the police station. When I learned that he wasn't on duty, I was relieved, but I knew I couldn't let myself off that easily. I dialled his apartment number, and as I listened to the phone ring, I imagined the familiar room with its clean, uncluttered lines and collections of Mozart. There was no answer. As I dialled Alex's cell, my face was flushed. I was certain he would pick up, but he didn't. I rang off without leaving a message – glad that I didn't have to ask questions with answers I didn't want to hear. But I was already asking myself a question. Lily Falconer had taken off. Was it possible that she hadn't taken off alone, that like her mother before her Lily had exerted a pull on the men in her life that she couldn't control, and that Alex had succumbed to what Morris, the man who had been around, termed her fatal attraction?

CHAPTER 7

I didn't have time to ponder Lily's history or her mother's. As they had since I'd arrived at Lawyers' Bay, events tumbled over one another, leaving me without time to do much but react. The head administrator at the College of Law called with contact information about Clare Mackey's Moot partners. It was holiday time, so finding people in the office hadn't been easy, but I did manage to track down one member of the team, a woman named Maggie Niewinski, who was working for a small law firm in Prince Albert, a city on the edge of our province's parkland. In less than an hour, Maggie had touched base with the other women from the Moot Team. None of them had heard from Clare. No one had been worried. They were all establishing new careers and lives in new communities; keeping in touch had been put on hold. But the sudden realization that no one had heard from Clare had been unsettling. When Maggie called me back to report, she tried to keep the edge of panic out of her voice, but I could hear it, and I felt an answering anxiety. Something was not right.

When a shiny black Ford pulled into my driveway and Detective Robert Hallam hopped out, waved, and smiled, relief washed over me. It was as if the Moot Team's collective anxiety had somehow conjured up this most reliable of officers. As always, Robert was dapper: black dress shoes polished to a high gloss, grey lightweight slacks with a knife-sharp press, a striped cotton shirt the colour of orange sherbet, and a grey silk tie.

When he came inside he gazed around at the shabby comfort appreciatively. "This is so nice," he said. "I've always thought knotty pine was exactly right for a cottage. And I like the family pictures, and the books and the stuff that belonged to the kids. This seems like a home where people have been happy."

"From what I hear, they were," I said.

"This is the kind of place I'd like Rosalie and me to retire to," he said. "And if I had my druthers, I'd keep a cottage like this just the way it is. But you know my bride. She'd be decorating. You wouldn't recognize that bungalow of ours."

"How's the wasabi-green bedroom working out?"

Robert blushed. "It's rejuvenated me," he said. Startled by the revelation, we both looked at our toes. In an effort to recover the situation, Robert walked to a shelf crowded with action figures. He named them carefully. "Batman. Aquaman. Spider-man. Mr. Freeze. Mr. Sinister. G.I. Joe. Han Solo. Darth Vader. C-3PO. Superman." He picked up a figure and chuckled fondly. "Lex Luthor," Robert said. "'He could have been a mighty force for good in the world, yet he chose to direct his great scientific brain into evil channels.' That's what Clark Kent said about him."

"Clark ought to know," I said. "Lex Luthor was always Superman's most dangerous enemy."

Robert regarded the figure in his hand. "I didn't think Lex and I would meet again this side of the grave."

"You should take a look around," I said. "You'd probably find a lot of old friends. This cottage is filled with heroes and villains. The moral lines are pretty strictly drawn around here."

"Maybe that's why I feel so at home." Robert smiled. "Today, everybody roots for the bad guys.

I never have. Even when I was a kid I thought the world was divided into two camps: there was good and there was evil."

"Superman and Lex Luthor," I said.

"You don't agree?"

"I guess I've seen too many shades of grey. But I'm glad you chose the line of work you did. We need police who still believe in good and evil."

"That's why it's a tragedy when one of them starts confusing things." Robert's eyes had grown steely. "Joanne, I'm a blunt man, and I don't like beating around the bush."

"Then say what you have to say, Robert. You and I have always respected one another."

"I wouldn't be here otherwise," he said. "You know I've had my differences with Inspector Kequahtooway. I thought he got promoted over guys like me because he was a member of a minority. I thought the department set the bar lower for people like him. To be honest, I still think that's true, but Inspector Kequahtooway turned out to be a good cop. He worked hard and he was honest."

I felt a sickness in the pit of my stomach. "But you don't think that's true any more."

Robert looked miserable. "I don't know what to think. There were . . . some questions . . . about the way a case was being handled. I was asked to check into things to see if an official inquiry was warranted." He made a sound of disgust. "It would be my badge if anyone knew I was telling you this. But once these investigations are set in motion, they're impossible to stop. I wanted to be sure of my facts."

"That's fair enough," I said. "So what are the facts?"

Robert tented his fingers. "The files on this case are incomplete. Items that should be there are missing. Inspector Kequahtooway talked to a number of people the day after Christopher Altieri died, but his records of those interviews seem to be hit-and-miss."

"Am I there?" I asked.

"Yes, and as far as I can tell the inspector's account of his interview with you appears complete."

"How about Lily Falconer?"

Robert cast his eyes down. "She's one of the problem areas. According to other officers who were present, the inspector interviewed her at length. In fact, he made certain he was the only member of the force who talked to her. But he didn't write up the interview."

"Alex was always so careful."

"I know, and that's why I'm talking to you, Joanne. Every cop knows there's a difference between what they teach you at police college and what you do on the job. In theory, you *are* supposed to keep a written record of everything, but every investigating officer carries material in his head. Sometimes there are good reasons not to put things down on paper. The information might just not feel right. You might be afraid of dragging an innocent person in. You might be working on a theory that you suspect could blow up in your face."

"If you're looking for an explanation about the problem with the records, why don't you ask Alex?"

Robert's gaze was steady. "I think you know the answer to that."

My heart sank. "You don't want to tip him off," I said. "But, Robert, why have you come to me?"

"As far as I know, you were the only friend he had."

Unexpectedly, tears stung my eyes. "I always assumed he had friends on the force, that he just believed in keeping his professional and personal lives separate."

"No. Inspector Kequahtooway has always been a loner – in fact, he's about the most alone human being I've ever known. He's always polite, but he doesn't mix with the people he works with – no beers with the guys when he goes off duty, no bar-becues or hockey games on the weekend."

"But as long as he does his job, why does that matter?"

"Because after a while, *not* socializing interferes with the job. Police work involves trust, Joanne. We have to be able to rely on the people we work with, not just when we're in a tight spot, but every day. For members of the force, talk is a safety valve – it keeps us from blowing a gasket. But we have to be able to trust the one we're talking to. That's rule number one."

"Alex didn't talk to me about his work," I said. "I wish he had."

"Maybe he would now."

"You think I should call him."

"I think he deserves one last chance to come clean."

I felt my nerves twang. I was not about to deny a good man his last chance.

"I'll call him," I said.

I walked Robert to the door, shook his hand, sent love to Rosalie, and invited them both to come out to the lake. Then, while the adrenaline was still pumping, I picked up my cell and called Alex. He still wasn't answering. I left a message asking him to call back, then I rang off and turned to look at my empty house. The prospect of being alone with my thoughts did not please me.

My salvation came, as it so often did, from Taylor. She roared through the door with Isobel and

Gracie, who were already in their swimsuits. As
Taylor raced to the bedroom to change into hers,
she carried on a conversation over her shoulder.
Rose's sister, Betty, had bought a new pair of shoes
with heels that were too high and she'd taken a
tumble. Rose was driving her into the city to get
X-rayed. Rose didn't want the girls to miss their
diving practice, but they needed an adult. Could it
be me? As we walked to the lake, Gracie confided
that Rose felt Betty had learned a valuable lesson
about acting her age. Then came the big news. The
girls had decided on a project. It might take them
a week to complete. After I'd established that the
project didn't involve danger or older boys, I let
them run ahead to buzz and make plans.

As we often were, the girls and I were alone on
the beach. Wealth had its privileges. The wind had
come up and cooled the air. As I kicked off my
sandals and walked into the lake, the water was welcoming. In my life, our cottages had always been on
northern lakes, and I was accustomed to bracing
myself physically and mentally for a shock when I
dove in. But even on a windy day, there was no
need to brace here. We all dove in quickly and
began to stroke through the choppy waters towards
the diving tower. I had always been a confident
swimmer, and as I moved through the waves, my

muscles relaxed and my mind stopped racing. In the days since the Falconer Shreve Canada Day party, I had been reeling; it seemed that finally I was ready, in my grandmother's stringent phrase, to take hold of myself.

A few metres away from the diving tower, I began to tread water while I waited for the girls to climb the ladder and begin their dives. I watched as, one after another, they came off the board, and when all three heads were bobbing safely in the waves, I yelled that I was going to do laps but I'd be in earshot. Then I swam back towards the raft that floated a hundred metres away. My stroke was the tried and trustworthy Australian crawl. Flutter-kicking forward, my arms cutting through the sparkle of foam on the waves, my gaze turning from the bright sunlight to the iridescent shimmer beneath the surface, I felt myself moving towards strength.

When I touched the side of the raft, I started back towards the tower, where I checked on the girls and began my next lap. Back and forth I went. Finally, I'd had enough. Exhausted but feeling better than I had in a very long time, I climbed onto the raft and lay on my stomach, my face resting on my hands, the sun caressing my back like a hand. The undulating waves rocked the raft like a cradle, lulling me into a state of equilibrium and the illusion that all was right with the world.

When Blake Falconer pulled himself onto the raft, the illusion shattered. He didn't impose himself. In fact, he made every effort to preserve the distance between us. He swung his body around, so he was sitting on the edge of the raft with his feet in the water and his back to me. For a minute or two, neither of us spoke, but we were aware of one another's presence. Finally, I pushed myself up.

"Hi," I said.

He turned around. There was something different about him. He was still a force to be reckoned with, but the assurance was gone.

"I didn't want to disturb you," he said softly. "I thought you'd earned your solitude. I was watching you do your laps. You were swimming as if your life depended on it."

"You're not far off the mark," I said. "I was trying to get a sense of being in control again. So much has happened."

"Being the victim of a break-and-enter can't have helped," Blake said.

"It didn't," I said. "It's disconcerting to think of someone watching your house and pawing through your things."

"But the only thing stolen was your laptop."

"As far as I can tell," I said.

"I have a replacement for you in the car," he said. "It's an Apple PowerBook. I've got one. It should be okay."

"I'm sure it's more than okay," I said. "But a notebook like that is way out of my price range."

"I wouldn't worry about it. We get a corporate rate."

"How much is the corporate rate?"

He shrugged. "That's Lily's department. We'll check it out when she gets back."

"Where is she?"

There was always something boyish about Blake, but at that moment he looked his age. "The social answer is that she went back to the city. The truth is I haven't a clue."

"That has to be worrying," I said.

"It was – the first fifty times it happened," he said. "But so far, she's always come back."

For a moment, the sentence hung in the air between us. Blake didn't take his eyes off me. "You don't look shocked."

"I learned long ago not to judge other people's marriages. If it works for you . . ."

"I'm not sure that it does," he said. "The reasons for staying together just outweigh the reasons for leaving." Blake's gaze was fixed on the diving tower.

In their identical navy swimsuits and red bathing caps, the three girls looked like sisters, but Gracie was clearly the tallest and the strongest. Obeying that sixth sense children often show when they're being observed, she turned and waved to us. As he waved back, Blake's face became young again.

"Your daughter is so much like you," I said, smiling.

The comment had been casual, but Blake's response was grave. "I always thought that was a source of sadness for Lily," he said. "I think she would have liked a child like her."

"In what way?" I asked.

"Physically," he said. "I always sensed that Lily would have felt more connected to a child who was unmistakably aboriginal." Blake's grey eyes were sad. "Not that we always get what we want in this world."

"What did you want that you didn't get?" I asked.

"Truthfully? I wanted to get the part that Lily always held back. Even when things between us were at their best, there was something in her I could never touch. It's been that way since the beginning."

"How did you two meet?"

His forehead crinkled. "Delia said it was like a Julia Roberts movie. The old days at Falconer Shreve were pretty loose. We were all busy trying to get those bright career arcs going, so we didn't pay a lot of attention to details like running the office, which incidentally was above a place that made dentures. The smell of false teeth was always in the air, and things were always in a helluva mess. Anyway, every Friday afternoon we had a happy hour for clients and people we knew from law school and anybody else who stumbled in, and one Friday afternoon Lily showed up."

"That is like a Julia Roberts movie," I said.

"It gets better," he said. "Anyway, I'd been drinking far too long and I'd reached that lost-in-the-funhouse feeling, and suddenly I looked across the room and there was this incredible woman with legs that went on forever and black hair that fell almost to her waist. She wasn't beautiful, but she was so much her own person. Everyone else in that room was sweating, busy pushing an agenda – trying to make a connection, trying to get laid – but Lily just stood there, observing. I'm sure you've noticed how she does that."

I turned my eyes to the diving board. Taylor was poised for a swan dive. I shut my eyes against the

inevitable belly flop, but she surprised me by enter-
ing the water cleanly.

"I've noticed," I said. "Lily's a very compelling
woman."

"Compelling," Blake repeated. "That's exactly
the word. And I was compelled. That afternoon I
went over to her, stroked her beautiful hair, and said
something so stupid that it still makes me cringe."

I smiled. "So what did you say?"

He bit his lower lip. "I told her I could make all
her dreams come true."

"Smooth," I said. "How did it go over?"

"My wife-to-be peeled my hand off her shoulder and told me she could make my dreams come
true, too — for a price. That flummoxed me, of
course. But as it turned out the price she had in
mind was a job, as office manager. She told me it
was obvious that Falconer Shreve needed organi-
zation. I looked around, saw the place through her
eyes, and realized she was right. It was amazing
that the board of health hadn't condemned us: files
spilling over the desks, wastebaskets overflowing
with containers from Chinese take-out and pizza,
dirty coffee cups and plastic plates and cutlery
everywhere."

Isobel Wainberg was on the diving board looking
as if she might change her mind. Her last dive had

not gone well, and Isobel took failure hard. Blake and I raised our arms in an exaggerated thumbs-up sign, then held our breath until she took the plunge.

"When we studied avoidance-avoidance conflict in university, I remembered that diving-board feeling," I said.

Blake nodded his head in agreement. "Damned if you do, damned if you don't. But good for Isobel – going off the high board is never easy."

"Is that what you did in your relationship with Lily?" I asked.

He laughed ruefully. "I'd never thought of it that way, but yes. From the night I met her there was no turning back. When she offered to organize my life, she made me an offer I couldn't refuse. I hired her on the spot. We had a drink. I made a pass. She told me to go to hell, and I gave her a key to the office and went home with somebody else. Monday morning when I came back the place was unrecognizable – spotless, organized."

"That is a Julia Roberts movie," I said.

"It would be," he said, "except that after Lily and her loutish boss finally got together, they didn't live happily ever after. He loved her, but she never quite came around." Blake turned to me. "I have no idea why I'm telling you all this."

"Because I'm here," I said.

It was a moment of silent communion that broke when Blake looked towards the shoreline. "Surprise, surprise," he said, pointing at the boat launch. "Company's coming."

Zack Shreve was gripping the device that allowed him to lower himself into his boat. The mechanism was sophisticated structurally, but simple. It depended not on electronics but on dexterity and strength. Zack was heavy-set, and I was struck again by the power his arms must have to hoist his body from land to boat. Blake and I sat in silence as he completed the manoeuvre, turned on the motor, and drove over to the raft. Zack was wearing Ray-Bans with grey mirror lenses that hid his eyes, making him seem even more unknowable.

"Perfect day for banana fish," he said. "Or for conversation. Joanne, you seem to have a reverse Scheherazade effect on my partners. They come into your presence and they feel the need to talk and talk. Is it a dark plot?"

Staring into the mirror lenses proved surprisingly disconcerting. I focused on the midpoint of Zack's forehead, above his glasses. "No dark plot," I said. "Just obeying a human need to say what's on their minds."

"Well, let's be human," Zack said. He reached up and removed his sunglasses. His green eyes were penetrating. "It appears that we're all without significant others tonight. Why don't we go out to eat? The girls might enjoy Magoo's."

"Never heard of it," I said.

"It's a restaurant across the lake," Blake said. "And it's fun. Nostalgia – jukeboxes, a little dance floor, a deck where you can get burgers with the works, greasy fries, milkshakes."

"And onion rings," Zack said, raising his forefinger. "Incomparable onion rings."

"That settles it for me," I said, standing. "Onion rings are one of my passions."

Zack gave my body a slow and intense once-over. "Obviously they do the job."

I felt myself colour. "So what time's dinner?"

"I should get some work done tonight," Blake said. "Let's eat early."

Zack put his glasses back on. "Good idea. While you're working, maybe I can get Joanne to listen to *my* story."

We met at the dock at six o'clock. The kids had decided it would be fun to get to the restaurant by boat and Zack was eager to oblige. I'd taken Willie for a quick run, so the girls had already taken their places by the time I arrived. As was often the case when they were together, they were huddled in conversation with Taylor, the youngest and the smallest, in the middle. I would have bet a box of Timbits that the subject of their conversation was the hush-hush project that had absorbed them all afternoon. When they came back to our cottage late in the day, they were dirty, sweaty, happy, and mum about their activities. I had a theory, but I hadn't mentioned it. Secret-sharing was obviously proving to be a lot of fun.

Blake was sitting beside Zack, so I stepped down into the back with the girls. Zack asked if we were set, and when we gave him the high sign, he turned on the motor and we nosed out into the lake. As we sped across the water, the girls fell silent, and I was able to catch them in a moment of rare repose. Dreaming their private dreams, their faces turned rosy by the slanting sun, they formed a striking triptych of privilege and promise. But young as they were, each of the girls carried a past, and I found myself wondering how heavily their personal histories weighed on their slender shoulders.

Gracie had tipped her head back so that her face was lifted to the sun. With her red-gold hair, her freckles, and her easy optimism, she was completely her father's child. Yet as someone whose own mother had been disappointed in her, I knew the burden of living with a mother's rejection, of knowing that your very existence was a source of sadness to the woman who gave you life. Gracie's blithe spirit would be tested.

Oblivious to my gaze, she leaned forward and threw her arms around her father. Blake twisted awkwardly to return the hug. It was a nice moment, and Taylor caught it. The longing in her eyes surprised me. Taylor had been very young when her own father died, and her memories of him were shadowy. I reached over and squeezed her hand, but the connection wasn't enough. She gave me a vague smile and turned away.

As she witnessed the moment, Isobel Wainberg's narrow intelligent face grew wary. Her reaction was no surprise. Isobel was a bundle of imperfectly insulated nerve ends. She had inherited her mother's cleverness, her odd squeaky voice, and her melancholy. Even her wiry black hair was like her mother's, shooting out from her head uncontrollably as if the impulses she carried in her brain had caused a short circuit. When she caught my gaze, her smile was hesitant. She knew Taylor had hit a bad patch and she wanted to help, but she didn't know how.

We could hear the music from Magoo's before we docked. Gene Chandler's classic "Duke of Earl" rocked out across the water. Gracie squeezed her

eyes shut in delight. "This is going to be so *wicked*!"
Isobel allowed herself a small smile of agreement,
but Taylor remained deep in the heart of darkness.

I leaned towards her. "Penny for your thoughts,"
I said.

My daughter raised her eyes to mine. "I was
thinking about what I'd leave behind," she said.

"I don't understand."

"I was wondering what I'd leave behind after I
died," Taylor said.

I tried to keep my voice steady. "Is something
wrong?" I asked.

"Everything's great," Taylor said.

"Can we talk about it later?" I said.

Her face was unreadable. "It was just a question,
Jo." The patient detachment in her voice was familiar. It was her mother Sally's tone. The boat docked;
the girls scrambled out, laughing as they raced
towards the music, and I was left to ponder the fact
that once again nature had trumped nurture.

It was early on a Tuesday night, but Magoo's was
crowded. It wasn't hard to figure out the secret of
the owners' success. They had chosen to recreate an
ideal of uncomplicated innocence that would make
people happy, and they had achieved their goal.
Everything was authentic. The big Wurlitzer jukebox that met you when you came into the room

was vintage. Its distinctive rounded top, bright columns of colour, and the glass front through which you could watch your musical choices slide into place were guaranteed to bring a smile – just as they had during their heyday in the middle decades of the twentieth century. The servers, too, had the bounce of an era before the age of irony. The walls were covered with cheerfully faked photographs of flesh-and-blood celebrities of the fifties and sixties posing with Mr. Magoo, the crotchety, myopic, W.C. Fields–like cartoon character who gave the restaurant its name.

Zack had reserved a table for us on the deck overlooking the lake, and as soon as we'd placed our orders, the girls hit us up for loonies to play the jukebox and gravitated towards the dance floor. Taylor seemed to have left her existential angst in the boat, so there was nothing to do but relax, listen to Jan and Dean sing "Dead Man's Curve," and enjoy the sunset and the Japanese lanterns.

When Blake excused himself to talk to friends he'd spotted across the deck, Zack gave me an opening I couldn't ignore. "So what have you been up to, Joanne? I know you were out of town, because I knocked at your door."

"I was in Saskatoon tracking down a former employee of yours," I said.

Zack raised an eyebrow. "And who would that be?"

"Clare Mackey," I said.

I watched his face carefully for a reaction. There was none. "You didn't have to drive to Saskatoon to find out where Clare was," he said evenly. "I could have told you."

"Good," I said. "So where is she?"

"Clare is in feminist heaven. She landed a job with an all-female law firm in Vancouver."

"What's the name of the firm?"

Zack shrugged. "I haven't a clue."

"Yet you're still comfortable with the official explanation," I said.

Zack rested his forearms on the table and leaned towards me. Like everything else he did, the move seemed calculated. His upper body was powerful, and braced against the table he had the controlled energy of an animal about to pounce. "What makes you think the official explanation isn't the truth?" he said.

"For one thing, no one seems to have heard from Clare. Her friends are getting anxious."

"Clare's an adult," Zack said. "She was offered a good job in an exciting city. She moved along. Do you have any more questions?"

"Not at the moment," I said.

"Then let's put that eager young server hovering behind you out of his misery and eat our onion rings."

"Perfect timing," I said.

"Perfect world," Zack said as the server placed the platter between us. "Take a bite."

Conversation during dinner was minimal. We were all hungry, and Magoo's food made talk a fool's option. The menu noted that the burgers were made on-site and sizzled on the kitchen grill; the oversized Kaiser buns were baked by the owner's mother; the lettuce and tomatoes on the condiment tray had been picked from the garden out back; the fries were hand-cut shoestrings; the milkshakes were so thick they were guaranteed to clog a straw.

We munched to the beat of the Shangri-Las, Sam Cooke, Gene Pitney, and Brenda Lee. Finally, Taylor pushed away her plate.

"Finished?" I said.

"I have to pee," she mouthed.

I waited a moment, assessed the situation, and followed her.

She'd been quiet during dinner, but Taylor had always been serious about food. That said, she was not a morbid child, and the fact that she'd talked about a legacy worried me. She was already in the stall when I got there.

"Everything okay?" I asked.

"I just had to pee," she said.

"Fine," I said. "I'll wait. We can go back together."

"As if I was two years old," she said.

"Taylor, one of these days you'll be a woman, and that means you'll be going to the powder room with other women for the rest of your life. Consider tonight your rite of passage."

Taylor was grinning when she came out of the stall. "*Powder room*." She rolled the words around in her mouth. "Who calls it that?"

In a photo above her, the cartoon Mr. Magoo peered nearsightedly at the spectacular cleavage of a life-sized Marilyn Monroe. "Women who need a place to talk privately about how their evening's going," I said.

"Cool," Taylor said. Her eyes held mine. "About that 'leaving behind' thing. Maddy's book about the Inuksuit said that once people all over the world built things like Inuksuit and left them behind to help the people who came after. I was just wondering what I was going to leave."

"I imagine you'll be like your mother and leave behind a lot of amazing art."

"But what if I'm like my father?" Taylor said. "He didn't leave anything behind."

"That's not true, Taylor," I said. "We all leave something."

"But what did my father leave?"

I put my hands on her shoulders and turned her towards the mirror. "He left you."

CHAPTER 8

After we left the ladies' room, Taylor went back to the dance floor to rock around the clock with Bill Haley, and I returned to our table on the deck and a *fait accompli*. Zack was alone, his fingers tapping out the beat on the Formica tabletop and his eyes fixed on the progress of a red canoe moving towards shore.

When I sat down, he gave me a satyr's smile. "Change in plans," he said. "Blake caught a ride to Lawyers' Bay with those people he was talking to before dinner. He's decided to drive back to the city tonight."

"So he can look for Lily?" I said.

"I imagine Blake can make an educated guess about his wife's whereabouts."

"Can you?" I asked.

He shrugged. "Anybody can make a guess, but Lily's wandering ways are Blake's concern. I never assume another man's burdens."

"Unless he pays you a retainer," I said.

"Good one," Zack said, raising his metal milk-shake container to me. "But back to the situation at hand. I didn't see any reason to end the evening. The girls and I are having a good time, and you looked as if you could use a little fun."

"You're very perceptive," I said.

"When it matters to me, I am. And since you matter to me, I'll do what I can to lighten your spirits. Would you care to dance?"

Taken aback by what sounded suspiciously like a pass, I hesitated a beat too long before answering. Zack picked up on my uncertainty.

"I *can* dance, you know."

I stood and extended my hand. "In that case, let's dance."

Zack took it. "A woman who leads," he said. "I like that."

The spectators around the dance floor were closer to Taylor's age than to mine, and they were agape. True to his promise, Zack really could dance. He manoeuvred his chair with skill and finesse, and he led me through the Twist, the Stroll, the Jerk, the Monkey, and the Swim before, sweaty and breathless, I raised my hand.

"I have to sit the next one out," I said. "It's either that or coronary care."

Zack was sweaty and breathless too. "Thank God," he said. "I was afraid you'd never give up."

"I didn't know it was a contest," I said.

"Everything's a contest, but I also wanted you to have a good time. You seemed preoccupied."

"Sorry," I said. "Just parent stuff. In the boat coming over, Taylor said something that bothered me."

"Fill me in," Zack said. "I'm a good listener."

"Is this going to be a billable hour?" I asked.

He grinned. "Nope. This hour's free. This is where I suck you in. Get you to like me."

"I already like you," I said.

"So the pressure's off. Let's talk about Taylor."

"There's not much to say. On the ride over, Taylor seemed a little down. I offered her a penny for her thoughts and she told me she was wondering what she'd leave behind after she died. That's why I followed her into the bathroom. But she assured me her concern about a legacy was no big deal – it was just a question she was mulling over."

In the candlelight, Zack's eyes were lustrous. "You don't believe her?"

"I don't know," I said. "Taylor has a complicated history. She was the daughter of a friend of mine – the artist Sally Love."

"Wow," Zack said. "I own a Sally Love. It's my favourite piece. It's also the most valuable thing I own."

"I'm not surprised," I said. "The price for Sally's work hit the stratosphere after she died, and it's stayed there. Taylor's a very rich young girl."

"But tonight she's a girl who's wondering whether she'll leave a mark on the world. A very human concern."

"Is it a concern of yours?"

"Not any more," Zack said.

A flotilla of ducks was moving towards shore. Twilight had calmed the winds and quieted the lake. As the ducks swam, each one left behind it a tracing, feather-delicate. Within seconds, the tracing was absorbed by the water.

Zack pointed to the ducks. "That's what we leave behind," he said. "Nothing. Once you accept that, everything else is easy."

"Then why does Chris's death matter so much to you?"

"Because he was special," Zack said. "A good man in a bad world."

"He didn't think he was good," I said. "The night he died he told me that he had done something unforgivable."

As a trial lawyer, Zack had years of experience keeping his public face unreadable, but a tic in his eye betrayed him. "Did our friend elaborate on his unforgivable act?"

I weighed the options: a pleasant evening or a painful discussion. Given the past twenty-four hours, there was no choice. I turned to Zack. "Chris told me a woman he'd been involved with had had an abortion. He couldn't get over it. More to the point, he didn't believe he deserved to get over it because there'd been something else – some previous sin. Does any of this ring a bell?"

I could almost hear Zack's brain click through the calibrations: I had information he needed; he had information that would interest me but that he didn't want to divulge.

"I didn't know about the baby," Zack said carefully. His words had the ring of truth, and I believed him. That said, I hadn't just fallen off the turnip truck. I knew his response had been selective.

"But you knew something was wrong," I said. "The night Chris died you tried to make me doubt what he'd told me. You told me that sometimes people confess to big things because they're burdened with guilt about little things."

Zack didn't answer. Seemingly, he was still trying to assimilate what I had just told him. "An abortion," he muttered as if to himself. "That's all it was."

"Chris didn't see it as a small thing," I said.

Zack sighed. "No, he wouldn't. But Jesus, to kill yourself over something like that."

The glass-shattering falsetto climax of Roy Orbison's "Only the Lonely" pierced the air. It seemed to bring Zack back to the moment, and he smiled. "That was the favourite song of a client of mine. He said it was so sad it could make a dog cry."

"Sensitive client," I said. "What were the charges?"

"He was alleged to have dropped a barbell on the windpipe of his sleeping grandmother."

I shuddered. "Guilty?"

"Absolutely," Zack said. "But he still had a good ear for a ballad of doom." He pushed his chair back from the table. "Ready to call it a night?"

"I am," I said. Then, like a long-married couple, Zachary Shreve and I collected the girls from the dance floor, rejected their pleas for just one more song, and shepherded them down to the dock for the trip across the lake.

It was a moon-drenched night, so serenely beautiful that it drew the giddiness out of the girls and
made them reflective. Except for the purr of the
motor and the squawk of the occasional gull, our
passage was silent. Continuing in our oddly parental
roles, Zack and I walked Gracie and Isobel home.
Gracie's cottage was nearest to the dock, so we
dropped her off first. Rose Lavallee met us at the
Falconers' door. Her grey hair was neatly pincurled
and she had covered it with a gorgeous scarf pat-
terned with the logo of a famous New York designer
and tied at the top of her head to make bunny ears.
The house smelled good, of spice and warmth.

"I made those spice cookies you like," Rose said
to Gracie.

Gracie planted a kiss on Rose's leathery cheek.
"You always do that when she goes away."

"It's to take the sting out," Rose said. She gazed
at the four of us still waiting outside. "Not a good
night for company. But I can bag you up some
cookies."

"We can get some tomorrow," Taylor said.

"They're better fresh." Rose disappeared into the
kitchen. In a flash she was back with four brown
lunch bags. She handed one to each of us.

"This is a treat," I said. "Thanks."

"You're welcome," Rose said. "Now if you don't

mind, I'm going to close this door. The bugs are getting in."

It was a night for threshold encounters. Delia Wainberg met us at her door. She was wearing orange velour pyjamas that looked roomy and comfortable. Her black hair was a nimbus and, for the first time since I'd met her, she seemed happy and relaxed. On the day Chris's ashes had been scattered, Lily Falconer had speculated that, with Chris out of the way, Delia and Noah might have a chance. Whether or not this was true, it was clear to me that the Wainbergs had been making love.

The same thought seemed to occur to Zack. After Isobel said her thank yous and goodbyes and the door closed behind her, he turned his wheelchair to go back down the walk. "It would be nice to have someone to come home to," he said, and his voice was full of yearning.

When Taylor and I got back to the cottage, there was a note on the table from Angus and Leah. They'd gone to a cottage down the shore for a wiener roast and a planning session for the Ultimate Flying Disc Tournament starting the next night, so Taylor and I were on our own. We got into our nighties, but when I went to tuck Taylor in, I didn't leave after prayers and a hug.

"Can we talk for a while?" I said.

Taylor surprised me by moving over in bed and making room for me the way she had when she was little. I slid in beside her.

"Let's turn out the lights," Taylor said. "It's nicer to talk in the dark."

I flicked the switch on the lamp on her bedside table and we waited for a few seconds until our eyes grew accustomed to the shadows.

"We haven't done this for a long time," I said.

"It still feels the same," Taylor said.

"You're right," I said. "It still feels good."

"I love it here at the lake," Taylor said.

"I'm glad," I said. "You and Isobel and Gracie seem to be having a lot of fun."

"We are," Taylor said. "But we talk, too. Gracie says she thinks her parents are going to get a divorce."

"How does Gracie feel about that?"

"She says it's for the best. She says her mother's unhappy – that's why she keeps running away." Taylor paused and took a hiccuping breath. "Was that why my mother went away?"

Over the years, Taylor and I had trod lightly around the subject of her mother. We had talked often about her art. Sally had given me one of her paintings as a gift, and friends in Regina had others. Taylor's hunger to connect with her mother through spending time close to the art Sally made had always moved me. I had once come upon her tracing the lines of one of her mother's paintings with her small fingers. "My mother touched this," she had said simply.

In truth, Taylor had probably spent more time gazing at her mother's art than Sally had ever spent gazing at her daughter. Sally Love had walked out of her daughter's life not long after Taylor was born. In the years before she decided to claim her now four-year-old child, Sally made some spectacular art and slept with enough men and women to populate a small town. Taylor had never asked me why her mother left, an omission for which I was grateful because I didn't have an answer. That night it seemed my luck had run out.

"Why did she go away?" Taylor asked softly.

"I don't know," I said.

"Did she and my father love each other?"

"Truth?"

"Truth," Taylor said.

"No," I said. "I don't think they did."

"Then why did they get married?"

"I think your mother hoped she could have a different kind of life. She wanted a child, and your father did too."

"If my mother wanted a child, why did she leave me?"

"Your mother was always searching for something."

"Is that why she made art?"

"No. She made art for the same reason you do."

"Because she had to," Taylor said.

"She loved that about you. When she came back and saw that you were an artist, like her, she knew that you were what she'd been searching for all along."

"And then she died."

"Yes," I said. "And then she died."

Beside me, Taylor stared up at the ceiling, her arms pressed against her sides, rigid as a soldier's. When I drew her into my arms, she began to cry. She was not a girl who cried often and the intensity of her grief frightened me. Her body convulsed with sobs, and for a while it seemed as if the tears would never stop, but her grief had been gathering force for a long time. She had never cried for her mother and father. I buried my face in the lakewater smell of her hair and held her tight until the sobbing ceased and her breathing quieted. Finally, she seemed to fall asleep. But when I inched towards the edge of the mattress to leave, she reached out to me.

"Do you want me to stay?" I asked.

"No. I'm okay."

I got out of bed. "You know where I am if you need me."

"And if I call you, you'll be there."

I kissed her forehead. "Yes, I'll be there."

I stood outside Taylor's room for a few seconds, listening, making certain that her reassurance wasn't just bravado, but all was silent. I walked down to the kitchen and poured myself a glass of milk. Our brown bags of spice cookies were on the counter. I picked mine up and carried it with me to the porch. I was sorely in need of something to take the sting out. Willie, ever faithful, lumbered after me. I'd just settled into the rocking chair and taken my first bite of cookie when my cellphone bleated from somewhere in the house. I almost let it ring, then I thought of Taylor sleeping, and I leaped up to answer and stop the noise.

My caller announced her name straightaway. "This is Maggie Niewinski," she said. I didn't make the connection immediately. Luckily, Ms. Niewinski helped me out. "I'm Clare Mackey's friend in Prince Albert."

"Right," I said. "I'm sorry. It's been a long day."

"That it has," she said. "Nonetheless, I thought I should call and give you an update."

"Has Clare been in touch with you?"

"No," she said. "That's the update. I've called everyone I could think of. All the women in the Moot Team have. Clare hasn't been in touch with anyone we know."

Despite the warmth of the evening, I felt a chill. "I guess there's still the possibility that she just decided to cut her ties here."

"Why would she do that?" Maggie asked.

"I don't know," I said. "I guess I'm just hanging on to the hope that there's a logical explanation."

"There isn't," Maggie said sharply. Clearly she respected unvarnished truth. "Clare wasn't an easy person to get close to. She was friendly with people, but she didn't seem to have a need for friendship. That's probably why it was so easy for her to simply vanish without anyone asking a lot of questions. But you asked questions. What's your connection with Clare?"

"It's tangential," I said. "Clare was the running buddy of a woman who'd once been my teaching assistant. Her name is Anne Millar. Anyway, when Clare stopped showing up for their morning run in November, Anne went to the police and she went to Falconer Shreve. Everybody gave her the brush-off. Anne and I spotted one another at Chris

Altieri's funeral, and she unloaded. I just agreed to do what I could to help."

Maggie's tone was withering. "So a stranger and a casual acquaintance took the time to do what none of us who were with Clare every day for three years at law school bothered to do."

"You had busy lives," I said.

"Nobody should be that busy. But we'll make up for it. You say the police gave Anne Millar the brush-off. Do you happen to know who she talked to?"

I hesitated, but I knew it was pointless to delay the inevitable. "Anne spoke to Inspector Alex Kequahtooway."

"Kequahtooway," Maggie repeated. "Okay, I've got it. He's obviously the place to start. We'll have to find out who's issuing the inspector's orders or who is paying him off." For the first time, Maggie Niewinski faltered. "November to July. Eight months. It may already be too late."

"You don't think Clare's alive?" I said.

"I hope she is," Maggie said. "But I'll tell you one thing. If anything's happened to her, Inspector Alex Kequahtooway is dead meat."

My mind was racing when I clicked off my cell. There was no way I could dismiss Maggie Niewinski.

A telephone call was not an infallible indicator of character, but Maggie had not struck me as a fanciful woman, nor did she strike me as a woman who made idle threats. Obeying the adage that one picture is worth a thousand words, I walked back to my bedroom and picked up the yearbook from Clare Mackey's graduating year at the University of Saskatchewan law school and returned to the comforts of the rocker on the porch and my bag of spice cookies.

I turned to the photo of the Moot Team. Maggie was at the centre of the picture, a fine-boned blonde with an air of fragility that, given her determination to leave no stone unturned in her search for Clare, was deceptive. I leafed through the book, looking for Maggie in other pictures. She was there many times, and always with the other members of the Moot Team. Clearly, they were women of parts: members of the staff of the *Law Review*; revellers toasting their tablemates at the Malpractice Mixer; exultant hockey players wearing skates and oversized sweaters with the U. of S. logo. According to the text on the page, their graduating year had been a good one for the women's hockey team. They had triumphed at the championships in Montreal. There was a picture of the team, beaming, arms draped around one another's shoulders. Beneath the photo the caption read, "Raising hell and kicking butt."

Seemingly, they were about to continue the tradition. I put on my glasses and brought the photo of the hockey team closer to my face. Together, the women had the relaxed stance and easy body language of team players. They did not look like people who would relish destroying another human being, but that was exactly what they were about to do, and in my heart I knew that if I'd been in their position, I would have been leading the pack.

The scent of nicotiana wafted through the screened windows. Unbidden, memories of other nicotiana-scented nights washed over me. Alex wasn't a faceless enemy to me. He was a man whose hands had caressed me and whose body I had loved. Our relationship had never been an easy one. There had been unasked questions and stupid arguments. We had quarrelled over small things because we both knew the big issue between us was beyond solution. But as problem-ridden as our personal relationship had been, I had never doubted that Alex was a good cop and an incorruptible one. Now it seemed that that assessment was being called into question.

The memory that drove me to pick up the phone and dial Alex's number was not one I cherished. It was of a time when the door to Alex's private world had opened and my cowardice had slammed it shut – perhaps forever. We had eaten dinner at my house and decided that, rather than driving, we would walk downtown to police headquarters. The night was unseasonably warm, and I hadn't worn a jacket. When we started home, I'd been chilly, and Alex had put his arm around my shoulders. As we'd crossed the intersection near my house, a man in a pickup truck yelled an ugly racial slur, not at Alex but at me. His words had branded us both. "When you're through fucking the chief," the man had said, "why don't you try it with a white guy?"

In the months afterwards, I replayed the scene a hundred times in my mind. Always in my revision, I behaved heroically. I raised my head and walked across the street with the man I loved. The truth was I had not been brave. Obeying an impulse as atavistic as it was unforgivable, I had shaken off Alex's arm and run to the safety of the sidewalk. The men in the half-ton had applauded the fact that I had allied myself with them. My apology to Alex had been heartfelt, and he had been understanding, but there was no denying the truth: that split second at the Albert Street Bridge had opened a chasm between us that we had never again been able to close.

I had failed him, and we both knew it. Tonight I had a chance to make amends. I picked up my cell and tried his number. Remembering what we had once been to one another, I wanted to warn him, but at another level I knew that I needed an explanation myself. The Alex I knew had been principled, a man of integrity who believed that every human being had an obligation to do what he could to make a difference. He had been one of the best things in my life. I needed to know that I hadn't been wrong to love him. I needed to know that, no matter what had happened on that icy November day, Alex was worth loving.

As the phone rang, images of the apartment I knew so well flashed through my mind. It was in a small old building downtown, not posh, but comfortable, with high ceilings and a bedroom with a small balcony where, after lovemaking, we would take our chairs and sit and look out across the street at the blank face of the church. The memories absorbed me. I didn't notice how many times the phone rang. When, finally, the phone was picked up, the voice on the other end was not Alex's. It was a woman's voice. "Hello," she said. "Hello," and then in a voice in which anger and fear were mixed, "Hello. Who's there? Hello."

I hung up. Those few words weren't enough to reveal whether the woman in Alex's apartment was Lily Falconer, but one thing was certain: the man I'd loved for three years had found someone else to come home to.

CHAPTER 9

The next morning the skies were grey and there was a drizzle that looked like it had staying power. It was a day to sit on the porch, wrapped in an afghan, reading Virginia Woolf, but Taylor, Isobel, and Gracie had other plans. Recognizing that it would be difficult to keep a scheme involving a quantity of rocks secret on a horseshoe of land from which all rocks except those in ornamental groupings had been removed, the girls decided to spill the beans about their top-secret project.

Taylor's enthusiasm for the Inukshuk book had infected her friends. Inspired by the tale of a man who had travelled almost two thousand kilometres guided only by the Inuksuit described in a song his father had taught him, the girls had drawn up plans for a series of Inuksuit that would lead a traveller around the land surrounding Lawyers' Bay. Each Inukshuk would have a sight hole in the middle. When a lost soul peered through it, he would find his bearings and be guided along the route to the next Inukshuk. Ultimately, he would end up where he wanted to go. The girls had chosen their sites with care, sketched each Inukshuk, and made a rough estimate of the number and sizes of the rocks they would need. They had done their homework, and, in my eyes, the value of their efforts was not diminished by the fact that it was unlikely anyone at Lawyers' Bay would ever get lost. Except for my ancient Volvo, every car there had a state-of-the-art global positioning system.

As if to offset the dreariness of the day, the girls were all wearing crayon-bright cotton shirts: Gracie's was tangerine, and she had gathered her red-gold hair in a ponytail held in place by an orange scrunchy. With her rosy freckled skin and bright blue eyes, it was impossible to imagine that her mother was a member of the Dakota First Nation. Blake Falconer had said that his wife's sadness at not having a daughter who was more in her image was enduring, but that morning Gracie seemed remarkably free of any marks of her mother's rejection.

Cheerful and practical, she identified the role I'd been called upon to play in the scheme. "We need you to phone the rock company," she said. "They won't accept an order from a kid – take my word for it. I tried the company my mother used when she got the rocks for the gazebo and they insisted on speaking to an adult. My house is short of adults at the moment, so we thought maybe you'd help us out."

"There's a place in Fort Qu'Appelle we could try," I said. "We might even be able to get what you need delivered today. Besides, I wouldn't mind doing a little grocery shopping."

Isobel gave me a puckish three-cornered smile. "You mean you're unable to meet all your shopping needs at the Point Store?"

"Every so often I just have a hankering for something that doesn't cost twice as much as it should," I said.

Peter's Rocks was one of those curious businesses that appear to spring up as backyard ventures, and then spill into the vacant lot next door, defying zoning laws and the dreams of fastidious neighbours. It might not have been nominated for any chamber of commerce awards, but Peter's seemed to be exactly what the girls had in mind. Despite the misting rain, they stormed the rock piles with a passion they typically would have reserved for a

sale at Old Navy. They argued good-naturedly over
their selections, replaced hotly disputed choices
with better choices, and generally settled in for a
morning of solid trading. They were dressed for the
long haul in waterproof ponchos, but the wind-
breaker I'd hurriedly bought at a discount house
before I came to the lake turned out to be worth
exactly what I'd paid for it. It wasn't long before I
hightailed it to the shelter of the corrugated plastic
roof that covered the concrete lawn ornaments.

All the usual suspects were there: jockeys, saucer-
eyed fawns, huddled gargoyles, gargoyles with
wings spread, Dutch girls saucily lifting the backs
of their skirts to reveal ruffled concrete panties and
sturdy legs, mother rabbits, bears wearing sweaters,
angelic doomed children, gnomes, a flock of plaster
owls that I glanced at only briefly, a solitary Sacred
Heart, three Holy Families, and a phalanx of Blessed
Virgins. Freed of the obligation to buy anything or
pass judgement, I gave the ornaments my full attention, listened to the rain bounce off the roof above
me, and tried to think of nothing at all.

It took the girls an hour to make their choices and
another half-hour to watch a buff young man in
jeans that appeared to have been put on wet load the
rocks they had selected into the back of a pickup and
tot up the bill. Then it was my turn. We hit the IGA,

where, in honour of customer-appreciation day, the manager had slashed 10 per cent from the cost of all purchases, excluding tobacco and drugs. A good morning's work all around, and we drove home content.

As we warmed soup and cut sandwiches, the girls dreamily revisited the many charms of the young man at Peter's Rocks. Clearly, breasts were not the only things budding that summer for my daughter and her friends. The goofiness and speculations continued during lunch, and I was relieved when the girls asked if they could skip dishes so they could start levelling the ground where the first Inukshuk would be built.

We were without an automatic dishwasher at the lake, and I'd just submerged my hands in warm sudsy water when I heard a car pull up. I grabbed a tea towel and headed to the front of the cottage. When I saw that the visitor trudging through the rain towards my front door was Detective Robert Hallam, I opened the door with a smile.

"Come in," I said. "There's still soup in the pot."

Robert was wearing a trench coat, a Tilley hat, and a look of abject misery. He stepped inside, but as he stood dripping on the hooked rug in the entry, he made no move to take off his wet outer clothes.

I reached for his coat. "Let me take that," I said.

"Come in and dry off. If you get pneumonia, Rosalie will never let me hear the end of it."

The mention of his wife's name brought a faint and fleeting smile to Robert's face. "Thanks," he said. "But this isn't a social visit, Joanne."

The penny dropped. "You're here to talk about Alex," I said.

Robert was clearly taken aback. "How did you know?"

"Maggie Niewinski called me last night. She said some friends of Clare Mackey's were going to force the police to find out why Alex quashed the investigation into Clare Mackey's disappearance."

Robert had adjusted his expression, but it was clear he was still genuinely dumbfounded. "Joanne, I have no idea what you're talking about. I've never even heard of Maggie Niewinski. I came out here today because Inspector Kequahtooway has gone missing. He booked off to attend to personal business, but he was supposed to be back yesterday. He still hasn't shown up, and no one knows where he is."

I felt as unsteady as Robert looked. "Come in and sit down," I said. "We need to talk."

Robert followed me into the kitchen. He perched on the edge of a chair, but he didn't take his coat off. His normally ruddy face was leached of colour.

"I might as well deal with this right off the bat," he said. "Joanne, I need to know exactly when you told Inspector Kequahtooway that there were questions about how he was handling the Altieri investigation."

"I never told him," I said. "I tried to call him a half-dozen times, but he was never there. The last time I phoned I left a message, but he never got back to me."

The colour returned to Robert's face. "Thank God," he said. He leaned back in his chair, tilted his head, and exhaled. "You have no idea what a relief that is," he said. "I could hardly keep the car on the road today because I felt so sick about what I'd done."

"You tried to give an officer you respected a chance to get things in place so he could defend himself," I said. "No one could fault you for that."

"I could fault me," Robert said, sitting upright again. "I must have gone soft in the head. Joanne, if the inspector had taken off because you'd warned him there was trouble brewing, I would have been responsible. After thirty-five years on the force I don't know how I could have faced that kind of betrayal of my fellow officers." Robert snapped his fingers. "And my sister officers," he added hastily.

"Rosalie tells me I have to watch that kind of stuff."
He took off his hat and placed it, dripping, on his
knees. "I'm making a mess," he said.

"It's only water," I said.

Robert gave me a small smile. "Is that offer of
soup still open? My appetite's come back."

"Then you're at the right place," I said.

I made tea and filled Robert in on Maggie
Niewinski's phone call as he ate.

After he'd finished his soup, Robert took his
bowl to the sink. He turned on the tap and, with
his back still to me, said, "Can I make a personal
observation?"

"Sure," I said.

Robert kept rinsing his bowl, and I remembered
how uneasy he had always been about dealing
with women. "I know you and the inspector are
no longer an item," he said. "But I thought you'd
be a lot more worried about him than you seem
to be."

"I probably would have been more worried," I
said, "except that last night when I called Alex's
apartment, a woman answered."

"Whoa," Robert said.

"Exactly," I said. "Robert, I think that bowl's clean
by now. You can probably stick it in the drainer."

Robert turned off the tap and faced me. "There

are always problems when a man lets his John Thomas do his thinking," he said sagely.

"His John Thomas?" I said.

Robert picked up on my confusion. "Husband-and-wife talk. I'm sorry. I crossed a line there. All I meant was that Inspector Kequahtooway isn't thinking clearly, and he needs his friends."

I poured more tea. "I don't think Alex considers me a friend any more."

Robert's eyes met mine. "Well, if he comes to you, give him a break – please. I know he disappointed you; he disappointed me too, but he's in a lot of trouble, and he needs a hand."

Detective Hallam's car had barely cleared the turn when Zack Shreve appeared at my door.

"Don't you ever work?" I said.

"I was working," he said. "But the case is problematic, and I'm procrastinating." Zack leaned forward, looking around. Finding nothing, he kept wheeling until he was in the kitchen. Willie, intrigued by the wheelchair, stuck with him. "So who was your company?"

"A detective from the Regina Police Force," I said.

Zack stroked Willie's head. "What did he want?"

I pointed to the cups on the table. "Tea," I said.

"One-forty klicks round trip," Zack said. "You must make a mean cup of Earl Grey."

"Can I get you one?" I asked.

"No," Zack said. "But thanks. I came to ask you to have dinner with me tonight. No kids. Just us. There's a place down the road that opened up on the May long weekend. A young couple runs it. They have a pleasant seasonal menu and, like Magoo's, they make everything from scratch. Unlike Magoo's, they don't have much of a clientele. I don't give the place six months, but we might as well enjoy it while we can."

"It'll have to be early," I said. "My son and his friends have an Ultimate Tournament."

Zack frowned. "What's Ultimate?"

"Come along and see for yourself," I said. "Is six o'clock okay for dinner?"

Zack winced. "That's when children eat," he said. "But beggars can't be choosers and I need a diversion."

"The problematic case?"

He nodded morosely. "My client is alleged to have taken a knife to the lover who betrayed her."

"Another case of a man led astray by his John Thomas," I said.

Zack raised an eyebrow. "Somehow you didn't strike me as a John Thomas woman. Be that as it may, the victim's John Thomas isn't going to lead him astray any more."

"Is he dead?" I asked.

"No, but he is without his John Thomas." Zack's smile was wolfish. "So I'll make a reservation for six o'clock?"

"Perfect," I said.

I saw Zack out, then turned to Willie. "What do you want to do for the next five hours?"

Willie didn't keep me on tenterhooks waiting for an answer. He went to the hook where I kept his leash, and we were on our way. We ran the horseshoe of Lawyers' Bay, stopping only to check on the girls' progress. Project Inukshuk was right on schedule. Seeing Taylor reminded me that I had to make some arrangements for her to have dinner, so Willie and I changed direction and headed for the Point Store. Through the screen door I could see Leah restocking the chocolate-bar display.

Willie hated being tied up, and I hated tying him up, so I just leaned closer to the screen. "How's it going?" I said.

Leah came over, pushed the door open, and stood on the threshold. "Great," she said. "I don't think I've found my life's work, but not many people have summer jobs that involve unlimited access to Werther's Originals."

"Since you're having so much fun, maybe you wouldn't mind doing me a favour."

"Anything," Leah said.

"Could you and Angus give Taylor dinner tonight before the tournament? I'm coming, but I'm going to have meet you at the field."

"No problem," said Leah. "So where are *you* having dinner?"

"With Zack Shreve."

Leah shivered theatrically. "Ooooh," she said. "The man who's mad, bad, and dangerous to know."

"That was Lord Byron," I said. "Someone who knew Zack in law school said he attracts women who want to get up close and personal with a chainsaw."

Leah grinned. "You can handle a chainsaw." She glanced over her shoulder. A customer had arrived at the checkout, and he had the air of a man who didn't like to be kept waiting. "Duty calls," Leah said.

"I'll catch you later," I said. "Is Angus around?"

"He took the truck over to Bonnie Longevin's to get strawberries. We're going to set up a stand out front here to lure the cottagers."

"Marketing 101," I said.

"Something like that," Leah said. "Anyway, Angus should be back any minute. Help yourself to a cup of our gross coffee and catch a few rays while you wait."

"I can expand my knowledge, too," I said. "I always learn something when I visit Coffee Row."

The old gents were already at their places when I slid into a spot at the picnic table next to theirs. Endzone was there, too. Morris had put a piece of rug on the ground so that the dog didn't have to lie on the wet grass. As Willie collapsed beside me, he gave me a reproachful look.

"Your dog's mad at you," Morris said. "Hang on. I'll get you something to put under him." He shoved the stub of his cigarette between his lips, walked over to his half-ton, pulled out a hunk of carpeting, and handed it to me. "Make him a little bed," he said, and watched until I did as I'd been told. Willie curled up happily. I picked up my coffee and the gents went back to their conversation. As always, I arrived *in medias res*.

"I'm betting he swallowed his gun," Morris said.

"Why the hell would anyone swallow his gun?" Stan Gardiner asked.

"He didn't actually *swallow the gun*." Morris hawked a goober disgustedly. "It's a figger of speech. Jesus, Stan, if you stopped mooning over the champagne lady on Lawrence Welk and watched a real man's show once in a while, you might join the rest of us in the twentieth century."

Stan glared at him. "The twenty-first century," he said. "That's where the rest of us live, Morris – in the twenty-first century."

Aubrey entered the fray. "Where we have VCRs that allow us to watch old TV shows and movies whenever we want."

Morris fixed his friends with a malevolent eye. "And you're so busy watching those old shows that you lose touch with how people today talk. Nowadays when people speak of a man swallowing his gun, they mean the man killed himself."

I was keen to see where this discussion of semantics would take us, but at that moment Angus's truck appeared, and Willie and Endzone got into a barking match. By the time Morris and I had calmed the dogs, the thread of conversation had been broken. As I left to greet my son, the old gents were talking about what would happen to a dog that had his bark removed, a good topic but not, in my opinion, a great one.

When Angus opened the truck's tailgate, the scent of fresh-picked strawberries was enticing. "Put a quart of those aside for us, will you?" I said.

"Help me unload the truck and I'll knock off a couple of bucks." He grinned, and I felt a rush of love for this handsome stranger with the easy ways and quick smile who seemed to move farther from me every day.

"Can we talk a bit first?" I asked.

My son frowned. "What's up?"

"Have you heard from Alex lately?" I asked.

"How lately?" Angus said carefully, and in that moment I knew there was something he wasn't telling me.

"Within the last few days," I said. "Robert Hallam came out to the lake after lunch. He says Alex booked off work to attend to personal business, and he hasn't come back."

Angus looked away. "That doesn't sound like Alex. He's Mr. Reliable."

"He is," I agreed. "That's why this unexplained absence is so puzzling." I stepped closer. "People are predictable," I said. "Take you, for instance. Whenever you answer a question with a question, I know you're holding something back."

The corners of Angus's mouth twitched. Once again I'd found him out. "Is this important?" he asked.

"I think it may be," I said. "So shall we start again? When was the last time you talked to Alex?"

He didn't hesitate. "The Sunday you went to Saskatoon to see Mieka."

"Did he just call you out of the blue?"

"No," Angus said. "We've kept in touch." He sighed.

"And you never told me."

"No, I didn't."

"How come?"

Angus was his father's son, tall and dark, with an unruly forelock and an easy smile. But his eyes, grey-green and unreadable, were mine. His gaze didn't waver. "Because I didn't want to have this conversation," he said. "But if you say it's important, I guess we should." He pointed to the tailgate. "Do you want to sit down?"

"I'm okay," I said. "Let's hear it."

"Last year, just before New Year's, I got into some trouble."

"What kind of trouble?"

"Drinking and driving."

My stomach turned over. "Oh God, Angus, how many times have we talked about that?"

"A million. I was a mutt. Okay, I know, but that's not the point. The point is I got pulled over in a spot check. I honestly thought I was all right. I'd eaten and I hadn't had anything to drink for three hours, but I blew above .04 – not that bad, but bad enough. The cop took my licence and got Leah to drive home."

"Leah was with you."

"And she was furious at herself, said she should have insisted on driving. We also had three people in the back who were really ripped, so the car smelled rank. That didn't help matters. Anyway, when I got home I called Alex."

"You didn't ask him to intervene . . . ?"

"Give me a little credit, Mum. The officer who pulled me over had been very clear about the consequences. I knew I'd lost my licence for a month and I knew I had to take a DUI class. But I was scared. I forgot to ask her if the charge was going to be on my record permanently. That's why I called Alex. I just needed – I don't know – reassurance, but Alex insisted on talking to me face to face."

"Where was I when all this was going on?"

"Upstairs in bed."

"Why didn't you wake me up?"

"It was late." Angus's tone revealed his exasperation. "Really late. Mum, give me a break here. I was scared. I hadn't had a chance to think through what had happened. I was hoping Alex would give me a piece of information that would sort of soften things when I talked to you."

"But you never did talk to me."

"Because Alex said you'd been through enough, and he was right. It hadn't been that long since you two broke up. Then Aunt Jill was in all that trouble at Christmas. I knew you'd been gritting your teeth through the holidays. I didn't think you needed me barrelling in to tell you I'd been arrested and your ex-boyfriend had come over to take me to Mr. Bean for coffee."

"Nice summation," I said. "And put that way, it sounds as if you were right. So what did you and Alex talk about?"

Angus shrugged. "Mostly about how people have to be careful about the decisions they make, because everything a person does stays with him. Pretty much what you would have said."

"That is pretty much what I would have said," I agreed. "I wonder why Alex felt he had to be the one to say it."

"You're angry," Angus said.

"A little," I said. "I wish Alex practised what he preached. He made a decision; he should have been prepared to accept the consequences."

"Not being part of your life meant he shouldn't be part of mine?" I could hear the resentment in my son's voice.

"Angus, I'm not the bad guy here. It was Alex's choice. He was the one who walked away. I wanted us to stay together."

"He wanted that, too, Mum. You wouldn't be so harsh if you'd seen him the night I lost my licence.

Alex has always been on top of things. When he came to drive me to Mr. Bean, he looked beaten down. And all the time that he kept talking about decisions and dragging everything along with you, it wasn't like a lecture. It was as if he was talking about himself."

"Angus . . ."

"Mum, let me finish . . . please. The day after Chris Altieri died, it was worse. Alex just kept looking at me. It was bugging me so I asked him to stop. He apologized, then he said he had to convince himself that I was okay."

"He was a day late and a dollar short there, wasn't he?"

"What do you mean?"

"I mean, if Alex had been concerned about our family, he could have called, and he didn't. Not once in all the months after he left."

"He wanted to, Mum."

"Then why didn't he pick up the phone?"

"I don't know," Angus said miserably. "All I know is, the day after Chris died, Alex told me that the best time of his life was his time with us, and he'd do anything to keep us from grief. Do you have any idea what he was talking about?"

"No," I said. "Maybe some day, when everyone's feeling less fragile, we can talk about it."

"That'd be good," Angus said.

"I agree," I said. "Now, reassure me. You really have learned not to get behind the wheel when you've had a drink?"

"I've learned," Angus said. "That DUI course I took sealed it. I made friends with this guy named Pedro who got picked up on his birthday. He was so drunk from his party that he doesn't remember getting behind the wheel. Wouldn't want to run into Pedro on the highway. Lots of other scary stories. We got treated like infants for the whole weekend, but we deserved it. Oh yeah, the guy who was my DUI instructor was also the guy who took me out for my driver's test. How about that?"

"Cosmic irony," I said. "So is the charge going to be permanently on your licence?"

"Nope," Angus said. "I was lucky. Didn't run into Pedro. Didn't hurt anybody else. Nothing on my record permanently. Horseshoes up my ass but I'm not going to push it."

"Good," I said. "I'll sleep better knowing that." Then I put my arms around my son and, despite the gawkers in the cars going by, I held him close for a long time.

There was a message on my cellphone when I got back to the cottage. It was Maggie Niewinski. I called her back.

She sounded breathless. "Glad you caught me," she said. "I was just on my way downtown."

"Shall I call later?"

Maggie laughed. "No, I'm not due in court for an hour. I thought, since I was in Regina, I'd check out the sales. I was just calling to bring you up to speed."

"Have you found something out?"

"Nothing encouraging. Sandra Mikalonis went to Clare's apartment building and talked to the super. He remembered Clare's leave-taking very vividly, mostly because it took place so quickly, and he didn't deal with Clare face to face. In fact, the super doesn't remember seeing Clare at all after the first week in November."

"Did he usually see her?"

"Yes. She lived at the Waverly on College Avenue. It's not one of those vast, soulless places. The super saw Clare most mornings when she came back from her run. He says what everyone says. Clare was pleasant but she kept to herself. He also says he was surprised that Clare never knocked at his door to say goodbye. He thought they were friends."

"Was the lease up?"

"It was a sublet. The original tenant came back on the first of January. Clare's rent had been paid until December 31."

"Smooth as silk," I said.

"Yes," Maggie said. "Someone arranged for a moving company to come in and pack for Clare – everything, right down to the toilet paper on the roll, the super said."

"Where did Clare's furniture get shipped?"

"A warehouse in Vancouver. Joanne, it's still there. Clare's things were never claimed."

I felt the last small wisp of hope escape. "Have you told the police?"

"Yes, and we think it's time we told the partners at Falconer Shreve what we know. They think they've pulled this off. We have to show them that they haven't – that we're carrying out our own investigation and that, unlike Inspector Kequahtooway, we can't be bribed."

My spirits sank. "You think that's what happened, that someone at Falconer Shreve paid the inspector to shut down the investigation?"

Maggie made no attempt to check the asperity in her voice. "Do you have a better explanation? Anyway, it's obvious that someone at Falconer Shreve knows something. They've got a firewall of administrative assistants and juniors at their office. We're thinking that if we come out to Lawyers' Bay, we can go for a walk on the beach, make ourselves conspicuous. Then maybe someone who needs a chance to talk will realize they can talk to us. What do you think?"

I remembered the calm determination of Clare Mackey's face in her graduation portrait. "I think it's worth a shot," I said. "And, Maggie, why don't you give Anne Millar a call and tell her what you're planning to do? She might want to be a part of it."

Maggie sighed. "Good idea. I'll need her number."

I gave Maggie Anne's number. "I guess the next step is to decide when you're coming. Zack's been working from his cottage and Blake and Delia both drive out after work. So I guess you can pick your evening."

"How about tomorrow around seven?"

"Tomorrow's fine," I said.

"Thanks for helping, Joanne. I know that Clare is just a name to you, but she was a decent human being."

"That's reason enough," I said.

CHAPTER 10

I dressed with more than usual care for my evening with Zack Shreve. I was under no illusions about the motive behind his dinner invitation. From the night that he manoeuvred his chair into the gazebo bent on discovering and discrediting what Chris Altieri told me, Zack had his sights trained on me. He wasn't sure what I knew or where I fit into the picture, but he wasn't about to let me disappear from his range of vision. Now I had my own reasons for establishing rapport. So when Zack called from his car to say he was out front, I smoothed the mauve-grey silk of my favourite summer shirt and slacks, freshened my lipstick, and took a deep breath. It seemed entirely possible that, to quote Bette Davis's stinging appraisal, we were in for a bumpy ride.

We got off to a good start. Seated behind the wheel of his white Jaguar, Zack could have been a GQ cover: great tan; jacket, slacks, and shirt in coordinated shades of taupe and coffee; dark hair still curling damply from the shower. He leaned across and opened the door on the passenger side. "You look sensational," he said.

I slid in beside him. "You're looking pretty tasty yourself," I said. "Shall we get started?"

The lake on which Lawyers' Bay was situated was one of a quartet known as the Calling Lakes, which wound through the Qu'Appelle Valley. The Stone House restaurant was on the lake next to ours. Zack had put the top down on his convertible, and we drove to the restaurant through the shimmer of heat in the colour-drenched world of high summer.

On the way there, Zack told me that the Stone House had once been the summer home of a wealthy American who had fallen in love with the history and legends of the Qu'Appelle Valley. Fired by tales of buffalo runs, the American had built his house not on the lake, but far above it at a point where a man could have stood and watched the buffalo pour like a mighty and endless river over the hills around him. The view from the restaurant was reputed to be spectacular, but the road there was steep and filled with hairpin turns, and as Zack negotiated them, my nerves were on full alert.

"Without setting foot in this place, I can already see one reason why it's doomed," I said. "Don't restaurants count on alcohol sales for a hefty source of their revenues?"

"They do," Zack said. "I've already decided I'm going to have one perfect martini and switch to water."

"You shouldn't have to be the designated driver just because you're the man," I said. "We'll flip a coin."

"Let's hear it for gender parity," Zack said. "If I win the toss, I get to drink as much as I like, and you get your way with my Jaguar and me."

"I can live with that," I said.

"Then you're on," Zack said as he pulled into the empty parking lot in front of the restaurant.

We were the only clients at the Stone House. The manner of the young woman who ushered us to our table in front of the window was as welcoming as the bright sunflowers hand-painted on her sleeveless shift, but her face was drawn and her eagerness to please brought tightness to my throat.

"Welcome," she said. "I'm Marian Doherty, and my husband and I own the Stone House. I know you're short of time, so I'll bring the menus and your martinis."

When Marian left, I turned to Zack. "You ordered for me when you made the reservation?" I said.

"Working on the assumption that Ultimate waits for no man, that's exactly what I did. If you don't care for your drink, reorder. We'll dump the martini on the potted plant. Fair enough?"

"Fair enough," I said.

Marian returned with the martinis and the menus. One sip and I knew the potted plant was safe. The martini was sublime. The food offerings were even better: homegrown and imaginative.

"Great menu," I said.

Marian beamed. "While we were renovating this place we planned our menus for an entire year. That was one of the really fun parts."

Zack put down his menu. "Do you need time to mull?" he asked me.

"No," I said. "Pickerel cheeks are one of God's great gifts to this province."

"So are rabbits," Zack said. "I'm going to have the braised bunny."

"With a side order of carrot sticks?" I asked.

Marian laughed. "If you two want to take your drinks and wander around while we get your meals, you'd make us very happy. We're really proud of this place."

After she left, Zack turned to me. "Care to wander? It's not as if we'd be disturbing anybody."

The Dohertys had done everything right. The hardwood floors gleamed; the deep chintz-upholstered chairs in front of the fireplace offered a seductive invitation to curl up and dream; the garden roses at the centre of each table were dewy, and the unmatched plates and cutlery on the snowy linen tablecloths evoked memories of family dinners generations ago. Everything was flawless, but Zack and I were the only paying customers in sight.

"In the best of all possible worlds, this place would work," I said.

Zack widened his eyes. "Whatever made you believe this was the best of all possible worlds? Come on, let's go back to our table and flip that coin. I'm feeling lucky, and I could use another martini."

Zack won the coin toss, and when his martini came he offered me a sip. When I shook my head, he frowned. "You're going to be eating, and you won't be behind the wheel for an hour and a half. I'm sure you could even have a glass of wine with impunity."

"I'll stick to mineral water," I said. "This morning someone with whom I share a surname told me he got into a lot of trouble using that logic."

"The Ultimate player?"

I nodded.

"So does he need a lawyer?"

"No. He's in the clear."

"Good. Then tell me about the game. Am I going to like it?"

"You'll love it," I said. "You're combative by nature. It's a cross between basketball and football but non-contact, played with a Frisbee. There are two teams, seven players each. In the RUFDC, the teams have to have both women and men."

"I'm in favour of that," Zack said. "What's the RUFDC?"

"The Regina Ultimate Flying Disc Club," I said.

"Sounds Trekky."

"Nothing could be further from the truth," I said. "Ultimate is about playing hard and not whining. The object of the game is to score goals. The thrower isn't allowed to take any steps, so the only way to move the disc is by passing. Any time a pass is incomplete, intercepted, knocked down, or sent out-of-bounds, the opposing team immediately gets possession. You score a goal by passing the disc to a teammate in the end zone of the opposing team."

"You've watched a few games, then?"

"And been in a few," I said. "Every so often if a team is short a female player, I'm the desperation draft."

Zack smiled. "That's flattering."

"It's annihilating," I said. "Those kids are in phe-nomenal shape. The last time I played, I had to mainline Ben-Gay for a week."

Our meals came and Zack and I talked of other things – music, travel, past adventures – the stuff of first dates. We both kept an anxious eye on the road outside. No cars came.

"I think the six months you gave the Dohertys may have been optimistic," I said.

"I'm afraid you're right," Zack said. "If they can't pay their suppliers they won't make it till Labour Day."

"Hard to watch your dream turn to ashes," I said.

"Isn't that what dreams do?" Zack said. "Marian and her husband will be tougher next time."

"And less hopeful and idealistic," I said. "Dis-illusionment is a terrible thing. It hardens the heart. I hate to think of that young woman with the sun-flowers on her dress turning into a cynic."

Zack put down his fork. "I hate to think of it, too. That's why I suggested we come to the Stone House."

"So Chris was right," I said. "You're one of the dreamers. The night of the barbecue he called you Don Quixote."

"I thought Chris knew me better than that,"

Zack said. "I never undertake a quest unless I'm sure I'm going to succeed. And I don't dream impossible dreams."

"But you do dream."

"Everybody dreams. Wise people know when to cut their losses. At one point in my life I wanted to be a baseball player. Obviously, that didn't work out, so I became a lawyer."

"It can't have been that simple," I said.

"It wasn't," Zack said. "But I didn't have a choice."

"What happened?"

Zack turned his gaze so that he was looking not at me but at the driveway to the Stone House. "One spring afternoon I was on my way back from ball practice, and a rich drunk ran a light. I was in the middle of the road at the time. I was ten years old. When my mother got the letter from the rich drunk's insurance company offering her five thousand dollars if she'd sign a full release, she dropped to her knees on our kitchen floor and thanked God for his many blessings. I imagine when my mother hand-delivered the signed release to the insurance company, their lawyers offered up a few prayers of thanksgiving themselves."

I reached across the table and covered Zack's hand with mine. The move was instinctive, but Zack was clearly taken aback. He stared at our hands as if they were something apart from us. Then he looked at me hard. "You know how to get a good vibe going, Ms. Kilbourn. Suddenly, I wish that I could spend the whole evening just sitting here holding hands with you."

"I'd like that too," I said. "But it's getting late."

Zack motioned to Marian for the check, then he leaned towards me. "For the record, I had a great time tonight."

"For the record," I said, "the evening's not over."

We left the restaurant together but, instead of going straight to the car, Zack moved his chair to the edge of the empty parking lot. I followed him.

"No use putting it off," I said. "At some point you're going to have to hand me the keys and slide into the passenger seat."

"I have absolute confidence in you," Zack said. "But this view always knocks me out."

"It is amazing," I said. I slid my hand along the back of Zack's chair and touched his shoulder.

He looked up at me. "The good vibes keep on coming," he said.

"So they do," I said.

On the highway below us, cars moved purposefully, taking people out to the cottage for the night or into Fort Qu'Appelle for a movie or a meal. But the lake beyond the road was glass, and the hills around us were solid and constant. Even at the crest of the hill where we watched and waited, no wind blew.

"This is such a beautiful part of the country," Zack said. "Nights like this make you understand the Twenty-third psalm – still waters and green pastures."

"And the Valley of the Shadow of Death is nowhere to be seen," I said.

"Do I detect a switching of gears?"

"Yes," I said. "Chris's death and all the ugliness that seems to have come in its wake are never far away."

"Specifically?"

"Some friends of Clare Mackey's are coming out to Lawyers' Bay tomorrow night."

"And their purpose in coming is . . . ?"

"They want the partners at Falconer Shreve to know that they're not buying the story that Clare left for a better job in Vancouver. They also want you to know they've gone to the police about Clare, and they're doing their own investigation. They're hoping one of you will talk to them."

"Quite an agenda," Zack said. "How come you're telling me?"

"I don't know," I said. "I guess I don't want there to be any secrets between us."

Zack stroked my hand. "I appreciate that," he said. "Truly, I do." He reached into his pocket and handed me his car keys. "You're in the driver's seat," he said. "Let's go."

The Regina Ultimate Flying Disc Club tournament was being played just outside Fort Qu'Appelle on the kind of grassy, low-maintenance field reserved for T-ball or games of pickup. There were benches for the opposing teams, some rudimentary bleachers, and a small playground close enough to the bleachers for a parent to keep one eye on a child swinging on the monkey bars and the other eye on a child rounding the bases. There were also bushes, mosquitoes, blankets, bug spray, and the air of pleasant lassitude that settles on spectators at an outdoor event on an evening in cottage country.

I had given Zack a thumbnail sketch of the rules of Ultimate, but words could not describe the game's poetry. To watch men and women who were more perfect than they would ever again be in their lives push themselves to their limits in the honeyed golden light of a fading day was to understand what it meant to be young, strong, fearless, and mortal. I'd once told Angus that Ultimate always made me think of the poetry of A.E. Housman. My son had looked baffled and slightly annoyed, but I knew that some day he would understand, more than most, the poignancy of Housman's line about all those early-laurelled heads.

Zack had positioned himself by the bench where Angus's team, Blackjack, had set up. He was watching the game intently – not cheering, just observing. Occasionally, he'd lean close to one of the kids on Blackjack and ask a question. He seemed perfectly at ease, as if there were nothing more pressing in his life than mastering the intricacies of a new sport.

Zack and I hadn't talked on our way back from the restaurant, but our silence had been companionable rather than awkward, and when I'd pulled up to park behind the ball diamond, he had leaned across and kissed me. It was a good and serious kiss with the lingering effects a good and serious kiss always has. I wanted more, but I could hear my daughter calling, and so Zack and I had touched fingers and gone our separate ways.

As soon as I found a place on the bleachers, Delia Wainberg joined me. Her hair was spiky, there was the faintest dusting of blush on her pale cheeks, and her outfit – black shorts, a white T-shirt, and white runners – was youthful and flattering.

"How're you doing?" she said.

"Fine," I said. "And obviously you're blooming."

"Thanks for noticing," she said. "I've decided Chris wouldn't want me to disintegrate, so I'm making an effort." She waggled her fingers theatrically. "No cigarette," she said. "I've quit smoking – again." Her voice made one of its appealing squeaky trills. "I haven't had one all day, but I'm not to be trusted. If I come up with some phony-baloney excuse to leave, sink your teeth into my leg and don't let go."

I laughed. "Just watch the game," I said. "Seeing the shape these kids are in will firm your resolve."

"Sounds like a plan," she said.

We settled back to follow the progress of the disc as it arced through the summer air. Like Zack, Delia had questions about Ultimate, and I did my best to answer them. At one point, her attention was diverted, and she touched my arm.

"Look over there," she said. "Hard to believe that an hour ago our daughters were asking us if they could have a party with the boys from the cottages down the shore."

The girls had found the playground, and with the Merlin-like ability of preadolescents they had become kids again, abandoning the mysteries of growing up for the sheer pleasure of daring one another to go higher, faster, and farther.

"I've missed so much," Delia said simply. "But no more. I'm going to do better. I'm going to be better."

Remembering the plans of Clare Mackey's friends, I felt a pang. Suddenly, I very much wanted Delia to have her chance.

In front of us, Leah, her face dirty and her hair soaked with perspiration, made a heroic leap, caught the disc, and hit the grass. The force of the impact knocked the wind out of her, and for an endless moment she lay motionless on the ground. When Angus ran over to see if she was all right, Leah shook him off angrily and pushed herself to her feet. The game continued.

"She's tough," Delia said admiringly.

"Not a bad quality in a woman," I said.

"I agree," Delia said. "Is she tougher than your son?"

"I'd say they were evenly matched," I said.

"Are you and Zack evenly matched?" Delia asked mischievously.

"I don't think that's an issue," I said. "We hardly know each other."

"I don't believe you," Delia said. "I saw that kiss he planted on you in the car. In all the years I've known Zack, I've never seen him be publicly demonstrative with a woman. In fact, I've never known any of his women. I know they exist, but he keeps that part of his life separate from us."

"Sometimes it's wise to keep professional and private lives separate," I said.

My only intention had been to switch the focus off the subject of Zack and me, but Delia seized on my words. "That's always been a problem for us," she said. "We've never been able to separate the personal and the professional. Noah and I can't. Blake and Lily can't. Chris and I couldn't."

Delia's reference to her relationship with Chris shook me. An image from the night Chris died flashed into my consciousness: Delia standing behind Chris, her arms encircling him as if to keep him from slipping away. Had she been the woman with whom he'd had the affair, the woman who'd chosen not to go through with her pregnancy?

Innocent of my speculations, Delia peered intently as the opposing team advanced the disc effortlessly down the field. When they scored, she pounded her fist into her hand. "Damn," she said. "Anyway, Noah and I have been lucky. We seem to have survived."

"Do you think Blake and Lily's relationship will survive?" I asked.

"I hope not," Delia said. She winced. "I know that sounds cruel. But that's a relationship that never should have been. Blake got far more than he bargained for with Lily. We all did."

"In what way?" I said.

"I shouldn't be talking about her," Delia said. "It's disloyal. More to the point, it's unfair. As much as any of us, Lily is responsible for the firm's success."

"That seems odd, since she's not a lawyer."

"You don't have to be a lawyer to have a brain," Delia said wryly. "Lily is one smart cookie. More significantly, she's able to see the big picture. There are a lot of sharp elbows and egos at Falconer Shreve. People are focused on their own work. There's not much glory in taking care of the day-to-day business of the firm. Most of us deal with office stuff on a need-to-know basis, but Lily's always understood what had to be done."

"That *is* a gift," I said.

"What's a gift?" Blake Falconer's question was casual, the kind of gentle repetition of a phrase that allows a newcomer a graceful entrance into a conversation, but Delia and I both jumped when we heard his voice. "Sorry," he said. "Noah and I just got tired of standing. We decided you two looked pretty comfortable. Did we interrupt something?"

"No." Delia patted the space next to her. "Lots of room here in the cheap seats," she said. "I was just telling Joanne how much Lily has contributed to the firm."

Blake looked abashed. "You know, sometimes I lose sight of that myself," he said.

Despite another heroic leap by Leah, Angus's team lost by a single point. It was a heartbreaker, but the RUFDC tournament had just begun. There would be other games, other chances. The members of Blackjack came over flushed and weary.

"We're going to get something to eat," Angus said. "We won't be long. Everybody has to work tomorrow."

"Have fun," I said.

"You've earned it," Noah said. "That was a good game."

"Not good enough," Angus said.

"So what prize are you playing for?" Blake asked.

Angus pointed to the parking lot. "See that puke-green shit-beater over there by the dumpster?"

Blake laughed. "The one with 779ULTI painted on the side?"

"Yeah," Angus said. "We're playing for the right to drive that for the rest of the summer. It's called the Bohmobile."

"Because Boh beer is the team sponsor," Blake said.

"Indirectly," Angus said, grinning. "Anyway, the Bohmobile is the prize for playing the hardest, bitching the least, writing the funniest post-game anthems, and generally demonstrating the spirit of Ultimate Flying Disc. All of which sounds pretty stupid now that I explain it."

"It doesn't sound stupid at all," Blake said. "It's a lot more sensible than always playing to win."

There was sadness in Blake's voice, and Angus, who wasn't always swift to pick up on the emotions of others, reacted. "Hey," he said softly. "There's no rule saying you always have to play to win." He tossed Blake the disc in his hand. "Go hard," he said.

"Point taken," Blake said finally. He turned to Delia. "Hey, partner, look alive."

With surprising speed, Zack wheeled himself over the bumpy grass to join them, and when he motioned to Noah and me to come onto the field, we didn't hesitate. The girls saw us tossing the disc around and came running. There was laughter on the field that night; there was also a sense of communion. We played until the darkness gathered and we were no longer able to keep track of the disc that was our prize. When Blake and I collided and hit the grass, Zack announced the inevitable.

"Game called," he said. "Before there's a lawsuit."

Laughing and grousing, we headed for the parking lot. Delia touched my arm in a sisterly gesture. "About those slacks of yours," she said, "they're raw silk, aren't they?"

"I got them on sale at the end of last summer," I said. "Even so, the only way I could justify buying them was promising myself I'd wear them for the next ten years."

"Maybe you could turn them into cut-offs," Delia said.

"Or a thong," I said. "I'd better make tracks. Zack and Taylor are waiting in the car."

"Tonight was fun, wasn't it?" Delia said.

"Yes," I said. "It was."

"We need more fun," Delia said, and her voice broke in one of those strange little cadences that made it impossible to tell if she was laughing or crying.

Zack kept the convertible's top down on the drive home, and Taylor provided us with spirited observations on the stars and on the signs sporting the whimsical names cottagers had given their summer homes. Suddenly, she fell silent. I turned around to check.

"Is she all right?" Zack asked.

"She's fine," I said. "In fact, if you listen carefully, you'll hear her snoring. Taylor is one of the few human beings I know who can move from full throttle to deep sleep in mid-sentence."

"Lucky Taylor," Zack said.

Our cottage was dark when we pulled up. "Damn," I said. "I forgot to leave on a light."

"I hate coming home to a dark house," Zack said. "I'll go in with you."

"You don't have to."

"I know," he said, turning and pulling his folded wheelchair from the back seat. In two minutes the wheelchair was ready for action and Zack was in it. "Want to give me the keys?" he said.

I fished around in my bag for the keys and handed them to him. Then I reached into the back of the car and wakened Taylor.

"We're home," I said. "But you're too big for me to carry."

"Okay," she mumbled.

Still more than half asleep, Taylor leaned against me and we walked into the house. I took her down to her room, helped her on with her pyjamas, and smoothed the sheets after she slipped into bed.

"Sleep tight," I said.

Taylor opened her eyes. "Hey, I forgot to tell you. Gracie's mum's coming home."

"Is Gracie happy?"

"I don't know. She just said her mother hasn't anywhere else to go."

"That's kind of sad, isn't it?"

"It's really sad," Taylor said, then she rolled over and burrowed deep into her covers.

Zack was by the sideboard in the living room, holding one of the action figures from Kevin's collection. I went to him and scrutinized the figure in his hands. "Darth Vader," I said. "I'm going to write a learned paper on how the action figures people choose reveal their inner lives."

"Darth Vader was the scourge of the Jedi and the master of the dark side of the force," Zack said. "Any new insights there about me?"

"No," I said. "That's pretty much my take on you."

"So who's your choice?" Zack asked.

"Wonder Woman," I said. "I love those bracelets, and it would be handy to have a lariat that compelled complete honesty and obedience from anyone I chose to snare."

Zack put Darth Vader back in place. "Is it okay if I stay for a while?"

"Of course," I said. "Would you like a drink?"

"Actually, I was thinking it might be nice to sit on that couch over there and neck."

"I'm sweaty," I said.

"So am I," Zack said. "We'll cancel each other out."

I went over to the couch. Zack slid off his chair into the place beside me and we started to make the kinds of moves I hadn't made since I was a teenager. They were still potent. Within minutes, it was pretty clear we were both aroused.

"If the kids come in and catch us like this, I'm going to lose my moral edge," I said.

"Can't have that," Zack said. He held me close, caressing my breasts. "Except for the obvious, I don't know where this is going, Joanne."

"Neither do I," I said. "But for tonight, I think the obvious will be enough."

"You'll come by my house after the kids get home?"

"Yes," I said. "I'll come by."

After Zack left, I sprayed my ruined slacks with Spot Shot and stepped into the shower. My mind was racing. The number of sexual partners I had had during my life could be counted on three fingers: my husband, Ian; a man named Keith Harris, who had always been more friend than lover and who was still a friend; and Alex Kequahtooway. I had never been casual about sex, and yet here I was, getting ready to towel off, dress, and walk down the road to spend the night with a man I'd known for less than two weeks. Seemingly, at the age of fifty-five, I was becoming a risk-taker.

After I'd stepped out of the shower, I looked at myself in the full-length mirror on the back of the bathroom door. Thirty-three years ago, when I was certain Ian and I would become lovers, I had stood on a chair in my room in the dorm and examined my body in the mirror above my bureau. The sun was pouring through the window and my flesh glowed firm and ripe as a pear. As I looked at my body that September afternoon, I had known that Ian was a lucky man. Zack Shreve would be less lucky. Still, none of us is perfect, and he had asked.

When I heard the front door open, I felt a moment of panic. It wouldn't be easy explaining to my son what I was about to do. As it turned out, the gods were smiling. Leah was alone in the kitchen.

"Where's our boy?" I said.

"Probably already asleep," she said. "There's a truckload of meat coming in early tomorrow morning." She sniffed the air. "You're wearing your best perfume and mascara and your second-best summer outfit. Want to tell me what's going on?"

"Actually, I have to ask a favour," I said. "I wonder if you'd mind keeping an ear open for Taylor. I have to go out for a while."

"Out as in out on a date?"

"I'm going over to Zack Shreve's."

The smallest of frowns crinkled her brow. "Jo, are you sure about this?"

"No," I said, "I'm not sure at all, but I'm going anyway."

Leah dimpled. "Well, good for you. My Aunt Slava always says that summer is for bad boys."

The front door to Zack's house was open a crack. I stepped inside.

"I'm here," I said.

Zack came in from the living room. He was wearing a white terry-towel robe. "I didn't think you'd come."

"You left the door open, and you're undressed."

"I'm an optimistic guy." He extended his hand. "Ready?"

The colours in Zack's bedroom were the same as those in the rest of the house – rust, metallic grey, and white – and the furniture was just as sleek, but this room was personal, with books, papers, and photographs. The bed was large enough to get lost in. On one of the bedside tables there was a bowl of apples, on the other, a white orchid in a graceful crystal vase.

"We can share the apples," Zack said. "But the orchid's for you."

"Where did you get an orchid at eleven at night?"

"I snipped it from the plant in the kitchen. Lights on or off?"

"Off," I said. "And thanks for the flower."

From the outset, we were surprisingly easy with one another. "This is going to involve a few adjustments," he said. "Tell me how you feel about what I'm doing." He slid his hand between my legs.

"I like that," I said. "So what do I do?"

He took my hand and guided it to his nipple. "Start here."

"Really?"

"Really."

And so we discovered one another's bodies. I had never been with anyone who understood a woman's sexuality the way Zack did. What we did was different from what I was used to, but it was sublime. We fell asleep in one another's arms, and I didn't wake until the first light of morning. I slipped out of bed and went into the bathroom, washed my face and cursed the fact that I'd forgotten my toothbrush.

Zack was awake when I came back. "Were you just going to disappear without saying goodbye?"

"I was going to let you sleep," I said.

"I don't want to sleep," he said. "Come here."

I sat on the bed beside him, and he drew me to him. When he started to kiss me, I turned my head. "I didn't bring my toothbrush."

"Use mine."

"I couldn't do that."

Zack looked amused. "We just spent several hours exchanging bodily fluids," he said.

"That was different."

"You're a woman of contradictions, Ms. Kilbourn, but I'll learn to live with them." He stroked my head. "So what are you going to do today?"

"I'll probably try to figure out what happened here tonight."

"Regrets?"

"None. At this moment, I'm very happy."

"Me too."

"And what are *you* going to do today?"

"I have to be in court by nine o'clock."

"You're kidding."

"No. I'm a lawyer. Appearing in court is part of the gig."

"Are you prepared?"

"Always." Zack pushed himself up so he was sitting. "Anything you want me to bring you from town?"

I kissed his forehead. "A toothbrush," I said.

CHAPTER 11

When I awoke for the second time that morning, my son was peering anxiously at me. "Are you okay?" he asked.

"I'm fine," I said. "What time is it?"

"Seven o'clock," Angus said. "You slept in."

"But I woke up, so you can stop worrying."

Angus was not reassured. "You always get up at five-thirty. Taylor said you were throwing the disc around last night. I thought you might have pulled something."

I sat up and stretched. "Everything's functioning," I said.

But my son's attention had wandered. Face down on the bed beside me was Harriet Hynd's copy of *To the Lighthouse*. The light bulb over Angus's head flashed on. "You were *reading*," he announced triumphantly. "You stayed up late *reading*. That's why you slept in." Once again the universe was unfolding as it should. He gave my leg a patronizing pat. "Gotta get you a real life, Mum," he said.

"I'll work on it," I said.

After Angus left, I showered, dressed, and realizing I couldn't live on the afterglow of passion alone, headed for the kitchen. Taylor was at the breakfast table, drizzling honey on her toast. Her hair was smoothed into a smart French braid.

I touched her hair. "When did you learn to do this by yourself?"

"Rose taught me last week. She says the fewer things you have to rely on other people to do for you, the better off you are."

"She's right about that." I peeled an orange and sat down opposite my daughter. "So what's on the agenda today?"

"This morning we're hauling rocks," she said. "We're going to build the Inukshuk out by the gazebo."

"That's quite a distance," I said. "Want me to put the rocks in the trunk of the Volvo and drive them out there for you?"

"No, that's okay. We'll use the wheelbarrow. We kind of want to do this ourselves." As she always did, Taylor cut her toast into the smallest of triangles.

"I'm supposed to ask you if it's okay if I go to Standing Buffalo later on. Rose wants to take her sister some lunch."

"Fine with me," I said. "How's Betty doing?"

"She's bored. *I'd* be bored if I had to sit around for six weeks with my leg in a cast."

"Maybe I'll come with you and visit."

"That'd be good," Taylor said. "But if Gracie's mum comes back, we have to stay here so she won't think we're mad."

"Why would she think you were mad?"

Taylor wolfed a dainty triangle. "I don't know," she said. "Gracie knows, but she won't talk about it."

I poured cereal into my bowl and went to the fridge to get the milk. The carton was suspiciously light. I opened it and held it over my bowl. Three drops of milk dribbled out.

Taylor and I exchanged glances. "Angus!" we said in unison.

I selected a banana. "A fruitarian's breakfast for me," I said. "But I might as well walk down to the Point Store and get a litre of milk. Want to come?"

Taylor shook her head. "I'm already late. We want to get the Inukshuk finished today."

"Okay," I said. "Don't forget to check in."

I picked up my purse and started for the door, but the mention of Lily Falconer had taken the bounce out of my step. I had no proof that Lily and Alex had been together during the days when they had both been AWOL, but logic suggested it was a strong possibility. If Lily was coming back, it was possible that Alex was coming back too. Our relationship was over, but the prospect of Alex losing the career he'd spent half his life building sickened me. When I picked up the phone and dialled Robert Hallam's number I was searching for reassurance that somehow the confusion and questions Alex had left behind had been cleared away.

Robert Hallam offered no comfort. He was pleasant but guarded when he heard my voice. We inquired after one another's families and then I asked if he'd had news of Alex.

I could feel the ice. "I can't talk about Inspector Kequahtooway, Joanne. It's an internal matter now."

"So Alex *is* being investigated."

Robert was edgy. "Joanne . . ."

"I know," I said. "It's an internal matter."

He sighed. "Rosalie and I still consider you a friend. I just can't discuss this."

"I understand," I said. "But Robert, is Alex all right?"

There was a silence. "I can't discuss it. Goodbye, Joanne." He cleared his throat. "Our door is always open to you."

As I walked to the Point Store, the realization hit me that, in the vernacular of another era, there was more than one way to skin a cat. Robert Hallam wasn't the only source of information available to me. I passed the store and went straight to Coffee Row. Three of the gents were already holding court and Endzone, flopped on the rug at her master's feet, was dreaming her old-dog dreams. The gentlemen raised their caps to me, but instead of continuing to my place at the next table, I joined them. The shock was seismic.

Morris took command. "You've sat in the wrong place," he said, turning up the volume the way he would for someone who didn't understand the language. He pointed to the picnic table under the tree. "That's your place over there."

"I want to sit with you today," I said.

Aubrey, the gnome with the dental-drill whine, leaped to his feet. "This is the men's table. We smoke. We use strong language. We talk about things you'd have no interest in."

Endzone, ripped from sleep by the ruckus, ambled over, sniffed me curiously, and fixed me with a baleful eye.

"It's all right," I said, stroking her jowls, "I'm just visiting." Mollified, she rested her chin on my knee and awaited developments.

I turned my attention to the men.

"I need some information," I said. "And I think you can help me. Once when I was having coffee here, I overheard you talking about Lily Falconer."

Aubrey sat back down and the trio exchanged glances.

"I'm not asking you to gossip," I said. "I just want you to tell me about Lily Falconer. That day you mentioned something about a tragedy involving her mother."

"Goddamn that daughter of mine," Morris thundered. "You could have read everything you needed to know if that girl had left my archives alone, but oh no, she thought they were a fire hazard. She gave me a choice – say goodbye to my Player's Plains or say goodbye to my archives. What the hell kind of choice is that for a daughter to give her father?"

Lear couldn't have been more cogent. It was a freighted question, and I waited for Morris to move on. It didn't take him long.

Tapping his temple with a forefinger brown as a cured tobacco leaf, Morris grew discursive. "My archives may be gone, but I still have my mind. I can tell you what happened, in my own words. It'll be – what do they call it, Stan?"

"Oral history," Stan said.

"Which is good," Morris said. "Except you lack the pictures."

"She can still see the damn pictures," Stan Gardiner said. "The newspaper has its own archives, Morris, and they don't use theirs to paper-train puppies. Mrs. Kilbourn can walk into the offices of the *Valley Gazette* and ask them to let her look at everything they've got on Gloria Ryder."

"Gloria Ryder," I repeated. "That was Lily's mother's name?"

"Yes," Stan said. "The date you'll be wanting is January 1968, and after you've gone through the paper's archives, come talk to me. It's only right that you get the full story."

In the months after I'd decided to rent the cottage at Lawyers' Bay, I subscribed to the *Valley Gazette*. It was a weekly that was clear in its purpose: to record the births, marriages, deaths, celebrations, follies, and accomplishments of its citizens and to keep a wary eye on governments, developers, and special-interest groups that might threaten the fine lives of the people of Fort Qu'Appelle and district.

The building that housed the paper was as solid and neighbourly as the *Gazette* itself. The brass plate that announced the paper's name was polished to a fine sheen and the red geraniums in the window bloomed with health. There was a bell on the counter that separated what was obviously the business part of the newspaper from the reception area, and when I rang it a very thin young man, wearing a jacket and tie, bluejeans, and John Lennon glasses came out to greet me. He didn't look much older than Angus.

"I'm doing some research," I said. "I wonder if I could look at your newspaper's coverage of a case involving a woman named Gloria Ryder. The events happened in January 1968."

"No problem," he said, and apparently it wasn't. He was back with the file within fifteen seconds.

"That was snappy," I said.

"You're not the first person to ask for that information today," he said.

"May I ask who else was interested?"

"The media are ever vigilant," he said, and his smile was impish. "Take as much time as you need. Ring when you're finished."

The reception room was a pleasant place to read: quiet, with sunshine filtering through the brilliant red petals and deep-green foliage of the geraniums. That said, the story in which Gloria Ryder unwillingly played the central role was grim, a tale of obsessive love that ended in the tragedy of a grisly murder-suicide.

Gloria was married to John Ryder who, like her, was a Dakota from Standing Buffalo. The newspaper described them as good people: hard-working, churchgoing, devoted to their only child, eight-year-old Lily. John was a mechanic and Gloria was a nurse at the Indian hospital in Fort Qu'Appelle. The problem started when a middle-aged white doctor at the hospital became infatuated with Gloria. The year was 1967. Indian women had had the vote for less than five years, and Gloria understood her position in the scheme of things. She needed her job, and she knew that in a case of he said–she said, she would be the loser. Afterward, she explained that she had done everything in her power to rebuff her unwelcome suitor, but that she hadn't wanted to risk telling either her husband or her employers. The doctor never made any physical advances towards Gloria. He was convinced that his destiny was to take Gloria from the life she knew and, as he put it, raise her up. One bitterly cold night in mid-January, Gloria's unwillingness to be raised up drove the good doctor to Standing Buffalo, where he shot John Ryder, who was sitting in his living room reading a *Maclean's* magazine. Then, apparently moved to pity by the presence of the daughter of the woman he sought to save, he turned the gun not on Gloria but on himself.

Thirty-seven years later, the soft pages of the *Valley Gazette* were still heavy with the tragedy of the event and the dark spoor of anger and recriminations that followed in its wake. The text of the stories was heartbreaking, but it was the anguish in the yellowed photographs of two people that stayed with me. The first pictures were of the woman at the centre of the tragedy. Gloria Ryder's face was stamped with the ancient misery of women whose lives have been devastated by forces beyond their control. It was also – unmistakably – the face of the woman whose likeness had been carved into the figure at the base of the gazebo. The second pictures were of Lily as a child. The photographer had caught her several times on the windswept, frozen playground of the residential school in Lebret. She looked dazed and frail, but she was never alone. A tall boy of perhaps twelve was always with her, his arm raised impotently as he tried to shield Lily from the camera's invasive eye. The boy was Alex Kequahtooway.

I took the file containing the stories to the counter and rang the bell. The young man in the John Lennon glasses appeared quickly.

"Hard to believe something like that could happen in a place like this, isn't it?" he said.

"Hard to believe it could happen anywhere," I said.

As I drove back to Lawyers' Bay, ideas swirled through my mind like the shifting shapes in a kaleidoscope. The question of whether Alex was Lily's lover was still unanswered, but there was no doubt that he had been her protector. When he stood at the window of the Hynd cottage and said, "Maybe we all would have been better off just staying where we were," his bitterness had not been directed at me. It had welled up from a source I never knew existed.

It seemed that the connection between Alex and Lily Ryder had never been severed. But if that was true, there were more questions. Why had Alex never told me about Lily? If she were simply a girl he had once known, why had he never mentioned her name and her tragedy? Other questions nagged. During the years when I believed Alex and I were as close as a man and a woman could be, what other secrets had he held back? What else hadn't he told me?

It was almost eleven when I pulled onto the shoulder of the road beside the Point Store and walked to the entrance. Angus was outside watering flats of annuals that had seen better days and were now being offered at seriously reduced prices.

"What's going on?" Angus said. "After you left, Mr. Gardiner came into the store and told me the moment you came I was supposed to tell you he was waiting. Then he went upstairs." Angus frowned. "I haven't screwed up, have I?"

I leaned over and picked a faded bloom from a wilting impatiens. "You're in the clear," I said. "This has nothing to do with you."

I could hear the strains of an accordion playing "White Christmas" as soon as I reached the landing at the top of the stairs. I tapped at the door and Stan greeted me. He was wearing a cardigan and slippers, master of his household. He motioned me inside. The living room was furnished with the essentials: a La-Z-Boy, a coffee table, a VCR, and a TV set on which Lawrence Welk was presenting his Christmas special. Stan turned the sound down but not off, walked into the next room, and returned with a chrome kitchen chair.

"Make yourself comfortable," he said, pointing to the La-Z-Boy.

I sank in, and Stan perched.

"So you read the articles?" he said.

"Yes," I said. "It was a terrible thing — for everyone."

"For her especially," Stan said.

"Lily?"

"I was thinking of the mother."

"What happened to her? The paper didn't say."

"She died of grief and guilt," Stan said tightly.

Stan was a man who meted out his words sparingly, but I knew he had more to offer. I fixed my gaze on Lawrence Welk. He was thanking his band. A quartet of young women in Victorian Christmas dress appeared on screen. They were fresh-faced and unmistakably related. I grappled for their name and, amazingly, came up with it: the Lennon Sisters. In voices that were sweet and true, they began to sing "Silent Night."

"She blamed herself," Stan said. "To this day I don't know why, but it was a terrible thing to witness. Are you familiar with the Catholic church down there at Lebret?"

"Yes," I said.

"Then you've seen those crosses on the hill behind the church."

"The Stations of the Cross."

"So you're Catholic."

"Anglican."

"But you know what those crosses are for."

"They represent things that happened during Christ's passion and crucifixion. Some people use the Stations of the Cross to help them pray and meditate on their sins."

"That's what Gloria did," Stan said. "You've seen how steep that hill is. Even in good weather it's a tough climb, and the tragedy happened in January. It was a bitter winter and that hill was sheer ice. Gloria went up that hill every day on her hands and knees. She stopped at every one of those crosses to pray. She blamed herself."

The image of suffering was as vivid as an illustration in a saint's tale.

"How long did she live afterwards?" I asked.

"A year to the day. She died on that hill. Of exposure, they said – and I guess you could take that in a lot of ways. When she died, some people said that she'd finally gotten God's attention and that He gave her what she prayed for." His gaze was piercing. "Do you believe in that kind of God?" he asked.

"No," I said. "I don't."

"Neither do I," he said. "Of course, I'm United Church."

I arrived home to the news that Lily still hadn't shown up, so the trip to Standing Buffalo was on. Gracie was uncharacteristically quiet on the way to the reserve. Her mood didn't alter until we came to Betty's house and saw Betty herself sitting on her porch, snapping beans. At that moment, Gracie became Gracie again, heedless of everything except her goal as she leaped out of the car and ran to Betty.

At Rose's direction, we loaded up the Tupperware containers of food she'd brought for lunch and headed for the house and a living room as fussily pretty as a midway doll. Under Rose's watchful eye, the girls began to set the table with the good dishes, but when I offered to help, she waved me off.

"Why don't you keep Betty company?" Rose said. "She's a talker, which means she can always use a listener."

It was an easy chore. I liked Betty. The family resemblance to Rose was marked but, in every way, they were very different women. Rose was wiry. She kept her grey hair in a tight, no-nonsense, wash-and-wear perm and limited her skin care to sunscreen. Betty was curvaceous. She was pushing seventy, but her long hair was still black and lustrous and her makeup was cover-girl perfect.

I pulled up a rocker and sat beside her. "So how are you doing?" I said.

"Fine. Except I'm mad at myself."

"Rose said you fell down your porch steps."

"And it was my own fault. Last time I was in the city, I went to Payless and bought myself a pair of backless shoes with stiletto heels. I knew it was foolish, but the shoes were on sale and they made my ankles look slim as a girl's. You know how it is – I just had to have them. Whoever said 'Pride goeth before a fall' knew what he was talking about. I was proud, and boy, did I fall."

"When do you get your cast off?"

"Not for five more weeks. Mind you, I'm not complaining. I'm still on the green side of the grass, and I've got Rose and I've got Gracie. Do you know that girl offered to come over here and stay with me for the summer if I needed her? She would have done it too."

"That's a selfless thing for a girl her age to offer."

"That's the kind of girl she is. She's never lost sight of who she is or where she belongs. Do you know that from the time she could walk Gracie has danced powwow? She still does. Red hair, freckles and she's a jingle dancer – a good one, too. She doesn't just do the steps, she understands their meaning and stays in time with the drumbeat. People on the reserve used to wonder why she bothered to learn. They don't any more. They respect her. I respect her too." Betty snapped the last bean and handed me the bowl. "Would you mind taking those inside? Beans shouldn't be in the heat."

I took the beans to Rose; she dumped them into a colander and ran cold water on them. "Ten minutes to lunch," she said.

I went back outside. "Ten minutes till we eat," I said.

"And I'm going to make the most of them," Betty said. "Come closer. I want to know what's going on over at Lawyers' Bay. Is Lily there or did she take off again?"

"Lily's been away," I said carefully. "She's supposed to be coming back today."

Betty's lips became a line. "I knew it," she said. "My sister didn't tell me because she thought I'd worry, and she was right. I worry about Gracie. I worry about Lily, too, but that doesn't mean I don't get frustrated with her."

"She's had a hard life," I said.

"So you heard about the tragedy," Betty said. "Well, lots of people have hard lives. They get over it. What happened to Lily happened a long time ago, and it's not as if she had to deal with it alone. Rose and I were there. So were a lot of other people on this reserve."

"I'm sure that's true," I said. "All I have to go on are the newspaper articles, and of course they focused on the deaths. But in the photographs of Lily in the schoolyard, there was always a boy. It was Alex Kequahtooway, wasn't it?"

Betty picked up a knitting needle, slipped it inside her cast, and rubbed. "I've never been able to leave an itch unscratched," she said contentedly. "To answer your question, I don't remember any photo, but it would have to have been Alex. He was just a kid himself, eleven or twelve. But he defended Lily against all comers, adults and kids alike. He walked her to school, and he walked her home. He was like a shield between Lily and the world."

"Not much of a surprise that he grew up to join the police force," I said.

"Not to me," Betty said. "Once a person gets that badge, people have to pay attention, no matter who's wearing it."

"Alex went through a lot, didn't he?" I said.

"Lunch!" Rose's announcement from inside the kitchen ended the discussion.

Betty's crutches were on the floor beside her chair. She stared at them with distaste.

"I'll get those for you," I said. I helped her to her feet and handed her the crutches. She positioned them under her armpits and heaved her body into place. She looked awkward, as if she didn't remember the next move in the sequence. "Is there anything else I can do?" I asked.

"Yes," she said. "Unlike my sister, you can remember that I broke my leg, not my brain. I can handle the truth. Keep me posted." And with that she lurched forward and made her torturous way into the house.

Despite her protestations that she was fit as a fiddle, Betty seemed weary after lunch. The girls and I cleaned up the kitchen while Rose shepherded her sister into the bedroom and gave her a sponge bath. When she emerged, Betty was dusted with fragrant talc and wearing a peach-and-pink cotton muumuu. Rose settled her sister on the couch and handed her a Barbara Cartland novel. Gracie poured her a glass of cream soda and adjusted the floor fan so Betty could catch the breeze. Given the circumstances, Betty was as comfortable as a human being could be, but Gracie's face was pinched with concern. She knelt beside Betty. "Are you sure you're going to be all right?" she asked.

"How could I not be all right?" Betty said. "I've got you."

Reassured, we said our goodbyes, piled into Rose's Buick, and set out for home. We didn't get far. As we were poised at the end of Betty's driveway, prepared to turn onto the road that led to Lawyers' Bay, Gracie leaned forward and tapped Rose on the shoulder. Her tone was beseeching.

"Could we go to the old graveyard, Rose? Please. There's something I want to check."

Rose craned her neck around so she could look at Gracie face to face. "Whatever do you need to check out there?"

"It has to do with our Inuksuit," Gracie said.

"Top priority," Rose said dryly. She glanced at her watch. "We've got time for a quick trip."

Taylor groaned. "I hate cemeteries."

Isobel played peacemaker. "I do too, but this one is neat in a tragic sort of way."

"Well, okay," Taylor said.

Rose and I exchanged glances. "Fine with me," I said. The vote was in. We were on our way.

Like all very old cemeteries, Lake View had an elegiac charm, but it possessed something more rare and valuable in cottage country: it was water-front property. On the open market it would have fetched the proverbial king's ransom, but respect for the dead or fear of public outcry had kept specula-tors at bay, and Lake View looked much the same as it must have looked when it opened its gates more than a century before. The girls scampered down to the beach and, after some excited point-ing and gesticulating, they resolved whatever ques-tion had drawn them to the shoreline and wandered back into the cemetery proper. Rose and I were walking among the graves too, and I wondered how the girls were reacting to these reminders of a past when entire families were wiped out by scarlet fever and brides not much older than the girls them-selves died in childbirth.

We stopped by a grave that was overgrown with weeds. Rose pulled the weeds up and shook the dirt off them.

"Is someone you know buried there?" I asked.

"No," she said. "I just hate an untidy grave." Rose took a plastic Safeway bag from her pocket and dropped the weeds in. "Compost," she said. She cleared her throat. "I want to apologize to you about Betty," she said. "I know she was on you like a hawk on a mouse, but I'm the one who should be blamed. My sister had a right to know what was going on with Lily."

"What *is* going on with Lily?" I asked. "Rose, I wouldn't be asking this if it wasn't important. Taylor told me that Lily was coming back because she had nowhere else to go. Is her relationship with Alex Kequahtooway over?"

Rose looked at me in amazement. "That relationship will never be over, but it's not what you think. It's not a man-woman thing. They're like one person, one blood."

"Betty told me Alex was Lily's protector after her mother died."

Rose made no attempt to hide her anger. Obviously, the wound I had touched was still fresh. "Did Betty tell you people in town blamed Gloria for what happened? They said she must have led the doctor on. They called her a squaw and a whore and worse."

"And Lily heard it all."

"Yes. And every day she had to watch her mother climb that hill, atoning for sins she never committed."

A breeze came up and rustled the grasses along the lake. Voices from the dead.

"Lily never got over it, you know." Rose thumped her heart with her hand. "Something broke in here. She should be happy – nice husband, wonderful daughter, good job, beautiful houses – but she isn't."

"The night of the fireworks, Gracie asked Blake why her mother couldn't just see how nice everything was."

"Lily does see how nice everything is," Rose said. "That's the problem. She can't believe she deserves a good life. So when things are going good, she unravels them, like that Penelope in the Greek story. Did you ever read that story?"

"Not since grade nine," I said. "It was a long time ago."

Rose laughed. "Longer ago for me, but I never forgot it. Penelope's husband went away and all these men wanted to marry her. She was weaving something, I don't remember what, but she told the men she couldn't get married until she'd finished her weaving. So the men waited and waited. They didn't know that every night Penelope went to her room and ripped out her weaving and every morning she started over."

"You think that's what Lily's doing with her life?"

"I know it. My sister always tries to get me interested in romance novels. I've read a few, but all those happily-ever-afters just don't ring true to me. Those Greek stories rang true – that's probably why I still remember them after sixty years." Rose squared her shoulders. "Would you mind herding up the girls? There are some graves I'd like to check on."

"You have family here?"

"Everyone around here does. My parents. The aunt I'm named after. Two of my brothers. More cousins than you can shake a stick at, and, of course, Gloria."

"I didn't realize you and Gloria were related."

"We're not – at least not by blood. But on this reserve you don't have to share a family tree to be considered family."

As soon as we got back, the girls marched off to work on their Inukshuk. Unencumbered by the obligation to leave signposts for future generations, I went back to the cottage. When I opened the front door, the heat hit me like a wave. The Hynds had not believed in air conditioning. The memory of Betty, cool and fragrant, propelled me. I turned on the ceiling fan, found a roomy cotton nightie in my drawer for the nap I needed, and made my way to the shower to wash away a morning of dust and melancholy. The phone was ringing when I stepped out. I grabbed a towel and ran to answer.

Zack's voice was teasing. "So were you out back milking the chickens?"

"Nope. I was just getting out of the shower . . ."

"That mental image may just get me through the rest of the day."

"Troubles in your kingdom?" I said.

"Well, let's see. The courthouse air conditioning fried itself this morning, so the building is hotter than hell. And the Crown is cleaning my clock. Apart from that, everything's swell."

"Come back to Lawyers' Bay. I'll let you sit next to the fan and score all the points."

"Best offer I've had all day," Zack said wearily. "I'll go back in there and throw myself on the mercy of the court."

I wasn't up to Virginia Woolf, and Harriet Hynd's library was short of trashy novels, so I chose a worthy book on birds of the Qu'Appelle Valley and was asleep before I turned the first page. I woke with a post-nap sense of well-being. It was three o'clock. I walked out to the road and looked towards the gazebo to check on the girls. They were toiling away in the mid-afternoon heat. Feeling guilty that I had been cool and lazy all afternoon while they worked, I sliced a loaf of banana bread, filled a Thermos with lemonade, dropped plastic cups and napkins into my beach bag, and went to assess their progress.

The girls were ready for a break. The Inukshuk was complete, but the wheelbarrow was full of rocks and more were strewn about the sand. Discovering the precise combination of stones that would fit the terrain and stack on top of one another without falling had proven difficult. Flushed with heat and effort, the girls made for the shade of the gazebo. It was the first time I'd been in the gazebo since the night Chris Altieri died, and the memories of Chris's sadness and of Zack's subtle menace that evening were sharp-edged and unsettling. Oblivious to anything beyond the moment, the girls poured lemonade, wolfed banana loaf, and discussed the engineering problem with which they'd been wrestling.

"When we were at the cemetery, we noticed that this arm of Lawyers' Bay was right across the lake," Gracie said. "We thought it would be neat to build this Inukshuk with a sight hole that pointed towards that huge cottonwood tree at the edge of the cemetery."

"My father says that, judging from its size, that tree must have been there forever," Isobel said.

Gracie rolled her eyes. "I thought *we* were going to be here forever trying to get the angle right," she said. "This is the third time we've had to take down what we've built and start again, but I think we've got it. Maybe you'd like to have a look, Mrs. Kilbourn."

"I'd be honoured," I said.

The girls came with me as I walked out to the Inukshuk and peered through the sight hole.

"Third time's the charm," I said. "You've got it."

They barely had time to exchange high-fives before we heard the squeal of brakes and the slam of a car door behind us. All day I had been carrying an image of Lily Falconer as frightened and vulnerable, a broken child who grew into a damaged adult. The wrathful woman who exploded out of the front seat of her Jeep and ran towards us was a shock.

Lily's face was contorted with rage and her voice was acid. "Put those rocks back," she said. "You don't know what you're destroying." She didn't give the girls a chance to obey or explain. Instead, she went to the Inukshuk and ripped out a flat stone from the base. Within seconds, the meticulously planned and executed structure collapsed.

Clutching her prize, Lily dropped to the beach and began exploring the support under the gazebo. She was desperate, as if she had to slide the rock into place before everything fell apart. She narrowed her focus on her daughter.

"Where did you take this from, Gracie?"

The colour had drained from Gracie's face. Her freckles looked painted on, like a doll's. I was afraid she was sliding into shock. I stepped between Lily and her daughter. My hands were shaking, but my voice was steady. "No one destroyed anything, Lily. We bought the rocks in Fort Qu'Appelle. I drove the girls in myself to get them."

Lily looked at me with loathing. "It's so easy for you to be the good one," she said. Her comment stunned me. So did the fact that she was still holding the rock she had ripped from the Inukshuk. For a moment it seemed entirely possible that she would hurl the rock at me. Instead, she dropped it on the beach, walked back to her Jeep, threw it into reverse, and sped off.

Gracie watched her mother's car disappear from sight. "Welcome home, Mum," she said. Then she picked up the stone her mother had dropped, placed it back where it belonged, and began patiently to restore the Inukshuk.

I stayed with the girls while they rebuilt what had been destroyed. Without discussion, they realized the importance of their task, and they worked silently and deliberately. Finally, it was done.

One by one the girls checked the sight hole, then Gracie nodded to me. "Your turn," she said.

I stared across the lake at the graveyard. When I spotted the cottonwood tree, I said, "Better than ever. Why don't we call it a day and go home?"

Gracie's smile was battle-weary. "Good plan," she said. "But can I go to your home, not mine?"

CHAPTER 12

N ot long after the girls had settled down with
  a video, Rose appeared at our door.

"I've come for Gracie," she said.

"She's in the living room with Taylor and Isobel
watching a movie," I said. "Before you get her, we
should probably talk for a minute. There was . . .
an incident."

Rose stepped inside, closing the door behind
her. "Lily told me," she said. "How bad was it?"

"Pretty bad," I said.

Rose's small body sagged with defeat. "More
unravelling." She took a deep breath. "I'd better
get my girl, see what we can salvage." She frowned,
seeming to turn something over in her mind. "Do
you think it would be easier for Gracie if Taylor
and Isobel came back with her? I could give them
all dinner."

"Makes sense to me," I said. "When in doubt, proceed as if life is going on as usual."

Not long after Rose and the girls left, Zack drove in. I walked out to the driveway to meet him. He was pale and clearly exhausted.

"Bad day?" I asked.

He grimaced. "You don't want to know."

"Would a large gin and tonic help?"

"I'm not certain," Zack said. "But I'm willing to give it a try."

We took our drinks out to the porch, where there was at least the chance of a breeze. The scent of nicotiana, heady and seductive, drifted through the screened windows.

Zack sipped his drink and sighed contentedly. "On the drive back I was thinking about how nice it is to have someone to come home to."

"Whoa, there," I said. "What's my favourite colour?"

He laughed. "You don't think I know enough about you to move in?"

"I don't think we know enough about each other to pass a couples' quiz in *Cosmopolitan* magazine."

"We can remedy that," Zack said. "After the Friends of Clare Mackey leave tonight, come sit on my deck. We'll watch the sunset – no sex, just the sharing of information. What do you say?"

"I've never been a big fan of either-or."

"Neither have I. So let's do both. Now, how was your day?"

"About as grim as yours," I said. My account of the scene with Lily was brief, but I didn't gloss over the punch-in-the-stomach gratuitous ugliness of Lily's attack.

Zack was visibly shaken. "How did Gracie take it?"

"She was stunned, of course. She was trembling and so pale that I thought she might be on the verge of shock. Lily either didn't notice or didn't care. Her only concern was where the rocks for the Inukshuk came from."

"Why would it matter?" Zack said. "The kids showed me what they've done. It looks like good work to me."

"I agree," I said. "And if there's a happy ending to this story, it's that Gracie didn't let her mother destroy what she and the other girls made. As soon as Lily left, Gracie started building again."

Zack's smile was faint. "Way to go, Gracie," he said.

"Kids have amazing resources," I said.

"But no one's resources are inexhaustible," Zack said. "Lately, Blake has been running on empty."

"There aren't many things more draining than a

bad marriage," I said. "Lily's clearly miserable. Why doesn't Blake just accept the truth?"

Zack shrugged. "He's in love with her, and once in a while she loves him back."

"And that's enough for him."

"I guess it is. I know he's absolutely faithful to her."

"I underestimated him," I said. "When I met Blake, I didn't like him. I had him pegged as a ladies' man."

"How did you have me pegged?"

"As the prince of darkness," I said.

"So you were wrong on both counts."

"Was I?"

Zack laughed. "Probably not entirely. But I have the rest of the summer to convince you that you were wrong about me." He finished his drink and placed the glass on the wicker table.

"Can I get you a refill?"

"Thanks, but no. I spent most of the lunch hour talking to my client, then I had an errand to run. I forgot to eat."

"You should have said something. I'll make us some sandwiches. Is ham okay?"

"Ham is perfect. I'm starving, and the prospect of going out to a restaurant does not appeal to me."

"Can't you cook?"

"Can't even boil an egg."

"Is that the truth or a ploy?"

"A ploy," he said. "I'd do anything to get you to make me that sandwich."

I brought back a tray with our sandwiches and a pitcher of milk. When we'd finished eating, Zack sighed with contentment. "You know, I might just live."

"That's good news."

"You don't look very happy about it."

"This isn't about you. It's about me. I wish Clare's friends weren't coming out here tonight. I feel as if I've betrayed them."

"Because you alerted me to the fact that they were asking questions? Joanne, if they want answers, you've helped them. You've expedited the process. Clare's friends don't have to jump out of the bushes and scare me. I'll stay here and answer any questions they have."

"I think your presence might just exacerbate matters."

"My presence has been known to do that," Zack said. "But I'm not sure why it would in this case."

"Because if you're waiting for them, it will appear that Falconer Shreve is trying to control events. Clare's friends are trying to create a situation in which people can come to them."

"Fair enough," Zack said. "But at least let me tell you what I know – just to clear the air."

"And I can pass this information along?"

"Every word. For the record, I believe Clare Mackey is working for a law firm in Vancouver."

"But you're not certain."

"You were at the Canada Day party, Joanne. You saw the number of juniors Falconer Shreve has. Unless I'm working with one of them, I don't keep track."

"So you didn't know that Anne Millar came to Falconer Shreve to find out why Clare had left so precipitously."

"No. I knew that," Zack said. "It came up at a partners' meeting. We decided that, out of respect for the privacy of those involved, we wouldn't disclose the circumstances under which Clare left. To be honest, two adults having a love affair that went wrong didn't seem to be anybody's business but theirs."

"Are you saying the woman in Chris's life *was* Clare Mackey?"

"You sound surprised," Zack said.

"I thought that Clare might be the one," I said. "But until this moment I wasn't certain."

"I guess each of us just knew half of the story," Zack said. "I didn't learn about the pregnancy and abortion until you told me that night at Magoo's. Then of course I put two and two together."

"But you didn't say anything to me?"

"You and I were just getting to know one another; Chris had been my friend for over twenty years. He'd kept Clare's pregnancy secret when he was alive. I didn't see any point in bringing it up after he was dead and Clare had started a new life." Zack moved his chair closer. "Does that make sense to you?"

"It makes sense," I said.

"Then we can watch the sunset together?"

I reached over and touched his cheek. "You look so tired. Go home and get some sleep. Willie and I will stop by on our walk in the morning. Sunrises are just as nice as sunsets."

He grinned. "And this time of year they come early. Lots of time to fool around before I have to go back to the city. Hey, I got you an electric toothbrush today at lunch. It's in the car. I'll plug it in as soon as I get home. Like me, the toothbrush will be ready when you are."

The members of Clare Mackey's Moot Team arrived on the dot of seven o'clock. Anne Millar had come with them, and it was clear from the outset that she had meshed easily with the other women. They were an appealing group. All were blond, all were fit, all were dressed smartly and informally – young professionals on casual Friday. Despite their smiles of greeting, they were sombre. When the introductions were over, I started to show them into the living room, but Linda Thauberger, who appeared to have been designated group leader, asked if we could use a room with a table. I led them into the kitchen. As generations of women had done before us, we took our places and began to talk, but our topic was not men, children, or the vagaries of our own flesh, it was Clare Mackey, and her story was murky and troubling.

"As far as we can tell," Linda Thauberger said, opening her smart red briefcase and taking out a file, "this is where it all begins." She placed the file at the centre of the table.

The name on the label made me blink. "Patsy Choi," I said. "That case was three years ago. What does it have to do with Clare?"

"Stay tuned," Linda said coolly. "I've had more than a few sleepless nights since we discovered the connection."

"We all have," Maggie Niewinski said. She still had the mop of blond curls she had in her law-school grad photo, but the shadows under her eyes were like bruises. It was clear she'd had her share of insomnia.

"And we know this is just the beginning," Sandra Mikalonis, a graceful woman with a ponytail, added.

"You're going to have to fill me in," I said.

"Since I'm the one who dropped the ball on this, I'll do it," Linda said.

Maggie shook her curls vehemently. "No hair shirts," she said. "We've agreed we all would have done exactly as you did."

"Which was nothing," Linda said quietly.

"Because no one asked you to do anything," Maggie said.

"You're still a terrier with a bone when you get an idea, aren't you?" Linda said. "Maybe we should let the facts speak for themselves. Last year, just after the August long weekend, Clare called me. She'd stayed in Regina for the holiday. At that point, she'd been at Falconer Shreve about four months, and she thought the long weekend might be a good opportunity to stay at the office and do some homework."

"Getting caught up on her files?" I asked.

Linda shook her head. "No. More just getting to understand the dynamics of the firm she was working for. Juniors are famously overworked. When you're slaving away twelve hours a day, it's hard to see where the snakes and ladders are, but if you're going to get ahead you have to be able to tell an opportunity from a dead end. Anyway, most ambitious young lawyers, and Clare was . . . *is* . . . ambitious, would have used the time to read through the files of their principals' more brilliant cases so they could drop a few fawning references to them later. But Clare's background is in accounting, so she went straight to the trust ledgers. They, of course, have their own tale to tell."

"Remind me about the trust ledgers," I said.

"That's where law firms keep records of their clients' trust funds," Anne Millar explained. "Monies paid in, monies taken out. Typically, monies taken out would be paid into general accounts to cover services from the firm. Any other withdrawal would require a written permission. In either case, there would be some sort of record in the file that the money had been transferred. At the end of every day, there's a trust reconciliation – that's just like balancing your chequebook. Everything has to be accounted for and justified."

"You haven't lost your skills as a seminar leader," I said.

"A seminar leader!" Maggie gave Anne a mocking smile. "You didn't tell us that on the drive out. I'll bet you were a tough marker."

A frown creased Linda's brow. "Let's keep our
focus here," she said. "Anyway, Clare was leafing
through the trust ledgers and she came upon something that set off the alarm bells. She noticed that
a number of trust funds were suddenly making sub-
stantial payments into general accounts, and they
were making them repeatedly."

"I'm guessing there were no permissions," I said.

"Bingo," Linda said. "No written record of any
kind. A clear case of defalcation – messing with
trust money. Anyway, the rest of the story is quickly
told. All the payments were made during a six-
week period. With Clare's background in forensic
accounting, she knew how to follow the money
trail. She went to the files and discovered that the
major case Falconer Shreve was handling at the
time was the Patsy Choi case. It was a civil case, tort
of assault, wrongful touching."

"My God, the uncle deliberately broke the girl's
fingers," I said.

"In the law, 'wrongful touching' was still the
charge. The plaintiff, Patsy Choi, had to prove her
damages, and it was not a slam dunk for her lawyer.
Clare made copies of the notes to the case. The
defence got great mileage out of the uncle's phi-
lanthropy, the fact that as soon as he'd heard about
Patsy's talent as a violinist, he spared no expense in

bringing her to Canada, giving her a home, paying for her lessons."

"And then smashing her fingers with a hammer," I said.

"Actually, it was a wooden mallet, the kind you use to tenderize meat," Sandra Mikalonis said mildly. "The uncle was tenderizing a piece of round steak when Patsy announced that she didn't want to practise any more – that she didn't want to be a freak, she wanted to be a normal girl. The defence scored some points on that little outburst too."

"But Patsy Choi ended up winning," I said. "She got a huge settlement."

Maggie snorted derisively. "Well, huge for Canada, and the appeal dragged on for a long time. But you're right. In the end, Patsy won."

Anne Millar gave a seminar leader's summation. "The point is that Patsy Choi proved her damages because her lawyer hired an array of professional experts who he knew were plaintiff-friendly, and they did their job. An entertainment lawyer and an impresario put a dollar figure on Patsy's loss of potential earnings. Three psychiatrists testified that she had suffered irreparable psychological damage when her fingers were broken. A partnership of psychologists who specialize in adolescents pointed out that no one would want to have their life determined by what they said during a tantrum when they were in their early teens. But expert testimony doesn't come cheap."

"And Patsy's lawyer paid the experts out of the trust funds of Falconer Shreve clients," I said.

"Bingo again," Sandra said. "In the normal run of things, the partners could have covered the experts' fees out of their personal funds, but Patsy Choi's case took place during a serious slump in the stock market. Clare's guess was that Patsy's lawyer knew his partners' circumstances and didn't even approach them. You have to hand it to Chris Altieri: when it came to the people he cared about, he was a class act."

An image flashed into my mind – Chris on the night of the barbecue whispering that he had done something unforgivable. But it didn't fit. In my mind at least, dipping into a trust fund didn't qualify as a mortal sin.

"What kind of disciplinary action did the Law Society decide on?" I said.

"None," Linda said. "Clare never went to the Law Society. She just made copies of all the documents and wrote up her notes. When she gave me the file, she told me to hang on to it until she'd made up her mind about what she was going to do. I told her that she had no choice. She said she wasn't talking about the Law Society – she was wrestling with a personal matter. She seemed very distracted, very un-Clare. Anyway, she never came for the folder, and she left town in mid-November without doing anything. A shocker, at least to me."

"She was just beginning her career," I said. "Chris Altieri had a lot of friends. Clare might not have wanted to be tagged as a troublemaker."

"She wouldn't have cared about that," Maggie Niewinski said. "Clare saw the world in terms of right and wrong. She had her own inner account book. It was like the trust ledgers Anne was talking about: at the end of the day, everything had be reconciled right down to the last word or deed. That's why I can't believe she left town with so many things unresolved – especially the defalcation. I mean, talk about black and white."

"Clare's relationship with Chris Altieri may have drawn her into a grey area," I said.

The women turned to me, alert and wary.

"Clare Mackey and Chris had an affair," I said. "Apparently, she became pregnant and terminated the pregnancy."

Anne Millar's grey eyes widened with disbelief. "How could you know that? You never met Clare. You'd never even heard her name until I told you about her at the funeral."

"But I met Chris," I said. "The night he died he told me he was haunted by a relationship that ended in an abortion. He didn't mention the woman's name. I didn't discover it was Clare until later."

Maggie was chewing her thumbnail. Sandra reached over absently and batted Maggie's hand away from her mouth, then she turned to me.

"Who told you the woman was Clare?" she asked.

"Zack Shreve," I said. "After Anne went to Falconer Shreve and put pressure on Chris to supply the name of the firm Clare had joined in Vancouver, there was a meeting. According to Zack, Chris told his partners that Clare left because she didn't want to be near him." I glanced around the table. "You all knew Clare. Is that behaviour consistent with the kind of woman she was?"

"*Is*," Linda Thauberger said angrily. "Let's try to hold on to a little hope here. And let's have a reality check. Clare would not have made the decision to have an abortion lightly."

"Because of her religion?"

"I never heard her mention religion," Linda said. "Just her own ethical sense. She would have lived with the consequences of what she had done."

"Not if she thought the father of her unborn child was immoral," Sandra said thoughtfully.

"Oh, come on," Maggie said. "I'll grant you that defalcation isn't exactly admirable, but it isn't as if Chris Altieri was diddling altar boys."

"I agree with you," Sandra said. "I'm just not sure Clare would. Don't you remember what she said about her father that night we celebrated passing our bar exams?"

Maggie groaned. "I don't remember anything about that night."

"I do," Linda said. "It's the only time I remember ever seeing Clare angry – actually, it's the only time I ever remember her revealing anything personal at all."

"It's coming back to me," Maggie said, narrowing her eyes. "Her father embezzled funds from the company he worked for."

"Right," said Sandra. "Then he skedaddled, leaving Clare's mother alone to raise her daughter. They lived in a small town. Everybody knew what had happened, and Clare felt that people were always watching her, waiting for her to slip up. That night at our little celebration, she was still bitter. I remember her saying, 'It took me twenty years, but I've finally proven to them that I'm not my father's daughter.' Maybe she was afraid history would repeat itself."

"But duplicity isn't a hereditary disease," Anne said.

"You know that, and I know that," Sandra said. "But when it came to questions of morality, Clare wasn't rational. I think it's more than possible that when she discovered she was carrying the child of a man who'd done exactly what her dear old dad had done, she just overreacted."

After that, there wasn't much to say. When Linda replaced the Patsy Choi file in her handsome red briefcase, it seemed to be a signal to us all that the meeting was over. We pushed our chairs back from the table and made our way to the front door. The evening we walked out into had the clarity of a Dutch painting: everything was bathed in the warm golden light of the setting sun.

"I guess it's time for us to take our stroll along the beach," Linda Thauberger said. "Not exactly a sacrifice. It's so beautiful here."

Anne Millar took a deep breath. "I think we could all use a little fresh air before we head back to the city."

Sandra Mikalonis kicked off her sandals and, ponytail flying, sprinted towards the lake. Maggie and Linda weren't far behind. With every step, they seemed to leave the years and the tensions behind.

Anne's voice was rueful. "They make me feel ancient."

"Your advanced age aside, how are you feeling about the way things are moving?"

"Rotten," Anne said. "I'm sure Clare is dead." The words, uttered baldly and without preamble, were a blow. Anne stared intently at my face. "You believe that too, don't you?"

"Yes," I said.

"So do the police," Anne said. "Of course, they're not about to make an official statement, but Linda says the officers she talked to really grilled her about how the case was handled. She also said the phrase she heard from everybody at headquarters was 'we needed to get to this sooner.'"

"They could have," I said. "You talked to Alex Kequahtooway at the end of November."

Anne laughed shortly. "The problem is Inspector Kequahtooway didn't talk to anyone else about what I told him."

"He didn't write up an official report of your conversation?"

"Apparently not. I guess there's some sort of internal investigation going on about what the inspector did or did not do. Frankly, I couldn't care less. What matters to me is that the police finally want to get to the bottom of this. Like everyone else involved in this very cold case, it's finally dawning on them that they failed Clare Mackey."

When Anne glanced towards the lake, something caught her eye.

"Who's that with our little group?"

I followed the direction of her gaze. "Let's see. The smallest of the girls in the navy bathing suits is my daughter, Taylor, the other two are her friends, and the man with them is Blake Falconer."

"Well, well, well," Anne said. "They landed a big one."

Blake and the girls had just come from a swim. The girls clearly had plans other than spending the evening jawing with adults, and it wasn't long before they hightailed it for the Wainbergs' cottage. As they darted off, Blake watched them fondly. He was bare-chested and barefoot, and his towel was slung over one shoulder. In the red-gold light, he seemed to glow himself, ruddy and handsome. We strolled over to where he was talking to the rest of the Moot Team.

"Hey," he said when he saw me. "I was just introducing myself to your company. More lawyers, just what we need around here." His smile was broad and genuine. Linda and Maggie and Sandra were smiling, too. It was a nice moment, and the part of me that longed for harmony wanted to ignore the ugly questions and ask if he'd had a good swim and if the water was still warm.

But the woman I had never met deserved better. "These aren't just lawyers, Blake," I said. "They're friends of Clare Mackey's from law school."

The wattage of his smile didn't diminish. "So how's she doing?" he said.

I pressed on. "No one seems to know."

"We haven't heard from her in months," Linda Thauberger said. "We were hoping someone from Falconer Shreve might be able to give us some contact information."

Blake chewed his lip. "I'm not the best one to talk to about this," he said. "You should get in touch with my wife, Lily. She and Clare were quite close there for a while. At least, they always seemed to be huddling."

"Could we talk to Lily now?" Anne asked.

"No," Blake said. "Lily's not well tonight."

"Tomorrow then," Anne said.

Blake's eyes met mine. "Maybe Joanne could call you when the time is right." There was such sadness in his face that my heart went out to him.

"Maybe that would be best," I agreed.

"Well, goodnight, then," Blake said. And he walked up the path that took him to whatever awaited him at home. The five of us watched until he disappeared from sight.

"For a guy who's supposed to have the world by the short hairs, he's not very happy, is he?" Maggie said.

"No," I said, "he's not."

She gave her curls a toss. "Well," she said, "you make a deal with the devil . . ."

The idea of making a deal with the devil might have been a throwaway line for Maggie, but after she left, the words stuck to my consciousness, persistent as a burr. Blake wasn't the only one who'd made a deal with the devil. Not many hours before he died, Chris Altieri told me he had committed an act that was unforgivable. By all accounts, Chris was a decent and principled human being, but he had also been involved in the rough-and-tumble world of the law for twenty years. He wouldn't have minimized his culpability about what he had done to win the Patsy Choi case, but somehow I couldn't imagine him characterizing the act as unforgivable.

The fate of his mizuko was another matter. Haunted by the memory of this child flowing into being, Chris had travelled halfway around the world seeking absolution. Yet the night of the fireworks he had made a point of telling me he had forced his lover to choose an abortion. What he'd said that night had nagged at me. Nothing about Chris Altieri suggested that he was the kind of man who would compel a woman to undergo an abortion she didn't want. And Clare Mackey certainly did not seem to be a woman who would cede control of her body to anyone. It simply didn't add up.

But there was another possible scenario, and it had its own cruel logic. Sandra Mikalonis had floated the possibility that Clare Mackey had chosen to abort her unborn child because she had decided Chris Altieri was morally unfit to be a father. If Chris had believed his unborn child had been denied its chance to come into being because of his own moral failure, he might not have been able to forgive himself. His responsibility for the abortion would have been the unforgivable act.

I had always believed the axiom that a burden shared is a burden halved, and the burden of my insight into Chris's state of mind was heavy. I wanted badly to talk to someone, and that someone was Zack.

He had seemed so tired it was possible he was already sleeping, so when I arrived at his front door I knocked softly. He came to the door almost immediately. He was wearing the white terry-cloth robe he had worn the night before, and there was a stack of folders on his knees. When he motioned me in, I saw the living room was littered with law books and papers.

"Homework?" I said.

"You bet. I don't like being humiliated, and to use a legal term with which you may not be familiar, I really stepped on my joint in court today."

"Sounds painful."

"You should have been there. Speaking of which, you're ten hours early – not that I'm complaining. I'm just glad you're here."

"So am I," I said.

He took my hand. "So do you want to go to bed or do you want to look at the sunset?"

"I think we need to talk first," I said.

"Fair enough. Follow me." Zack led me through his house to the deck. It was large and uncluttered and it faced west onto the spectacular light show of a Canadian sunset in cottage country.

"How did things go with Clare's friends?"

As I gave my account of the women's visit, Zack leaned forward in his chair. He didn't interrupt or comment until I was finished. When he did speak, he was pithy.

"Fuck," he said. "Why didn't he come to me? He didn't have to go through this alone. If he'd let me help with the Patsy Choi case, none of this would have happened. I must have offered to give him a hand a dozen times. I saw how he was throwing the money away. I just assumed we had it to throw."

"What would have happened to Chris if he'd been caught – I mean, after he'd put the money back?"

Zack rubbed the back of his neck. "Probably not much," he said. "The Law Society is the Law Society. No matter who's involved, they have to investigate and decide on appropriate disciplinary action. But this is a small province, and Chris had a boy scout's reputation. He was loyal, trustworthy, courteous, kind, clean, and obedient."

"Don't forget reverent," I said. "After Chris died, one of the gents at Coffee Row said Chris went to Mass every day."

"He did," Zack said. "But the daily attendance started after the Patsy Choi case. Before that, although he never missed Mass, he went only once a week. Guilt, I guess."

"Why did he feel such guilt?" I asked.

"I don't know. Maybe something happened when he was a kid that convinced him he had to take on the sins of the world."

"Who was it who said, 'Childhood lasts forever'?"

"Probably someone at social services," Zack said sardonically. "But whoever it was, they were right on the money." He brightened. "I'll bet *you* had a real Norman Rockwell childhood."

"Don't bet anything you value," I said. "Because you couldn't be more wrong."

"You're one of the walking wounded?"

I nodded.

Zack moved his chair so that our knees were touching. He leaned forward and placed his hands against my cheeks. "Then maybe you've had enough," he said. "Falconer Shreve is in for some rough times, Joanne. If you want to walk away, now's the time."

I covered his hands with my own. "Isn't there a song called 'Too Late Now'?"

"Frank Loesser," he said. "One of my favourites. Want me to play it for you?"

"I'd like that," I said.

"Then let's go inside."

It was a little after ten when I got back to the house. Angus and Leah were in the living room watching a video. Angus tapped an imaginary watch on his wrist. "So what were you up to at this hour of the night?"

"I was with Zack Shreve," I said.

Leah grinned, and raised her thumbs in a gesture of approbation.

Angus was less enthusiastic. "Come on, Mum. Zack Shreve? He is *way* too much for you to handle."

"You may be right about that," I said. I gave my son a friendly punch on the arm. "Then again, you may be wrong."

CHAPTER 13

Shortly after two that morning, a violent storm began. One volley of thunder was so ear-splitting that I sat bolt upright in bed. Heart still pounding, I went down to check on Taylor. Despite flashes of lightning bright as daylight, Taylor continued to sleep the sleep of the just, and I wandered back to my room intent on catching a few more winks. I would have been more usefully employed trying to jam toothpaste back in the tube. No matter how diligently I pounded the pillows, smoothed the sheets, breathed deeply, sought my mental good place, assumed the shava-asana position, and willed my mind to free itself from thoughts of past and future, sleep eluded me. Finally, I gave up, took my blanket to the chair by the window, and sat back to watch the show and see if I could make sense of the revelations that had been coming like hammer blows, one after another.

It turned out to be a profitable night. By the time the worst of the storm was over and the bleak light of dawn seeped in my window, I hadn't come up with any answers, but I was certain I knew what questions to ask. Eager to get started, I dug out my slicker and snapped on Willie's leash. Like Maggie Muggins, I had places to go, people to see, and things to do.

It was a day to believe in the pathetic fallacy: a gunmetal sky, a driving, hostile rain that stung my face and legs, and a keening wind that tossed the gulls around like pieces of tissue. Oblivious to the warnings from the elements, Willie pounded through the sloppy gravel, barking happily as we rounded the road by the gazebo and he spotted the Inukshuk, a new friend. I would have turned back but there was something I needed to check. When I found what I was looking for, I felt the rush that comes when the pieces of a puzzle are beginning to fit together.

My exhilaration was short-lived. As we passed the Wainbergs', a vehicle shot out of the driveway. Willie and I were right in its path. When I jerked him out of harm's way, I lost my footing in the gumbo of the gravel road and fell. The car skidded to a stop and Delia jumped out. She was dressed for the city: a smart black suit with a very short skirt, black stockings, pumps with serious heels.

"God, are you all right?" she said.

I stood up and checked for damage. There didn't seem to be any. "I'm fine," I said.

"You and Willie look as if you've been mud-wrestling. Come on. Get in the car. I'll take you home."

"We're an upholstery hazard," I said. "We can walk. A little more rain's not going to hurt us."

Delia frowned. "I just about killed you. The least I can do is get you out of this monsoon."

"Sold," I said. I opened the back door of Delia's car and turned to my dog with a command. "In, Willie." He stood, riveted to the spot. "In," I repeated. Willie cocked his head, perplexed but immobile. I lifted his bum and gave him a push. "In," I said. Accepting the inevitable, he lumbered up, threw himself belly down on the upholstery, and pressed his nose against the window.

When I got into the passenger seat, Delia looked at me hard and shook her head. "All the women who've been after Zack, and you're the one . . ."

"I'm not 'the one,'" I said, "but I *do* clean up nicely." We looked at one another and laughed.

"Hey," Delia said, "a good start to what will no doubt end up being another crappy day." She turned the key in the ignition. "Zack and Blake have decided the partners have to go through the trust ledgers together. More beating up on ourselves. It's not as if we don't know what we're going to find. Zack filled us in last night." She pulled a tissue from her bag and blew her nose. "At least we know now why Chris killed himself, but what the hell was up with Clare Mackey? Chris would have been the best father."

"I guess Clare didn't agree," I said.

"Forgive me if I don't lead the applause for Clare and her ethics," Delia said icily. She pulled into my driveway. "Here you are," she said. "Home sweet home."

"Muddied but unbowed," I said.

She gave me a faint smile. "Guess what? I'm still not smoking."

"I'll lead the applause for *that*," I said. I had my hand on the handle of the car door, but I didn't push it down. "Delia, did Noah build the gazebo?"

Her eyes widened. "Where did that come from? Anyway, the answer is no. He did the carving of the woman, but not the rest." She reached over and gave my shoulder an affectionate pat. "Watch out for traffic. Now that I'm a non-smoker, maybe you and I can get up our own Ultimate team."

Angus greeted me at the front door with a whoop of laughter. "You and Willie look like you've been mud-wrestling."

"You're the second person to tell me that," I said. "That means you win the big prize – the opportunity to take Willie out back and hose him down. I'm going to hit the shower."

The phone rang before I'd kicked off my runners. Angus answered it and handed it to me with a lascivious wink. "It's the Man," he said.

"I'm outside your house," Zack said. "Have you got a minute to say goodbye?"

"As long as you don't make any mud-wrestling jokes," I said.

"I don't get it."

"You will."

When he saw me, Zack raised an eyebrow. "Hop in."

"I'll wreck your upholstery."

"I'll take my chances."

He was dressed for work: white shirt, striped tie, and a suit that probably cost as much as my entire wardrobe. He put his arm around me. "What's the punchline to that joke about how porcupines make love?"

"Very carefully," I said. And for a few lovely minutes, we were very careful.

When I got out of the shower, Taylor was sitting on my bed, knitting. The hyacinth scarf was finished, and she was practising the moss stitch before she moved on. "Rose would like you to call her. She has a favour to ask. The something-or-other on her car is broken, but she wants to visit Betty because Betty gets blue when it rains. Gracie's mum is still sick, so Rose wondered if you'd mind driving us over."

"I don't mind," I said. "You and the other girls are going too?"

"Rose says we're as good as a tonic for Betty. Besides, we always have fun there."

I called Rose and we agreed that, given the driving conditions, we should get an early start. As we set out, I was glad we were in my car. Rose's Buick was a boat, and the road to Standing Buffalo was filled with turns that were hair-raising on a good day, and this was decidedly not a good day. In fact, the weather seemed to be growing uglier by the hour. Visibility was poor to non-existent, the roads were slick, and the ditches were filling. When we drove between the white-painted tractor tires that marked Betty's driveway, my tires spun ominously and I wondered if I'd be able to make it out. We sent

Rose inside, and the girls and I scurried between car and house, carrying Tupperware containers of food, a fresh supply of magazines, a case of pop, and pyjamas and a change of clothes for everybody "just in case." As soon as everyone was settled, I asked for a rain check on Betty's offer of tea, and, cleverly navigating the ruts, I drove straight to the Point Store.

Stan was watching an *I Love Lucy* classic when I arrived. As he had before, Stan turned down the sound, dragged a chrome chair in from the kitchen, and directed me to the La-Z-Boy. That morning, the plush contours of the chair were as comforting as a warm bath. On TV, Lucy was starting her job at the chocolate factory.

Stan tore himself away from the screen and turned his attention to me. "More history?" he asked.

"Recent history," I said. "When was the gazebo at Lawyers' Bay built?"

"Last year, middle of November. Late, but we had that mild winter, remember?"

"I remember," I said. "We had a green Christmas."

Stan nodded. "I never liked those. They don't seem right."

"Did a local company do the work?" I asked.

Stan made of moue of disgust. "She'd never hire local."

"She?"

"Lily Falconer," Stan said. "She got a company in the city, and I'll tell you, men never worked harder for their dollar than those men did."

"It was a difficult job?"

Stan shook his head. "It shouldn't have been. Pretty straightforward piece of construction except for that fancy stonework. Of course, there was that statue of Gloria, but Noah Wainberg carved that. In my opinion, Lily should have got Noah to do the whole thing. He could have, but maybe it was his good luck that she didn't ask him. Lily was in such a state about that gazebo. She was there every day, supervising. It got so's they were afraid to move a shovelful of dirt. 'Build it to last forever.' That's what she told them. The man in charge told her his company built everything to last forever, so she could relax and go home, but she wouldn't budge."

"The workers talked to you about the job, then?"

On TV the conveyer belt was moving more quickly and Lucy was saucer-eyed with desperation. Stan and I exchanged smiles. "The coffee pot's always been on at the Point Store," Stan said. "The bottomless cup's not something your son's girlfriend dreamed up, although to be fair she's made it a lot nicer. But to return to my point, when the gazebo men were on the job, they came into the store to warm up, have a cup of joe, and talk. Lily was a tough taskmaster. One of the men said she carried on as if they were working on holy ground."

Lucy and Ethel were growing more frantic, popping chocolates into their mouths until their cheeks bulged, shoving chocolates under their factory caps, dropping chocolates down the front of their uniforms, and still the conveyer belt kept on moving. Nothing could stop it.

I pulled myself out of the La-Z-Boy and thanked Stan.

He waved at me absently. He was mesmerized by the screen where, once again, Lucy was about to get her comeuppance.

The rain had stopped by the time I reached the gazebo. Even from fifteen metres away I could see that the stone-and-concrete outcropping on which the gazebo had been built was the perfect crypt. The world had suddenly become very small. I walked to the carved woman, reached out, and touched her cheek. It was cool and wet. "How much do you know?" I asked.

"How much do *you* know?" When I heard Lily Falconer repeat my question, the marrow in my bones froze.

I whirled around. She had made no effort to protect herself against the weather. Her bluejeans and the soft leather bag slung over her shoulder were dark with rain, her white shirt clung to her breasts, and her beautiful hair hung lank against her shoulders. The family likeness between Lily and her mother shocked me. The faces of both women were carved with the lines of those who have known too many sorrows and carried too many secrets.

Startled, I answered without thinking. "How much do I know about what?" I said.

Lily raised her arm and brought the flat of her hand against my jaw with full force. The pain brought tears to my eyes. "Don't pretend you don't know," she said.

I touched my jaw to see if it had been dislocated. It hurt, but it appeared to be where it should be. I started towards my car.

Lily stepped in front of me. "Where do you think you're going?"

"Home," I said.

She shook her head as if to clear it. "No," she said. "You're not." She reached into the bag slung over her shoulder. "I have a gun."

The weapon she pulled out was a Glock 22, the German-made semi-automatic pistol used by the Regina police. There was no way Alex would willingly have handed this gun to anyone. I could feel the first stirrings of hysteria.

"Lily, you didn't –"

She cut me off. "I could never hurt Alex. I knew I'd need a gun, so I took his while he was sleeping."

She held the gun expertly, aimed down at the sand. There was no doubt in my mind that she was capable of pulling the trigger. Out of nowhere a memory surfaced: Alex and Angus watching a TV cop show, and Alex telling my son that the Regina police had adopted the Glock because it was so fast and safe that it allowed the shooter to concentrate on the target. Now that I was the target, I did not find the memory cheering.

Lily raised the gun. If she pulled the trigger at that angle she'd shoot my kneecap. No more runs with Willie.

"You haven't answered my question," she said.

"I know where Clare Mackey is," I said.

"And you're going to tell the police."

I looked at the pistol. The pain in my jaw was excruciating. I'd have to make every word count.

"Maybe not," I said. "Make me understand."

"You're trying to buy time," she said flatly.

"No," I said. "I just want to know more."

"I had to protect the Winners' Circle," Lily said.

"No matter what?"

Lily frowned, annoyed at my thick-headedness. "It gave me my life," she said.

The night I met him, Zack told me that when he

joined the Winners' Circle, he'd been like a drunk discovering Jesus. His words had been sardonic; Lily's were not. Her lips were slightly parted, and there was a fanatic's glow in her grey eyes. When it came to the Winners' Circle, she was clearly a true believer. She was also scarier than hell.

"Tell me about it," I said. I took a step towards her. "Lily, you're important to so many people at Lawyers' Bay. They're good people and they respect you. I want to know you better."

Lily met my gaze through eyes that were as forlorn as those of a lost child. "I wish Alex had told me about you earlier."

"So do I."

"You know, we might have become friends."

"Perhaps we still can," I said. "But, Lily, you're going to have to put down the gun."

She looked down at the Glock. "If I throw this away, will you stay with me?"

"Yes," I said. "I'll stay."

Lily raised her perfectly toned arm and pitched the gun along the shore behind me. When I heard it hit the ground, my pulse slowed.

"I kept my part of the bargain," Lily said. "Now it's your turn."

"I'm still here," I said. "Tell me about the Winners' Circle. What did it mean to you?"

"Everything," she said and suddenly her face was washed of care. As she talked, Lily was in the past, discovering her identity, building her life. "The first time I heard the word 'entitlement' I thought of the way the partners were the afternoon I met them. It was at this drunken happy hour in the old Falconer Shreve offices. The place looked as if it had been strafed, but the five of them were perfect, so sure of themselves. They knew that they were the best and that they were entitled to the best."

"And that's why you wanted to be part of their world."

"That's why I *deserved* to be part of it," Lily corrected. "I didn't just marry into the Winners' Circle. I earned my place. As much as any of them, I made Falconer Shreve a success. I knew if we wanted to get platinum-card clients we needed prestigious offices. I found that heritage building where we are now, and I made all the decisions about the renovations. I've hired every administrative assistant and sat in on the interviews for all the juniors we've hired. I know when someone is Falconer Shreve material. I've made sure the bills are paid and the clients are handled with care – we entertain the ones who matter twice a year, Christmas and Canada Day. That party you were at was my idea. It was my idea for us all to build summer houses out here.

When Kevin's parents were alive, we'd just camp on the beach, but I knew if we were going to be a top law firm, we had to have houses, big expensive houses that said Falconer Shreve was a presence in the community.

"After we built the houses at Lawyers' Bay, the people in town who had looked down their noses at me my whole life, who had called me names and treated me like dirt, like less than dirt, started treating me with respect. And I treated them with respect. There was nothing to be gained by holding a grudge. I had to make certain everything ran smoothly."

I met her gaze. "Rose said that from the time she taught you to knit, you never dropped a stitch."

Lily shook her head sadly. "I couldn't afford to. I always knew that if I dropped a stitch everything would come undone."

"And Clare Mackey was going to take away everything you'd worked for."

Lily looked at me gratefully. "You *do* understand."

My jaw was swelling. It was difficult to get out the words. "What happened with Clare?"

"She brought it on herself," Lily said. "That business with the trust ledgers was old news. Every account had been balanced to the penny. Everyone in the firm took a lot of crap jobs to make sure we got back on top again."

"So the partners knew."

"About the trust accounts? No," she said. "Chris was the only one who knew. I told the others we were in a slump because of the market. I said that, for a while, they'd have to take whatever cases came along, and they did."

"Without question?"

"They trusted my judgement. If Clare had trusted my judgement things would have been different. I was the one she came to when she discovered the problem with the ledgers. I tried to convince her that since there were no victims, we could all just move along. I said that if she didn't want to stay at Falconer Shreve, I'd make inquiries about other firms."

"But she didn't agree to that."

"Oh but she did — at first." Lily's voice was thick with contempt. "And when she agreed, I arranged an interview with a really good law firm in Vancouver. Everything was taken care of. Then she missed her period, and things fell apart. I'd always gotten along well with Clare. She was like me — realistic, able to keep her focus — but the pregnancy threw her. It was almost as if she saw it as some sort of punishment. She arranged for the abortion. She didn't tell Chris until it was over. He was devastated. Clare didn't help matters there. She put the blame for the abortion squarely at his door, said that the poison of dishonesty seeps into everything and that if she was going to start a new life, she had to excise the poison by going to the Law Society. That's when he came to me.

"He was in terrible shape. He felt he was responsible for the death of his child and now he was going to bring shame to the firm. It was just before the Remembrance Day holiday, so I went to Clare and begged her to take the weekend to think about her decision. I said she could use our place out here. I was certain if she just had a chance to consider, she'd realize that there had been enough grief."

Lily's eyes were beseeching. She was desperate to make me understand the forces that had driven her to kill Clare Mackey.

"Clare wouldn't listen to you," I said.

"No. When I came to pick her up on that Sunday night, she hadn't changed her mind." Lily laughed softly. "Did you know she couldn't drive? Three university degrees and Clare Mackey couldn't drive a car. If she had a driver's licence she'd be alive today." Lily shook her head. "But there's no going back, is there?"

"How did it happen?" I said.

"I choked her to death with my bare hands," Lily said. "We were standing on that spot where the gazebo is now, looking out at the lake. She just wouldn't listen. No matter what I said, it was the same old tune – she had to get the poison of what Chris had done out of her life. No thought at all about how it would affect the rest of us. I was so angry. When it was over, I couldn't believe what I'd done. Then, of course, I had to take care of the . . . aftermath . . . myself."

"Did you have to take care of Chris, too?"

Lily's smile was faint. "No. Chris took care of Chris. After he talked to you the night of the fire-works, he came to me. He said he was going to 'atone.' He'd already made some phone calls and he'd gotten up his nerve to call Clare."

"He believed the story about the 'dream job'?"

"No, he believed Falconer Shreve was paying Clare to stay away and stay silent. But all of a sudden he had to cleanse his conscience. He was as stub-born as Clare was. He was prepared to go to the ends of the earth to find her and ask her forgive-ness, regardless of the consequences for the firm. So I told him what I'd done. I told him that I'd killed Clare to protect Falconer Shreve. I told him that all that time he'd been talking to you in the gazebo, he'd been standing on her burial ground. I thought that might shock him into understanding that his first loyalty should be to us, to the Winners' Circle. But he said he had to go to the police." Lily's grey eyes met mine. "Do you know what he told me? He said he couldn't live with the knowledge of what I'd done. So I said, 'You don't have to live with it.' All I meant was that *I* was the one who had to live with what I'd done, but he heard it differently. He gave me a hug and said, 'Point taken.' The next thing I knew he'd driven his car into the lake."

"The ultimate act of loyalty," I said.

"Yes," Lily said. "At the critical moment, Chris knew exactly what to do. Maybe that's something members of the Winners' Circle are born with, like their sense that they're entitled to the best." Her face crumpled. "I never quite managed to convince myself of that one."

I remembered Chris telling Taylor that nothing lasts forever. He'd been wrong. Childhood lasts forever.

When I saw Alex's Audi drive up, I felt a wash of relief. It was over. As Alex approached Lily, his voice was gentle and reassuring. "Time to go home, Lily," he said.

In an instant, the pain and confusion were wiped from her face. "You always find me."

"Yes," he said. "I always do."

She shivered. "I'm cold."

He put his arm around her shoulders. "Better?" he asked.

Silent, she nodded and drew closer to him. The moment triggered the memory of a night of changeable weather when a wind had come up, and Alex had put his arm around me. Something inside me broke.

For the first time Alex looked at me. "Are you all right?" he asked.

My jaw was so sore I could barely speak. "Just remembering," I said.

Two words, but they were enough. "That night on the Albert Street bridge," he said. "The beginning of the end." I turned away because I couldn't bear to look at his eyes. "It was probably for the best," he said. "It would never have worked for us, Jo."

I waited till they'd driven off before I went to my car. When I called Zack on my cell, I was prepared to leave a message, but he answered.

"Hi," I said.

"Hey, this is a nice surprise," he said.

"I'm afraid it's not," I said. "Lily's been arrested for Clare Mackey's murder."

"Oh Jesus," he said. "What happened?"

"Zack, I've hurt my jaw. It's hard for me to talk. But Lily will need a lawyer."

"What about you?"

"No lawyer, just an ice pack," I said.

"I'm calling a doctor," Zack said.

"Don't. Just make sure someone's with Lily."

"Was Gracie there when Lily was arrested?"

"No," I said. "Rose took the kids over to Standing Buffalo for the day."

"Thank God for that," Zack said. "Hang on, Ms. Kilbourn. I'm on my way."

When I got back to the cottage, I changed into dry clothes, lit a fire, and made myself a hot drink. Then I went over and picked up Louis L'Amour's *Buckskin Run*. The book jacket told me there were over 110 million copies of his books in print around the world, and assured me I would be spellbound. I wasn't, but it wasn't Louis L'Amour's fault.

Rod Morgan and Jed Blue had just agreed to be partners because they were cut from the same leather, when the phone rang. It was Zack.

"Something's screwy, Joanne. I'm at police headquarters. They don't know anything about an arrest – especially not one involving Alex Kequahtooway. He's been suspended from the force."

"But Lily confessed to everything. They left together. I assumed . . ."

Zack sighed. "Never assume. Don't talk to any-body until I get there, okay? There are a hundred cops looking for Lily and the inspector, and they're sending someone to Lawyers' Bay to talk to you. I'll be there as soon as I get some ice for your jaw."

"If you brought some single-malt Scotch to go with that ice, I wouldn't take it amiss," I said.

I hung up the phone furious at Alex for deceiv-ing me once again, and at myself for being stupid enough to believe that he had suddenly remem-bered the oath he'd taken when he'd graduated from the police college. He and Lily were clearly on the run. Like everything else, that decision made no sense. Alex knew me well enough to know I would follow up on what happened after Lily was taken to the police station. And he knew that the moment the police realized he and Lily had fled, they would deploy every available officer to track them down. There was no way they could escape. Then, like Paul on the road to Damascus, the scales fell from my eyes, and I knew.

It was a short drive to the church at Lebret. Not more than fifteen minutes, and for the first time that day, the skies had cleared. The silver Audi was parked behind the church, facing the Stations of the Cross on the hill that Lily's mother had climbed every day during the last year of her life. My legs were weak as I picked my way through the puddles towards Alex's car. Bathed in the watery sunlight, the vehicle already seemed unearthly.

I think I had realized all along that I would be too late. If I hadn't known the truth, I would have mistaken Lily and Alex for lovers. Her head was against his chest; his arm was around her shoulders, shielding and protecting. Later, forensic testing would determine that Alex had fired both shots. There was no way out for either of them and they hadn't wanted to take a chance that one would live without the other. But at that moment, all I could see was the blood that flowed from their wounds, mingling and mixing like tributaries of a larger river, two lives that had run their parallel courses and come together in death. At long last, Alex Kequahtooway and Lily Ryder were home.

There are few sites that have the emotional resonance of a fresh grave in summer: the moist dank scent of earth and the too-sweet smell of cut flowers curling with heat and the onset of decay. The week after the tragedy at Lebret, I was present as two people were put in their graves and a third was removed from hers.

Lily and Alex were buried in Lake View cemetery across the water from Lawyers' Bay. In an act of generosity that made it possible to believe in human decency, Blake Falconer arranged to have the woman he had always loved buried next to the only human being she had ever cared for. Both Lily's funeral and Alex's were private. Both were marked by the bruised bewilderment of mourners forced to deal with the fact that a human being's final act had been to throw a grenade into the careful construction that housed everything that those who loved them believed them to be.

From the moment Eli Kequahtooway arrived back from Vancouver, where he was studying art at Emily Carr, Angus was at his side. There had been a time when the boys had been like brothers, and I was glad to see that the bond between them was still strong. Eli had chosen to stay at Standing Buffalo until his uncle's funeral, and Angus had, without comment, simply moved in with him. They bunked together at Betty's house, and the night before the funeral, Betty made tea and fried bannock for the boys and me and then withdrew to her pretty, frilly bedroom so Angus, Eli, and I could talk.

We sat at Betty's kitchen table until the small hours. Eli was haunted by the fact that there had been no suicide note, no final telephone call, and that night, in an attempt to explain the unexplainable, the three of us tried to piece together what we knew. It wasn't enough. As I watched the hope in Eli's eyes turn to despair, I knew that it would be years before he would trust again. When finally we said goodnight, I drew Eli to me and whispered that his uncle had loved him deeply, but that events had overtaken him and he simply hadn't had time to say goodbye. The words were cold comfort, but they were all I had.

Clare Mackey's funeral was the same day as Alex Kequahtooway's. Had there been no conflict, I might have gone. Then again, I might not have. I'd said my prayers the day the machines ripped up the hill where Clare was buried. The workers had been careful as they disassembled the gazebo. One of the men assured me that not a pane of glass was cracked. The wooden carving of Gloria Ryder had been placed to one side. It lay on the beach, its back to the gazebo as the police dug up Clare Mackey's remains.

Sandra Mikalonis sent me a copy of the eulogy she had delivered at Clare's funeral. In it she praised Clare's integrity and remembered her passion for Bach and her joy when she scored the winning goal at the national law games in her graduating year. Sandra ended her eulogy by noting Clare's steadfast dedication to her principles. Clare's life, Sandra said, had been fired by her commitment to the motto of the University of Saskatchewan's College of Law: *Fiat justitia* – let justice be done.

A week after the funerals, Rose and I visited the Lake View cemetery. We came with flowers, jam jars full of petunias from Betty's garden. Lily's were pink; Alex's purple. "Better for a man," Betty had declared.

As we always seemed to be, Rose and I were in step. We were silent as we placed our flowers on the graves and unhurried as we thought our private thoughts. It was a gentle day, cool, sunny, and breezy.

"So how are you doing?" Rose asked finally.

"Truthfully, I feel as if someone ripped away my top layer of skin."

Rose nodded sagely. "I know that feeling. But we have to stop. The old people say if you mourn too long they get stuck, the ones who've passed away. They can't get on with their journey."

"I've heard that," I said. "I always thought it made a lot of sense."

"And you and I have to get on with it, too. We're not young women."

"No," I said. "We're not."

"And we've got responsibilities," Rose said. "I've got Gracie and her dad."

"And I've got my kids and my job. Did I tell you my daughter and her family are spending the month of August here?"

"Is that the daughter I met at Alex's funeral?"

"Yes," I said. "My daughter Mieka."

"How old are the kids?"

"Maddy's three and Lena's seven months."

"That's good," Rose said. "We could use some babies around here."

I stopped to pick a weed from a grave. Rose took the Safeway bag from her pocket and held it out to me. I dropped the weed in and she nodded approvingly.

"That Zack Shreve's an interesting man," she said.

"He is," I agreed.

"Tough."

"So they say."

Rose raised an eyebrow. "They also say that sometimes the toughest nuts have the sweetest meat. I wonder if that's true."

"I don't know," I said.

Rose shoved the Safeway bag back in her pocket. "Well," she said, "isn't it lucky that you've got the rest of the summer to find out?"

ACKNOWLEDGEMENTS

Thanks to Jan Seibel, B.F.A., LL.B., a great artist, a fine lawyer, and an incredibly patient and generous teacher; to Joan Baldwin, who continues to care for our family with consummate skill; and, as always, to my husband, Ted, for making everything possible.

New from Gail Bowen

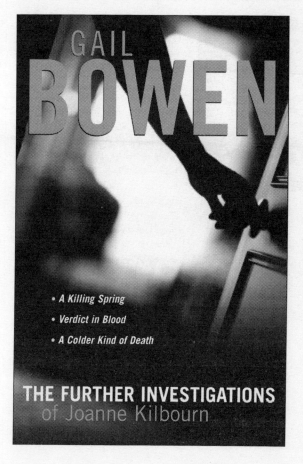

GAIL
BOWEN

- *A Killing Spring*
- *Verdict in Blood*
- *A Colder Kind of Death*

THE FURTHER INVESTIGATIONS
of Joanne Kilbourn

Spring 2006

THE EARLY INVESTIGATIONS
OF JOANNE KILBOURN

"THESE REALLY ARE SECRETS TO DIE FOR."
– KIRKUS REVIEWS

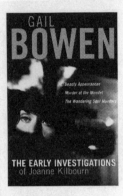

0-7710-1467-8
$24.99

Award-winning mystery writer Gail Bowen's first three masterful mysteries featuring amateur sleuth Joanne Kilbourn are now collected in a single volume. In *Deadly Appearances*, a successful politician sips his water before a speech at a picnic on a sweltering August afternoon and, within seconds, he is dead; in *Murder at the Mendel*, Joanne's childhood friend may have a far more complicated and deadly past than Joanne knows about; and in *The Wandering Soul Murders*, a centre for street kids holds a dark and disturbing secret, forcing Joanne to act when her own children are drawn into a web of intrigue. This book is a must-have for readers coming to Gail Bowen for the first time, as well as for her large and devoted audience who want to reread the early novels in this handsome collector's edition.

"Gail Bowen's Joanne Kilbourn mysteries are small works of elegance that assume the reader of suspense is after more than blood and guts, that she is looking for the meaning behind a life lived and a life taken."
– Catherine Ford, *Calgary Herald*

"Bowen has a hard eye for the way human ambition can take advantage of human gullibility."
– *Publishers Weekly*

A COLDER KIND
OF DEATH

When the man convicted of killing her husband six years earlier is himself shot to death while exercising in a prison yard, Joanne Kilbourn is forced to relive the most horrible time of her life. And when the prisoner's menacing wife is found strangled by Joanne's scarf a few days later, Joanne is the prime suspect.

To clear her name, Joanne has to delve into some very murky party politics and tangled loyalties. Worse, she has to confront the most awful question – had her husband been cheating on her?

0-7710-1495-3
$9.99

A KILLING SPRING

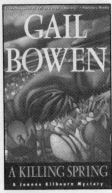

0-7710-1486-4
$8.99

The fates just won't ignore Joanne Kilbourn – single mom, university professor, and Canada's favourite amateur sleuth. When the head of the School of Journalism is found dead – wearing women's lingerie – it falls to Joanne to tell his new wife. And that's only the beginning of Joanne's woes. A few days later the school is vandalized and then an unattractive and unpopular student in Joanne's class goes missing. When she sets out to investigate the student's disappearance, Joanne steps unknowingly into an on-campus world of fear, deceit – and murder.

"This is the best Kilbourn yet."
– *Globe and Mail*

"*A Killing Spring* is a page-turner. More than a good mystery novel, it is a good novel, driving the reader deeper into a character who grows more interesting and alive with each book."
– *LOOKwest Magazine*

"Fast paced . . . and almost pure action. . . . An excellent read."
– *Saint John Telegraph-Journal*

"*A Killing Spring* stands at the head of the class as one of the year's best."
– *Edmonton Journal*

BURYING ARIEL

> ## "A RIPPING GOOD MYSTERY."
> – CATHERINE FORD, *CALGARY HERALD*

Joanne Kilbourn is looking forward to a relaxing weekend at the lake with her children and her new grandchild when murder once more wreaks havoc in Regina, Saskatchewan. A young colleague at the university where Joanne teaches is found stabbed to death in the basement of the library. Ariel Warren was a popular lecturer among both students and staff, and her violent death shocks – and divides – Regina's small and fractious academic community. The militant feminists insist that this is a crime only a man could have committed. They are sure they know which man, and they are out for vengeance. But Joanne has good reason to believe that they have the wrong person in their sights.

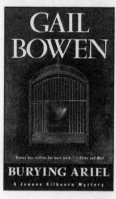

0-7710-1498-8
$9.99

"A study in human nature craftily woven into an intriguing whodunit by one of Canada's literary treasures."
– *Ottawa Citizen*

"Excellent . . ."
– *National Post*

"The answer to the mystery . . . remains tantalizingly up in the air until the entirely satisfying finale."
– *Toronto Star*

THE GLASS COFFIN

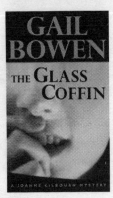

0-7710-1477-5
$9.99

This chilling tale about the power of the ties that bind – and sometimes blind – us, is Gail Bowen's best novel yet. Set in the world of television and film, *The Glass Coffin* explores the depth of tragedy that a camera's neutral eye can capture – and cause.

Canada's favourite sleuth, Joanne Kilbourn, is dismayed to learn the identity of the man her best friend, Jill Osiowy, is about to marry. Evan MacLeish may be a celebrated documentary filmmaker, but he has also exploited the lives – and deaths – of the two wives he lost to suicide by making acclaimed films about them. It's obvious to Joanne that this is stony ground on which to found a marriage. What is not obvious is that this ground is about to get bloodsoaked.